Co

The Vengeance Trail ii
Prologue 1
Chapter 1 3
Chapter 2 13
Chapter 3 23
Chapter 4 35
Chapter 5 46
Chapter 6 60
Chapter 7 72
Chapter 8 80
Chapter 9 92
Chapter 10 103
Chapter 11 115
Chapter 12 128
Chapter 13 141
Chapter 14 153
Chapter 15 164
Chapter 16 175
Epilogue 190
The End 191
Norse Calendar 192
Glossary 193
Historical Note 196
Other books by Griff Hosker 197

The Vengeance Trail

Dragonheart's Heir

By

Griff Hosker

Published by Sword Books Ltd 2020

SWORD
BOOKS

Cover by Design for Writers

Prologue

I am Sámr Ship Killer and I am the heir of Dragonheart. I have led the clan since we laid his body to rest in the cave of Myrddyn under the watchful eye of Ylva, his granddaughter. I had thought that I had been a good leader who led the Clan of the Wolf well. The three sisters who weave and plot proved to me that I was wrong. *Wyrd.* It had been Harald Finehair, the Norwegian King, who sent warriors to take my land. He did not fight fairly; that was not his way and I did not have The Dragonheart's clever mind; perhaps his faith in me had been misplaced. My father and uncle were killed, and I was captured in the war which made the Clan of the Wolf the prisoner of King Harald of Norway. Had it not been for Ylva and her powers then the Clan of the Wolf would have been completely destroyed. We were hurt when his men took over Whale Island, Cyninges-tūn, Hawk's Roost and Windar's Mere. Many great warriors died. My best friend, Baldr, was slain along with his family and I was made a prisoner, in a cage, in my own home! That might have been endured but Aethelflaed, my wife, along with my children, Ragnar Sámrsson and Ylva Sámrsdotter, were taken as hostages or as playthings. While I was a prisoner I did not know. I just hung suspended each day in my cage and endured the taunts, insults and injuries inflicted upon me by the Danish Skull Takers who were my guards and tormentors. That time was the lowest in my life and I lost all hope. I think that it was then that The Dragonheart, now in Valhalla, would have wondered at his decision to make me his heir. Better a swineherd than the great-grandson who had lost all.

As I hung in the cage I believed that the King of Norway took them to his rocky home in Norway but I did not know. I still do not know what would have happened to me and my family had not Ylva summoned Fótr the Wolf from the land beyond the western seas. Even now I cannot believe that any man, let alone a clan, sailed that mighty ocean but Fótr did it, not once but twice. When he came and landed on the western coast of the Land of the Wolf, it was like the rolling of a single rock down the slopes of Úlfarrberg and the impossible happened. We destroyed the hold Finehair had on the Land of the Wolf. That was almost a year since. It has taken us since then to scour the land of every one of Finehair's men. My people have spent the time rebuilding our lives and our defences so that we can make our enemies fear the Clan of the Wolf once more. The Danes from the land of the east are ever eager to take our land. Now that we do not have the sword which was touched by the gods then they believe we are weak. They took Eoforwic from the Northumbrians and, it is said, were even trying to take the land of the West Saxons and their King Aethelred was hard-pressed. Perhaps that was why they had, in the last fighting season, lessened their attacks.

Now that I am older I see that the year I spent in scouring my land of enemies was a year wasted. At the time I thought I was doing the right thing. I was making my land strong but I was not. I was delaying in seeking my family for I feared what I might find. When a man marries and has children then they are his responsibility and I had failed in mine. As much as I appeared to be busy, leading my men to seek rumours of Norwegians and Danes still hiding in my land, I knew that I was putting off the inevitable. One day I would have to find my family. If I did not, then I would never enjoy a night of sleep again. Each night, in my empty hall at Hawk's Roost, I tossed and turned. Only mead and ale helped me to sleep and that was a fitful sleep. I was not strong enough and, once again, it took the threads of the three sisters, the Norns, to either hang me or find me salvation!

All of that meant that a year after my release I could begin to think about rescuing my family. I could take a crew and sail to Norway and beard King Harald Finehair. I would take the first steps on the vengeance trail, but it would take others to move me. King Harald had taken the heart from Sámr Ship Killer.

Chapter 1

Fótr the Wolf lived close to the coast on the far side of the high pass and the old Roman fort. When he had first come to our land he and most of his people had lived at Úlfarrston but it had not been for them. There were too many they did not know and they had joined the two Hibernians, Aed and Padraig on the west coast of the Land of the Wolf. There were few people there for the Hibernians raided the coast for slaves. He had asked for a home which looked west for his brother still lived in the land of the Skraeling. I had made him lord of that land and his people had become part of the Clan of the Wolf. When that happened those of his people who lived by the Water rejoined him. It was *wyrd* and we were all happy. I wondered at the time why he had only given the place a month but I had other things on my mind. Men make plans and look for perfection. As much as I wished to rescue my family I saw too many obstacles in my way.

I looked around the warriors of my land and saw that all of those I would have chosen to follow me to Norway were either dead or even older than I was. The last few years had seen a few grey hairs in my beard and my hair. My great grandfather's old Greek servant, Atticus, would have said that was normal in a man of my years but I still saw myself as the young warrior sailing with The Dragonheart. Many of their sons and even grandsons had fought in the war to free our land, but none had gone raiding. The three warriors with experience of sailing and fighting at sea were the three who had come from the New World: Fótr, Ebbe and the Skraeling, Bear Tooth. There were others in their clan, like Æimundr Loud Voice, who were too old now and it would not be fair to take them with me. The others who had come, like Harald of Dyroy and Danr, would not wish to uproot themselves. I knew that I was waiting for a sign or perhaps a miracle, or it may have been that I made an excuse, if I did not sail to Norway then I could not fail, again! There was little point in sailing to rescue my family if it was doomed to failure from the beginning. So it was that I found reasons to stay in the Land of the Wolf. Had I been serious about going to rescue them then I might have begun work on a drekar to take us there. I told myself that I still planned to go but I was telling that most hateful of lies, to my heart and my head!

That all changed when Erik Black Toe returned to Whale Island. It was many years since Whale Island had ruled the seas between Mercia and Hibernia: my great uncle and my father along with Pasgen were long dead as was Pasgen's brother Raibeart. Now there was not even a drekar there. A few knarr and threttanessa from Dyflin used its facilities and its strength lay in the defences built by my father and Raibeart. There would have been a time when a rider would have galloped up the road by The Water to bring us the news of his arrival. Now Erik, who had followed The Dragonheart and carried his shield, walked the fourteen miles to Cyninges-tūn and reached there just after dark. A boat came across The Water to fetch me.

They just said that a weary warrior called Erik had staggered in to the stad and had said that there was news of my family. That was enough for me, but I think I knew who the Erik they spoke of was. He had been Erik Shield Bearer but when he and Haaken One Eye had been to Wyddfa he had been injured and it was Ylva who had renamed him. He was now Erik Black Toe and that was also strange for he lived, for a while, with Erik Short Toe, the Captain of Dragonheart's drekar! At the end, he had not only protected my great grandfather, The Dragonheart, but he had also stood to guard Ylva and I owed him much. I had not seen him since my capture, and I had thought him dead. I knew that this was the work of the Norns. They had spun and he had returned but whence from? I remembered that it was he who had composed the last saga of Dragonheart. Haaken One Eye had passed the mantle of the singer to him. He had been little more than a youth then and now he would be a man grown and more.

Haaken Ráðgeirsson was the head man of Cyninges-tūn. Bjorn Asbjornson had been the one who led the men to help rescue me, but he had lost family and now ruled Windar's Mere for me. Haaken Ráðgeirsson lived in the hall that had been The Dragonheart's. His father, Ráðgeir, had been a mighty warrior who had fallen in the war of King Finehair. If the King of the Norwegians had been an honourable man and fought a battle to see who ruled the Land of the Wolf then we would have won for our army was made up of heroes but instead, he used mercenaries and allies to draw our men into an ambush where they were slaughtered. It was then that I realised my shortcomings. I was Dragonheart's heir, but I was not and could never be, Dragonheart. The glory days were long gone and the best that Sámr Ship Killer could hope was that I would be able to hold on to the little land we still had and hope that the world would pass us by.

Haaken had a large family and lusty sons. I was greeted by Ráðgeir Haakensson. He was the image of his father. "Lord, the man who came to us is Erik Black Toe. My mother recognised him. He is weary and has hurts. We have put him in the chamber used by Germund. Would you like to speak to him?"

I nodded for my mind was too full of questions for me to contemplate conversation.

Erik had been undressed and put to bed. Gertha, Ráðgeir Haakensson's mother, was feeding him stew. Erik saw me and tried to rise. Gertha was the matriarch not only of the family but also of Cyninges-tūn, "Lie down, Erik! First, you eat!" She continued to feed him but spoke to me, "I know not what the people of Whale Island and Úlfarrston were thinking, Lord Sámr! This is a hero of the battle with the Danes and yet they let him walk, not ride mind, but walk, all the way here and he is starved enough as it is! They did not feed him but, from what he said, just showed him the gate and then slammed it behind him! Things have changed in the Land of the Wolf! If The Dragonheart…" She realised that she was about to criticise me, and she shook her head, "I am sorry, lord, that was wrong of me!"

"No, Gertha, you are right, and I have let down the people. It is a year since I was freed, and I have not even begun to do all that I intended."

Anya, the wife of Ráðgeir Haakensson, brought me a horn of ale, "Do not think too badly of her, lord, her brothers were slain by the Danes."

I sat by the bed and looked at Erik. He was barely recognisable. There was a long scar down one cheek and he looked like a skeleton with little flesh upon him. His skin was sallow and almost grey. This was not the lively youth who had guarded my great grandfather's back. He finished the stew and Gertha gave him a horn of ale. He drank it and Gertha stood, "Do not question him too long, my lord, for he needs rest. One night cannot make much difference, can it?"

I nodded, "And if it was your family you sought?"

Her eyes met mine, "If it had been my family lord, I would have left a year ago and not rested until they were returned!"

That hurt but I took the criticism for it was right. I had not known where to begin looking and I feared failure.

I waited until we were alone and said, "Erik, you were ever a loyal warrior and I am sorry that after the death of Dragonheart I did not accord you the honour which you were due."

He smiled and I saw that he had lost teeth, "Lord, I expected nothing. I was Dragonheart's shield-bearer and you had much to do."

"Then tell me your story but when you are tired then stop for Gertha is right. I should not make you suffer for my tardiness."

"I fought alongside the men of this stad when the Norse came, and I was taken prisoner. Because I was young, I was not killed but taken as a thrall by a Norwegian, Egil Seal Breeks, back to his home in Norway.

5

He was not a kind lord and I was beaten. It was on the voyage to Norway that I heard your family had been taken and I confess that I assumed that you were dead. The hersir's home was at Hringariki, north of Kaupang, where King Harald sometimes has a court. I had a yoke around my neck, and I tended his pigs." He drank deeply from the horn of ale and shook his head, "You berate yourself, lord. as do I. I did nothing for quite a while. I fed the pigs and I endured the beatings for I thought I was being punished for failing. I felt sorry for myself and, I believe, I might be there still, but I had a dream." He drank some more and then said, after shaking his head, "Not a dream, a vision. I slept close to the sty and one night, Lady Ylva came to me. She told me I had to find Lady Aethelflaed and your family. She told me that they would be close and that the spirits of Old Ragnar and his family would aid me. It shocked me into action. Perhaps they thought they had broken me for they removed the yoke. It was not kindness, it just allowed me to be worked even harder. I stole a knife; it was not hard for they thought I was not a warrior. They called me a girl and a lover of boys. Now, I can see why. I waited until I had managed to steal enough food to keep me alive for a while and I escaped. I headed for Kaupang. I knew where it was as we had landed there, and I assumed that would be where they kept your family. I soon discovered that they were not there, and it was not a place for me for Egil Seal Breeks sent men to find me and I took a knarr which plied the waters of Norway." He sighed.

"If you are tired then this can wait."

He gave me a wan smile, "Lord, you know not the meaning of tired until you have been a thrall." He took another drink of the ale which had been brought. "Each place we landed I listened for a word which might tell me that your family was close. There was little plan to my search for we went wherever there was cargo to be delivered and some places we did not visit. It was almost half a year since I had managed to escape, and the nights were so long that the captain spoke of paying us off until the spring when we visited the coast of Nordr-Agadir and Rogaland. We passed the entrance to a narrow fjord and landed at Flekkefjord. The narrow fjord is important, lord, but I did not know so at the time. We landed our cargo and the captain paid us off. The others in the crew seemed to have been expecting this for there was a widow of a warrior who was an alewife and the captain spent the winter with her. The other three crew took ship south, but I heard a rumour of a family of three who were kept captive at a place called Moi. As the crow flies it was just fifteen miles north of Flekkefjord, but it was up the narrow fjord we had passed. It seemed to me that I should investigate. The odds were that it was not your family for there was

6

nothing spoken to suggest that they were anything other than folk taken from the lands to the west of Norway. I told the captain that I would seek work and after buying myself food, a fur and a sword with the money I had earned I set off north. The fifteen miles took me almost three days for there was snow and I was still not healed from my beatings. The journey took longer for there was a huge expanse of water the size of The Water. I might have risked the frozen ice-covered short cut, but I did not. I had not become brave then. When I reached Moi, I did not expose myself but watched the stronghold for that is what it was. Above the town at the head of the fjord, it had a strong gatehouse, wooden towers and a fighting platform. While the town lay close to the water the lord lived behind wooden walls with a pair of sentries at the gate." He smiled, "Your great grandfather taught me well, Lord Sámr. I did not simply walk up to the walls and ask if there was a family of captives, I spent a week walking through the snow until I had circumnavigated the stronghold. The sisters were spinning for I found a farm with an old couple. Their son had gone a-Viking and not returned. The old man was ill and the woman could not run the farm herself. They happily employed me as a farmhand for the winter. Geirahǫd was younger than her husband and laughed a lot. Dagstyggr had been a mighty warrior once but was clearly not a farmer. I think that if I had not arrived then the animals that they kept might have died. Geirahǫd was another who was not cut out for farming. It was they gave me most of the information which led me to find your family."

I could not help myself, "There were there, at Moi?"

He smiled, "Haaken One Eye told me that I was the new teller of tales, lord, let me tell the tale." I nodded for he was right and deserved to be heard. "Uddulfr the Sly is the lord of Moi. He had been the one who had cheated Dagstyggr out of his better lands leaving him with the uplands only and they did not like him. They said that he had been a lieutenant of King Harald and served him in his wars. He had been given Moi and a drekar as a reward and given the honour of keeping a family in his stronghold. I had heard of other families of captives taken by King Harald and his men. Geirahǫd liked to gossip with the other women at the market. It was the wives of raiders who told her that many of those close to King Harald now had numbers of slaves taken in the west, Viking slaves. She told me that the last time she had been to the market in Moi, she had heard a rumour that the woman kept captive was a Saxon princess!"

"Aethelflaed!"

Erik nodded, "A week later I was sent to Moi to buy at the market there. It was in the market where I saw your son."

7

I held my breath, Ragnar was alive!

"He had a yoke about his neck and was being used to carry heavy goods. There were other slaves too, but I recognised Ragnar for he looked just like you."

"Thank you Allfather." I could not help smiling.

Erik shook his head, "Lord, he had been hamstrung. One of the men at the market told me that he had tried to escape, and they had hamstrung him to stop him running. Over the winter I visited the market every week and I saw your daughter too. She had no yoke, but she was heavily guarded. The folk with whom I spoke, for I got to know them, told me that she was used as the slave of the lady of the hall, the wife of Uddulfr the Sly."

"And my wife?"

"I never saw her but all in the town knew that she was a captive."

I now saw that Erik had been more than Dragonheart's shield-bearer, he was the link to our life in the past and in the future. He was the child of the three sisters.

"I spent every visit looking for weakness in the defences. There is a river which runs through the small settlement to the sea. They have a bridge over the river which leads to the wooden stronghold. Towards the end of winter, I tried to get close to the bridge and the wooden palisade and it was a mistake. Two men were watching the walls and they saw me and realised what I was doing. They tried to apprehend me, but I ran. I was faster than one of them and thanks to my weekly visits I knew the trails better than they did. I almost managed to escape them. The one who was closest to me was as fast as I was, and he caught me. While his friend was labouring behind, we fought. We could not use swords, but I had a seax." He rubbed his scar. "He went for my eye and did this. I went for his groin and gutted him. I fled before his companion reached us. I knew I could not stay with the old couple. Geirahǫd sewed my scar and I left like a thief in the night. I had not told them whence I came, and I took the mountain paths back to Flekkefjord. It was harder than the journey there and I had little food, but I made it. The knarr captain was actually pleased to see me as he was preparing his ship and the other crew members had not yet returned. When the sailing season began, we sailed first to Kaupang. My new scar and the changes time had wrought meant that none sought me. Egil Seal Breeks must have given up the search. The knarr and its captain only sailed the waters of Norway. I needed to escape King Harald's Kingdom. I resolved to make my way back here and tell you my news. That took time. I left the first knarr which took me on as crew when we docked at some small port in Jutland. I spent a month sleeping in the streets before I found a ship which took me across the sea and I landed at Lundenwic. From there I worked on a knarr which went to Om Walum and from there to Dyflin. The last voyage was the one which was the easiest. I paid for a passage to Whale Island."

I put my hand on Erik's, "You have done well, and I cannot repay you. Why are you so thin? Did they not feed you on the knarr?"

He closed his eyes, "Lord, Lundenwic is a cesspit! I should never have gone there. It is a place filled with every villain both Saxon and Dane. I was robbed and cheated. Had I not managed to find a captain whose crew had been decimated by sea raiders then I might have died there. It was why I went to Om Walum first. All that I now own is on my back. The last of the coins I was paid was used to sail home, but I am here now." He closed his eyes. "And the ale has worked, lord, I am tired."

"Then sleep, Erik the Hero, and tomorrow you shall come to Hawk's Roost. We have plans to make. I have a family to recover!"

I joined Ráðgeir Haakensson before the fire. His sons were there also. They looked at me expectantly and I was obliged to tell them Erik's story. Ráðgeir was angered by the attitude of the people of Whale Island. I shook my head, "That is my fault for I looked inward. The Water is like a sanctuary. It has healing properties and Old Olaf looks down and guards us. The spirit of Dragonheart and Ylva protects us and I was seduced by the peace." They each nodded for they knew that what I spoke was the truth.

"And you will fetch your family back?"

I nodded, "Erik did not tell me how many men were in the stronghold and I will ask him tomorrow but as I know well you need more men to assault a stronghold than defend it and I am not sure how many men we have to go to war."

Ráðgeir Haakensson said, quietly, "It is not just the lack of men, lord. We have no drekar. King Harald took our best ships. How will you get there?"

I smiled for I had thought of this already. "Ráðgeir, the sisters have been spinning. They sent Erik to find my family and they sent Fótr the Wolf to bring us a drekar. I will ask him if we can use '*Gytha*.'"

Ráðgeir nodded, "Yet they are not warriors."

"This is for the Clan of the Wolf. We drove King Harald to find other places to grasp but until we fetch back my family and, if we can, those other slaves that he took, then his presence still hangs over our land."

"I will come with you."

9

"I only want volunteers and we will need to leave men here in the Land of the Wolf. I will ask Bjorn Asbjornson to watch my people." I shook my head and drank some of his wife's most excellent beer. "Time was we would have had Ketil, Olaf and Ulf to watch my land. Now it is left to their children and grandchildren for Finehair took a generation of warriors."

Ráðgeir gazed into the fire, "And now we have no Ulfheonar!"

"Even without Finehair, they were doomed to die with my great grandfather. He, Aðils and Haaken were the last. I was not trained as they were, and none are now left. The crew I take will be, I think, like those who first came with Jarl Buthar when they went to carve out their home on Man." I laughed at the thought, "And now we sail back to the land of Harald Blue Eye to fight his descendants again. The threads of the Norns are strong."

"So, my lord, what would you have me do? This is still the heart of your land and here your men are the most loyal."

"After I have spoken to Erik Black Toe, I will travel to speak with Fótr. If he will not let us use his drekar then we cannot sail."

He shook his head, "Surely he cannot refuse! You let him live here in our land!"

"And if he had not rescued me then this land would be Finehair's yet. I am not too proud to beg. I am paying for the mistakes my family made after The Dragonheart died. Ylva did her best but the rest of us…" I stared into the fire. It was like a picture of the Land of the Wolf. The haven had been burned and scoured because our family did not stay together. My grandfather had named me his heir but that was not enough. When he was killed old ambitions surfaced. I stood, "I will sleep. Old Germund was a warrior and perhaps his spirit and that of The Dragonheart will inspire me."

I did not sleep well. Ráðgeir Haakensson's words had raised doubts in my mind. I was up well before dawn and went down to the Water. Despite the chill I walked into it naked and plunged my head below the surface. I knew that Dragonheart believed the spirit of my great grandmother flowed through the water and allowing her spirit to bathe me could only help. I then stood and with a cloak around my shoulders faced west to look at the Old Man, Olaf the Toothless. I was patient and as the sun rose behind me, I saw his features form as the first rays of dawn seemed to paint them on the rock. When I saw his smile then I knew that the spirits of the clan were with me.

Erik was seated at the table and Gertha was ladling porridge into a bowl She smiled, almost apologetically at me, "I thought I had offended you, lord, and you had gone back to Hawk's Roost."

"No, Gertha, I am not Dragonheart, but he taught me well. You were right to chastise me and I was too eager." She nodded and left. I nodded to Erik, "You look better."

"Being back here in the home of Dragonheart was like a feast for me. I feel like I could take on the world. When do we return to Moi?"

"You are not yet in a condition to return and I have no ship. Atticus taught you to use the scribe and wax tablet?"

He frowned, "Aye, but what has that to do with the rescue of your family?"

"You are not a sailor, but you know the places we seek. I need you to make a map of the land through which we will travel. I will then make it into a chart." He nodded. Gertha brought in some small beer and porridge with honey. As I ate, I gently questioned Erik. "You say there were other slaves from the Land of the Wolf?"

"That is what I heard but I saw none." He put down his spoon and began to smear butter on the still-warm bread Gertha had fetched in. "I would not have known them, lord, would I?"

He was right, of course, and I would probably not know them. They would know me. "You say there are warriors who guard the stronghold. How many?"

"I did not manage to get inside, lord, and so it would be a guess. Perhaps forty?"

"Mail? Weapons?"

"Only a few had mail. Uddulfr and his oathsworn all had mail byrnies and good swords although they did not normally wear them. I saw them wear mail when he was visited by another hersir who came in a drekar. There was also a jarl who regularly visited. He had a large drekar. Uddulfr had eight oathsworn who guarded him. The rest wore metal-studded leather or simply tunics. Most had spears."

"And archers?"

"I saw few of them."

"And the other places where you were, what of the men there?"

"There were not large numbers of mailed men. The hersir who ruled them and their oathsworn were the ones I would fear."

I smiled, "Then you know why I ask these questions?"

He nodded, "It could be The Dragonheart asking them."

"Except he would not have got himself into this position, would he?" It was an unfair question and Erik just ate his bread. "And what of drekar you saw? Were any as big as *'Dragon's Breath'*?"

He shook his head, "I sailed the waters for many months, and I saw a number of drekar and snekke. Most of them were threttanessa with twelve or sixteen oars on each side. I saw none of them double crewed.

11

There was just the one large drekar which visited Moi. Uddulfr's is a threttanessa, '**Loki's Revenge**'. To the north of Moi, perhaps a hundred mile or so is Hafrsfjord where Finehair won his kingdom. Stavanger is the town where he keeps many of his ships. When we traded there, I saw many drekar. Not all were manned but it was an indication of how many men are under his command."

I smiled for Erik showed that he had not forgotten anything my great grandfather had taught him. A double crew meant two men to each oar. Larger drekar could be tripled crewed. I had seen drekar with twenty oars on each side and if they were triple crewed then there would be a hundred and twenty men!

"I will leave today and after going to my home I will ride to find us a ship."

"I will come with you!"

"I need you to regain your strength and to make me my map!" He nodded. "I will see Bacgsecg the weaponsmith and see if he has a byrnie for you." Bacgsecg and his family had been making weapons and mail for the clan since the time of Prince Butar. The greatest of them had made the sword that was touched by the gods. Although Bacgsecg was good his namesake had been the best.

He shook his head, "I was a shield-bearer lord. My skill is with a bow."

"A metal-studded jerkin and a helmet then. I would have you protected!"

I left Ráðgeir Haakensson with my commands. I wanted the word spreading that I needed warriors who would go raiding with me. I did not specify the destination. I had been burned once by spies in my land and as only Erik and Ráðgeir Haakensson knew what I intended then I would keep it that way. I sailed across the Water to my home at Hawk's Roost. It was no longer the stronghold it once had been, but it was still my home and, when I fetched back my wife it would be a stronghold once more. I would rescue my family or die trying.

Chapter 2

Barely twelve people now lived in Hawk's Roost and they reflected my mood. Valborg was the widow of Ulf who had died in the Finehair wars. Her son, Uggi, had been wounded and acted as my steward. There were just four servants and two oathsworn who lived in the huge halls and stronghold. Farbjorn and Halfgrimr were both young warriors. They had come from Cyninges-tūn when Fótr had rescued me. They had impressed me with their courage for despite having neither mail nor helmet, they had fought with spear and seax as fiercely as any Ulfheonar might have done. They had stayed by my side when we had scoured the land of the Norse and asked to be my oathsworn. They had not let me down, I had done little about rescuing my family, but I had made myself stronger and trained the two during my indolent time. Now I was happy that they would watch my back.

All of my household was keen to know what had kept me in Cyninges-tūn overnight. I told them of the return of Erik. All knew of the young standard-bearer who had stayed with Dragonheart and Haaken One Eye. It was he had composed the saga of their death. I did not tell them that I might be heading to Norway for I needed to speak with Fótr the Wolf first. "Halfgrimr, you will come with me when we ride to the coast. Farbjorn, you need to make my home strong for if we do sail then I want Hawk's Roost protected!"

We did not wear mail when we rode the horses west. The land was quiet, and the journey was not a long one. The days when the road would have passed through prosperous farms were long gone. Farms needed men to tend the animals and to sow crops. The women and children who had survived the wars had fled to the safety of towns like Cyninges-tūn; the Land of the Wolf had changed when the Norwegians had won. Ylva's mother had run a hall for women who were widows or had a similar calamity and it still provided a refuge. The women there were given work to do and they prospered. Often they remarried but Kara's hall was still necessary.

Halfgrimr had seen twenty summers and he was strong. It was his grandfather who had brought his family to the Land of the Wolf when they had fled the islands where Finehair had first begun to exert his influence. With his blond hair and beard, he was everyone's vision of a Viking. I did not look like a pure Viking. The Dragonheart had the blood of the old people, the Walhaz, in his veins as well as the Saxon from his father and that had passed to me through my father. My mother was from the people of Om Walum. Although we had not taken our

13

mail, we had brought our helmets and shields. It marked us as warriors and warned any bandits who might inhabit the quieter trails that we would be a dangerous mouthful to take. Although the journey would be safe the lack of farms and farmers, not to mention lords to rule the land meant that there were bandits and men who lived outside the law. If their presence was reported then we did something about them but often the bandits preyed on isolated families. While we rode the road to Fótr's stad we would watch for deserted buildings and signs of trouble. Skelwith was the last place which could be considered occupied and the headman of the small community had been crucial when Fótr had come to find me. Egge tried to make us stay the night, but I was anxious, now that I had begun the journey, to reach Fótr as soon as possible. Travelling north to Skelwith had added seven miles or so to our journey but it would tax our animals less for it was a flatter route and would also allow me to see more of my people. There was little point in taking the high trails over heath and moor.

Following the Esk, we passed a few small farms where families still made a good living. I was relieved, as we spoke to each one as we watered our horses, that there had been little sign of brigands. It was getting on towards the setting of the sun when we came across people I did not immediately recognise. These were Fótr's folk who had come east with him from the New World. They knew me and the red dragon on my shield marked me as Dragonheart's heir. Fótr had told me that when they lived in the New World, the land of the bear, they had not used a stad but had been spread out so that none lived on top of a neighbour but were close enough for them to visit. So it was here and there was no one place which could be defended except for the land around Fótr's hall. Having said that the leading warriors, Æimundr Loud Voice, Aed, Padraig, Ebbe, Fótr and Bear Tooth each had a hall with a ditch around it and a single entrance. By the time the two of us had reached Fótr's hall, some of the other warriors had come from their own homes to see who had come to visit. I saw that Fótr's hall now had a stone path which led to a wooden dock where the drekar was moored. There were houses and halls lining the stone path. I did not see the snekke and assumed she was fishing, and I wondered what had happened to the Hibernian ship they had captured.

Fótr had been young when he had first returned to this land but the war we had fought and his experience in Myrddyn's cave had made him grow older quickly. However, I still saw the young man who had rescued me in his eyes, his smile and his warrior's clasp.

"Lord Sámr, it is good to see you. You will stay the night?"

"Of course. This is my oathsworn, Halfgrimr."

"And you are welcome too." He turned to his wife, "Reginleif, we have guests. Fetch some of Ada's mead."

The hall was well made but did not look like our halls. Fótr later told me that they had developed this style of building on Bear Island. Not for the first time I yearned to visit this mysterious land. I knew I never would.

Even before we had sat down in front of the inevitable fire, which was kept burning every day of the year, the other senior warriors entered. Fótr was that kind of leader. He did not need men to bow and scrape. He had led his people across a whole ocean. They knew that he was their leader. Ebbe son of Ada had also helped to rescue me and, along with the Skraeling, Bear Tooth, the three of them were the heart of the clan. Æimundr Loud Voice was the old man of the clan. He had fought at Hawk's Roost but that would probably be his last battle; he would not go to war again. He was grey and looked like an old man, but I knew that Fótr valued his opinion and his advice for he was a connection with the past and his father, Lars the Luckless.

When Bear Tooth came in, I barely recognised him for they had shaved part of his head when he had rescued me and now he looked like a Viking; a dark-haired one but a Viking nonetheless. Reginleif and, what looked like Fótr's son, Erik, came in with a jug of mead and some horns.

Ada, who was Ebbe's mother, stood behind Erik and she beamed, proudly, "Here, Lord Sámr, have some of the finest mead you will ever taste. We missed having great quantities of honey when we were on Bear Island but here the bees enjoy the wild thyme and flowers. Now we can not only make it but have enough to be generous with it. On Bear Island, we eked out the small quantity we were able to produce. Taste it and tell me I am wrong!"

When the drinking horns were filled Fótr raised his, "Dragonheart's heir and the Lord of the Land of the Wolf!" As the toast echoed around the hall, I felt a fraud!

It was a delicious mead. Good mead was a fine balance of the sweetness of the honey and a sharpness which I appreciated. "You are right, Ada, I have never enjoyed so golden a mead and one which was as tasty. You should be proud!" I knew I had said the right thing when she hugged Erik, Fótr's son. I turned the conversation from me to Fótr and his people, "You prefer it here to Whale Island and Cyninges-tūn?"

Poor Fótr looked a little embarrassed, "I am sorry, Lord Sámr, if we caused offence but we are a close clan and while we now feel part of the Clan of the Wolf, we are more comfortable with neighbours with whom we have endured hardship." He paused, "I confess that we might have been able to live at Cyninges-tūn but it was too far from the sea."

"And Whale Island?"

He paused and I could tell that he was worried about offending me. I became suspicious. Had my indolence caused other problems? "The hersir there, Pasgen Sigtrygg, seemed to me to be one who liked power and the abuse of it and he did not make us welcome. If we had stayed there would have been blood. I am sorry if that offends you."

I smiled, "I am not offended, and you have done us a favour for this part of the land was always empty and subject to raids from Man and Hibernia but I wish that you had mentioned this to me. I need all of my folk to be happy."

Æimundr Loud Voice growled, "Aye, well the Hibernians learned of the danger of trying to raid us. There were twenty heads at the high tide mark until the last spring storm took them."

I liked Æimundr Loud Voice for he reminded me of some of the Ulfheonar, Olaf Leather Neck especially.

"And where are your own Hibernians?"

Fótr frowned and then smiled, "We do not think of Aed and Padraig as Hibernians. They have been with us so long we regard them as our folk. Aed is fishing and Padraig has taken the *'Hibernian'* to Dyflin to trade."

"*'Hibernian'*?"

"It is the name we gave to the ship we captured. She can carry cargo and it puts her to good use."

We chatted for a while and I learned that Bear Tooth was now a father. His son was called Aed and was quite a healthy child. Erik Fótrsson was also growing while Ylva Fótrsdotter was a heartbreaker. I saw that around her neck she wore the dragon token which Ylva, Dragonheart's granddaughter, had given to Fótr. The threads which bound us were strong.

Reginleif came in and asked, "Are you all eating with us?" It was spoken bluntly and was the signal for the others to return to their own halls. The hall seemed huge when they had all gone, and I sat with Halfgrimr and Fótr's family. It was a long time since I had eaten with a young family and it brought it home to me that I had been absent from my own home for too many times. Halfgrimr helped Reginleif and Erik Fótrsson clear the table. Fótr took us to the fur-covered chairs which were on either side of the fire. I did not recognise the animal which had become one of the furs. I guessed it had come from Bear Island.

"This is not a courtesy visit is it, Sámr Ship Killer?"

"No. I have discovered where my family have been taken and I intend to fetch them back."

He smiled and I was reminded what a calm character he was. He was not a wild Viking. From what I had learned his brother Arne was the wild one. "I promised that I would help you and I shall."

This was difficult for me as I was asking much of Fótr and I already owed him and his people my life and my land. "I will not hold you to that, but I would like to use your drekar."

He did not react but smiled and said, "And I am guessing that they are not held in the land of the Danes?"

"No, they were taken to Norway. Erik Black Toe found them."

"You do not wish me to come with you?"

I shook my head, "You have done so much for me already and you have a family. I would not tear you away."

He smiled and said, "But it is my choice if I come?"

"Of course."

"Then I will come. *'Gytha'* is special for although she is a drekar she comes from a New World. The blood of my clan lies within her. The prow was carved by my uncle. My aunt put her spirit within the keel and Erik and I built her. If any other than I sailed her then I do not know what the result would be. It is like when I used the sword of The Dragonheart. I did not feel in control. I know we won, and men said I fought well but that did not feel like me and if it was a ship then... I will come and although I am not my brother Erik and not a navigator, I will steer."

I could not help laughing, "You who were out of sight of land for so long are not a navigator? Of course, you are."

He nodded and continued to stare into the fire. "I would not bring my warriors. As you know Man and Hibernia are still threats. I would have my family protected. Have you a crew?"

"Not yet and when we do have one then they will have no experience of rowing a drekar."

"That matters not for we have until we reach Orkneyjar to train them."

I was surprised, "You have a route already?"

He laughed, "Perhaps I am a navigator then for all the time we have been talking I was working out a course which would take us to Norway. It is the reverse of the one my father took when he fled Orkneyjar and came to Larswick. I was but a child and do not remember it clearly, but I have the charts for Erik gave them to me. From Orkneyjar I do not know the way but unlike travelling west I know that, eventually, we will reach land!" He drank deeply from the ale, which was, in truth, very good and then said, "Despite the fact that I saved you I am no warrior. That was my brother Arne. I am not sure how much use I will be and, if as you say the crew will be inexperienced then it is warriors that you will need."

I nodded. "That has been on my mind too. This is where I miss a galdramenn or a witch, Aiden, Kara and Ylva were always able to see through things hidden from ordinary warriors. You see that I must do this, Fótr?"

"Of course. There is nothing more important than family. We have witches but they are not witches like Ylva. I can have them spin for us. That cannot hurt. I know that when we sailed here it was the spells which Helga, Ada and the others spun which helped."

Unbeknown to us Reginleif had entered. She held in her hand a seax, "Lord, if you would allow me, I would cut some of your hair to put into the spell."

I should have thought of that. It showed how long it was since I had been able to talk easily with a witch. "Of course."

She cut a good handful. My hair would look odd for a while, but I knew that the more strands and the longer the strands the more powerful would be the spell.

She left us and I knew that she would seek the witches and they would begin the process of spinning a spell to protect us and their ship.

"How many oars does the drekar boast?"

"When we built her, we made her a threttanessa, but she is not as narrow as most ships. That was Erik's doing. He knew she had to brave the deep oceans. '*Njörðr*' was built here in the east and she did not survive the return. '*Gytha*' can be double crewed and, in places, triple crewed if you wish. The hold is wide and deep. As we will not be trading, we can take plenty of supplies."

"And how long for the voyage?"

I saw him rub his chin and he smiled, "I was a child when my father sailed the clan away from Finehair's grasp. The journey seemed interminable, but I think it would take no more than five or six days to reach Orkneyjar. There are currents from the south and west which will help us but the passage to Norway?" He shrugged, "I know not."

"The Dragonheart said that the voyage across the open sea would take up to five days. I have Erik Black Toe making a map for he sailed the seas around the coast in a knarr."

"The sooner I can speak with him the better. I know the questions which I must ask."

Just then Reginleif returned and with her, she had Ebbe and Bear Tooth. Fótr stood and frowned. It was then that I realised that the three of them were little more than youths. For all that they had done was I expecting too much from Fótr? I needed a greybeard. And then I remembered Erik Short Toe who had been trained by a Greek Captain, Joseph. He had been the captain of Dragonheart's drekars and there was none better.

"You thought to leave us, Fótr?"

"Ebbe, Bear Tooth, this is not your fight. I owe Sámr Ship Killer. You two can stay and watch the clan."

Bear Tooth shook his head, "We are brothers of the blood. Your brother saved my life and I have left my home to follow this clan. Do not dishonour me by leaving me here. I am a warrior!"

Ebbe nodded his agreement and added, "And I have neither wife nor children. I will voyage with you."

"You have your mother."

"And she has your brother's children now. She needs not me; besides you need someone to watch your back and that will be Bear Tooth and me! This is not a matter for a Thing, Fótr. We have decided and we will come."

Despite his apparent protest, I could see that Fótr was happy at their inclusion. This was *wyrd*. Three was a magical number and the three of them might make the Norns less vindictive towards our enterprise.

The next day I went aboard the drekar. I had not been aboard a warship for some years and yet there had been a time when I had led my small fleet of drekar to keep the seas off our coast safe! How things had changed. It was a well-made vessel, but I noticed that I did not recognise the wood of the keel. The deck and the mast were a pine but the strakes, the withy and the other wood was a redder wood than we used. I saw what Erik the Navigator had done. He had sacrificed a little speed to give the vessel more stability. If we had to flee then that might come to hurt us. The broader beam, however, had allowed them to make the mast a little higher than was normal and that meant that if there was a wind then they might be able to outrun an enemy. The ship was an enigma, but I liked the feel of her. I ran my hand along the steerboard and even though she was young for a drekar I could feel that the voyage across the sea had worn the steering board as smooth as a veteran.

Fótr said when I had been all around the drekar, "We have spare oars. They can be carried below the deck."

I nodded and saw that while the captured Hibernian ship had not returned the snekke had. "Did your brother make that one too?"

He nodded, "We made that in Orkneyjar, and I helped him. She is a lovely boat and she survived the storm in the Great Sea which destroyed our other drekar. She is a ship of war but a small one. We will not leave the stad without defences."

I left before noon. We had a long ride home and I had much to do. "I will bring Erik back the next time I visit."

"Aye, and by then the spell should be finished and we can sew it on to the sail."

I was in such a positive mood that we made it back to Hawk's Roost before the sun had set. We could begin to prepare for war. I used Halfgrimr and Farbjorn to take messages to those who were the lords of my towns. I asked them to come to speak to me. It was courtesy. I had a responsibility to the land of the Wolf and I was keenly aware that I might not return. I would be sailing with a single drekar and an untried crew into the heart of King Harald Finehair's lands. The odds of our survival were slim!

My hall still felt empty and deserted. When Baldr and his family had lived there it seemed impossible to find space to even think. Now I yearned for such noise. Had my son and daughter not been taken then, by now, they might have been considering marrying and having children of their own. Ylva would be ready to bear children and Ragnar to father them. If Finehair had not sent his men then I would be a grandfather. Baldr had had plans for his children too. At least I knew that mine lived and where they were. As I sat and ate the food which Valborg had prepared, I wondered how many others of the Clan of the Wolf were slaves and thralls. Mine had been taken to Norway and I knew why that was. The Norwegians had feared Ylva. Even in death, they feared her spirit. Loughrigg and the Rye Dale had been assiduously avoided by Finehair's men. They had decimated the land and then stayed south and north of it. Perhaps they feared the spirit of The Dragonheart.

I called over Uggi, "I need my mail cleaning, Uggi, and weapons preparing. I want my Saami bow and arrows. Both of my swords will need to be sharpened and I want my father's spear, Blood Letter, sharpened and burnished."

"Aye lord. You will be leaving?"

"I seek my family, Uggi. Until I return then Bjorn Asbjornson will be lord of the land."

He started to leave and then turned, "Lord, do not throw your life away. The land has begun to recover, and people return to the Land of the Wolf."

I shook my head, "My family comes first. I have tarried too long and even now it may be too late."

"Then stay!"

I patted my heart, "Here is empty, Uggi. The Land of the Wolf is great, but it cannot fill it. Do you know the story of Dragonheart and the Hibernians?"

He shook his head, "I have heard all of the great sagas and the story of the sword but not that one."

"Sit, and hear it while I finish off this ale. When The Dragonheart lived on Man his family was taken as slaves by the Hibernians. Even though they were outnumbered he took a handful of men, Ulfheonar, and he rescued them. Not only that he found Aiden."

"Aiden!" Uggi's hand went to his hammer of Thor. "He was a powerful wizard."

"And it was he and Kara the witch who protected this land. That protection is gone. So, you see I must go and fetch back my family. How else can I face Dragonheart in Valhalla?"

"You think that you will find a wizard or a witch there?"

I downed my horn of ale, "The sisters spin and their threads are long. I am a warrior and I follow my sword and fight for mine. That is all that a man can do. That was Dragonheart's way. He chose his end and he thought to save his land. His faith in me was misplaced."

I sailed to Cyninges-tūn the next morning. I met Erik Black Toe at the Water. He was waiting for me. "I was told a boat had put off from Hawk's Roost and I came to greet you." He pointed to the steam hut. I do not think any had used it for years, "I recall sitting in there with Haaken One Eye and Dragonheart." He chuckled, "The two were like an old married couple. They would argue all the while, but they were as close as brothers. I was honoured to be allowed to sit there with them. I learned much. If I had learned more, I might have acted sooner to try to save your family."

"I am more remiss for it was my family and I was the steward of the land." I waved a hand as though to dismiss the negative thoughts. " I have a ship! When I have spoken with Ráðgeir Haakensson we will fetch your belongings and return to Hawk's Roost. That is where I will begin the muster. I will send you with Halfgrimr and Farbjorn to Fótr's stad. He wishes to speak with you."

"I have heard this warrior's name, but I know little about him."

"He comes from a clan which is as important as the Clan of the Wolf; perhaps more so. They fled Finehair many years ago and sailed across the empty sea to the north and west." I smiled when Erik clutched his hammer of Thor. "They found the Land of Ice and Fire and when they left there, they found land which was so green that they found vines and so many animals that they thought it was a paradise."

"Yet they returned."

21

"The Norns, Erik, they spin, and they weave. I will let you ask Fótr about that and he will tell you the reason. He has crossed a great sea where he sailed for weeks without sight of land so you can be confident that we will reach Moi." I hesitated, "Will you come with us?"

"Of course. This Fótr may be the navigator but I have seen the stronghold and know where they are kept. I will come and this time I will have a sword and shield. They will pay for what they did to me and to your family. A Viking does not forget and never forgives."

When I reached the hall in which Dragonheart had lived I found that there were men, young men, who wished to go a-Viking with me. It was not simply the adventure they sought. The eight who were there all came from Cyninges-tūn and their fathers and even a grandfather or two had been butchered by the men of Finehair. It mattered not to them that the men who had killed them had, in turn, fallen in battle when we had reclaimed our land. They wanted revenge on the King who had caused the pain their families had endured. I told them to make their own way to Hawk's Roost and I told Ráðgeir Haakensson my plans.

"I would come with you, Lord Sámr."

"No, Ráðgeir Haakensson, you must stay here. When men learn that Dragonheart's heir has taken the vengeance trail then they might seek to take my land. I go with the untried and untested. I go with the young. It is a gamble, but I will not gamble with the Land of the Wolf. Bjorn Asbjornson will help. I will speak with him before I leave but I will leave a ring of steel around the heart of my land."

He smiled, "I can hear Dragonheart in your voice." He nodded towards one of the young men who was hoisting his war-gear upon his back, "That is Ráðulfr Ráðgeirsson, my second son. He will represent my family. He is a good warrior but untested in battle."

"Then you know that he may not return."

"Aye, but if he fights alongside you and dies with his sword in his hand then his place in Valhalla is assured and he can tell Dragonheart that his father serves him still."

"When others arrive send them to Hawk's Roost. I will leave as soon as I have a crew. This will be the last conversation we have before I leave. When next you see me, I will have my family. If you do not, then the Norns have cut my thread and the last of Dragonheart's family will be gone!"

Chapter 3

Hawk's Roost began to fill up with the new warriors and servants Valborg felt we needed for the increased number of people we had to feed and house. They were all from across The Water and I knew that they could be trusted. Pay was not a problem for the Norwegians had not found Dragonheart's fortune which was well hidden. I would never be able to spend all the coins he had left to me. The warrior halls which had last housed the Danes who had tortured me had been cleaned and filled with fresh bedding. The young warriors began to bond. After my two oathsworn had returned I sent them with Erik to Fótr's Stad and I began to work with the young warriors. They knew how to use weapons; every Viking could do that but they had no idea how to battle. The three sisters had determined who would be the heart of my men for the first eight were the ones I first worked with. We began with the wedge.

"I will be the tip of the wedge. Behind me will stand Halfgrimr and Farbjorn. They are not with us yet and so two others will take their place. Behind them will stand, Ráðulfr Ráðgeirsson, Danr Danrsson and Ulf Olafsson. Come take your places." They did so and I showed them how to lock their shields together and how to present their spears. "Next comes, Gandálfr Eriksson, Qlmóðr the Quiet, Hrólfr Haakensson and Ketil Arneson. That leaves you, Asbjorn Ulfsson. The next four warriors who join us will flank you. Now let me see you all present your weapons." As they did so I went around to make adjustments. "Now push your shield into the back of the man before you." They did so. I smiled, "Now comes the hard part. I dare say that some of you will end up with wounds and bruises. They are the price you will pay to become warriors. Now we march. When we go to war we will sing a song of the clan but for now, we use the words shield foot and spear foot. We march around until I am happy and then we run around until you are one!"

I was right, of course, and when we ran, they tumbled. No warrior has a blunt spear and there were cuts. We were lucky that none lost an eye but by noon they could manage to run even over rough ground. As they ate the food and drank the ale which Valborg and Uggi brought, Ráðulfr Ráðgeirsson asked, "Lord, why did we not begin with the skjalborg, the shield wall? We have practised that."

"And that is one reason why I did not start with that. The other reason is more important. You are the first to be here and you will be the ones who follow me into battle. The eleven of us must think and act

23

as one. This formation is the one which we will have to use to break down the enemy. We will be outnumbered when we reach our destination." I let that sink in. I wanted no misunderstanding. "We will break their line by using this formation. We have no time to learn how to run at a skjalborg and jump high into the air to break it. We use the wedge and our bodies like a battering ram. My oathsworn will protect me and you three, Ráðulfr Ráðgeirsson, Danr Danrsson and Ulf Olafsson will thrust your spears over our heads to help us. The deeper into the enemy line we go the more of you will be needed. The ones at the back use their weight in the fight. When a man falls then the next one steps up to take his place. We do not stop for wounded. When we win, we will return to tend to you."

The afternoon saw their skills improve and I had them spar with shield and spear. I spent time, in the evening, talking with each of them to learn about their special skills. All warriors have skills and a good leader uses them. I learned which ones were good archers and who could use a sling, I found out the ones who preferred an axe. I learned of the reasons for their presence. Each told me, in gory detail of the death of the family member which had made them choose this route and that gave me an insight into their character. When we went to war I would know what made each of those behind me fight! I allocated their duties as guards. I did not think that we would need them, but it was good to become used to that skill. I wanted them to see the phantoms here in the Land of the Wolf and not when we anchored on some lonely island.

The next morning four more recruits arrived along with my two oathsworn who had ridden since before dawn from the coast. We were now able to practise the wedge with more men. I decided to wait until the others arrived before I taught them a chant. We would have the march to Fótr's stad to do that. During the day another eight men arrived and the first thing we did was to put them in the wedge. The evening was a repetition of the first but now the ones who had been there a day longer were able to pass on their stories. We were becoming a warband. We had more men on duty. We did not need it but I wanted them to get used to losing sleep and still working hard the next day.

Bjorn Asbjornson arrived the next day with nine warriors and two of his oathsworn as bodyguards. My own oathsworn continued the training, this time using the shield wall. I stood with Bjorn on the gatehouse. I remembered him bringing the men of Cyninges-tūn to our aid and I could never repay him for that had saved the Land of the Wolf.

24

"Lord Sámr, let me come with you. The ones I brought, as you asked, are young men. You need some grey hairs amongst them!"

I flicked my own beard, "This is all the grey hair we need. Besides, I fear that our enemies will take advantage of our absence to raid us. There will still be spies in our land; of that, I have no doubt. There is another reason. When The Dragonheart was a young man he and the other young men, Haaken One Eye, Bjorn the Scout, the Shape Shifter and all the others were young men. They had no mail, but they fought as one. We remember them as old men but they began as young ones. I train the next generation. I do not know how many will return but they will be better warriors for it and they will have fought together. There are few like you and Ráðgeir Haakensson left. You hold on to what we have and then pass it to the young."

"I had not thought of that. Then I will do as you ask but I fear for you. I know why you have to do this, but you have set yourself a mighty task."

"A task such as The Dragonheart would have undertaken? Like going to Om Walum? Fighting Egbert in Lundenwic? It is what we do, Bjorn, my family and my warriors." He nodded, "I would have you, if you will, keep men riding the land and watching the borders. If all goes well then in two moons, we should return but if we are not back in half a year do not worry."

Bjorn stayed the night and left the next morning. As I was preparing my horse another twelve men arrived and I left Halfgrimr and Farbjorn to train them.

"Where do you go, lord?"

"I go to Myrddyn's cave to speak with Ylva and The Dragonheart."

"One of us should come with you."

I laughed, "There I am close to Úlfarrberg and do you think that Ylva's spirit would fail to protect me? I will return by nightfall. Perhaps I will test the mettle of our new sentries."

I took a cock with me to make a blót. Its noise kept me entertained all the way to the Rye Dale. I spoke with Egge at Skelwith and Arne at the Rye Dale, but they were the only ones I saw. When I left Skelwith I saw, in the distance, Bjorn Asbjornson and his two oathsworn as they headed back to Windar's Mere. Our paths diverged when I turned north to the Rye Dale. I walked my horse up the scree-covered path. When Fótr and I had been there last, Ylva's final act had been to cause a landslide and bury the cave. None had been there since as the rocks which had cascaded down the slope still remained. I knew that at some time in the future the stones would be moved as they could be used for building but so long as the memory of Ylva lingered at Loughrigg then no Viking would touch them. I tied the horse to the last tree and carried the cock to what had been the entrance to the cave. It was now a mass of fallen rocks. I saw a large flat one and I climbed up to it.

I intoned the words for they were for the dead. "Ylva and Dragonheart I come here today to apologise for failing to protect the Land of the Wolf. I swear that I will make amends. I come here to make a blót and I beseech you to protect our men as we go to rescue my family!"

I used my seax to slit the throat of the bird and laid it on the rock. I took my sword from my sheath and squatted with it across my legs. I closed my eyes and began to breathe slowly. I had no idea if Ylva would be able to speak with me. In a perfect world, I would have built a steam hut and waited until dark, but this would have to do. If she did not come, I would just accept it. The times I had spent in the steam hut with Dragonheart had taught me how to enter my own mind and shut out the world. I saw blackness and then images appeared. Even though my eyes were closed I still saw the Scar of Nab. And then I heard a voice. Until then I had heard my own voice and my questions. Now I heard Ylva. I did not see her, but I heard her in my head.

'Sámr, kinsman, you do yourself a disservice. Since you retook your land there has been peace and our people prosper. The new blood in the clan has made it stronger. The Clan of the Wolf is returning to its proper dominion. What is it that you wish?'

I said the words in my head, 'Ylva, great sorceress and witch, we sail to the place where Dragonheart was named. I ask you to invoke the help of the spirits. The crew I take are young and untried. I do not wish to waste their lives.'

'And you will not. Fótr the Wolf was sent for a purpose. Had he not returned across the seas then what you contemplate would be impossible. Use the Skraeling and use Fótr. He is not just a navigator. He is a warrior although he does not yet know it. Now you must go. All the time I can give you is gone but the spirits will listen. Trust in me. Trust in yourself and trust the warriors you lead.'

I opened my eyes and was amazed at the time which had passed. It was now the middle of the afternoon. I returned to my horse which had grazed happily beneath the tree and I headed for Hawk's Roost. I would have one more night there and then the great adventure would begin.

I did not ride my horse to the coast for we did not have enough for all of my men. Another five had arrived during my absence and I wanted all of us to be as one. I told Uggi that any more who arrived should be used to guard my walls. I would need more men if and when I returned. We used my eight ponies to carry our war gear. Only three warriors, apart from my oathsworn, had mail. They were short byrnies handed down from dead warriors. All had their swords, helmets, shields and spears. We marched west.

I began to sing the song of the birth of Dragonheart as a warrior. Some had heard it, but none knew it. It took six miles for them all to be able to sing it but that was good for we were at the bottom of the high pass which led to the sea and it was a hard slog to climb it. The song gave us rhythm and brought us all together. I would teach them more but this one honoured my great grandfather and it was right that this one should be their first.

From mountain high in the land of snow
Garth the slave began to grow
He changed with Ragnar when they lived alone
Warrior skills did Ragnar hone
The Dragonheart was born of cold
Fighting wolves a warrior bold
The Dragonheart and Haaken Brave
A Viking warrior and a Saxon slave
When Vikings came he held the wall
He feared no foe however tall
Back to back both so brave
A Viking warrior and a Saxon slave
When the battle was done
They stood alone
With their vanquished foes
Lying at their toes
The Dragonheart and Haaken Brave
A Viking warrior and a Saxon slave
The Dragonheart and Haaken Brave
A Viking warrior and a Saxon slave

We were still singing it when we wearily walked towards the sea and the drekar which awaited us. There was still no sign of the Hibernian ship but the snekke was tied up. Fótr, Ebbe, Bear Tooth and Erik greeted us. Fótr waved a hand at the warriors I had brought, "We cannot accommodate all of these warriors in our halls. Some will have to sleep on the drekar and others, outside."

I smiled, "It matters not for there will be far greater hardships when we sail."

"We know that, but Erik has told us that the men you lead have not been to sea. Will they be able to do so? I know that we had some folk

27

who thought the voyage west would be easy and many had to be persuaded not to turn back."

"These are volunteers and they will manage. Halfgrimr, see to their accommodation."

"Aye, lord. Unpack those ponies and when I call your name come to me. Half will sleep on the drekar and the other half on the dock! We will make Vikings of you!"

I hid my smile; Halfgrimr had never been to sea but he was my oathsworn and as such he would not show either fear or discomfort. He would endure it.

"Come inside and see the map we have made. Erik and I have worked closely since his arrival and we have worked out a route to take us there."

The change in Erik since he had first arrived from Whale Island was nothing short of remarkable. He now looked full of life and eager to sail once more. The two of them obviously worked well together and they showed me the route as though the two men were one. It did not matter to me what our route would be as I simply wanted to get to Moi and my family. We would be sailing for days out of sight of land and while these two had done that I had not. I had to trust them. I allowed them to go through the whole voyage before I spoke.

"You have done well, and I have complete faith in your plan. When can we sail?"

It was Fótr who spoke, "Lord Sámr, the men you bring are a new and raw crew. They have never rowed and never sailed together. We need to spend at least a couple of days with them rowing. I would go to sea and have Harald of Dyroy allocate the oars. When we sailed from Bear Island the oars were easy to allocate as we knew each rowers' strengths."

I nodded, "You are right, and I have forgotten that. I can see now that I have become old and did not realise it. Then tomorrow we row."

That night, as we ate, I learned that Padraig and Aed had taken their Hibernian ship north to buy seal oil, some of which they intended to trade at Dyflin. They would also buy some of the hardy sheep of the north and outer islands. They had learned much in the New World and one was the value of the right animal in the right place. Fótr told us of some of the animals they had found like the horse deer and bjorr. "Each had its own place and nature was in harmony. Here the valley bottoms suit cattle but the uplands have lush grass. If we had hardier animals, then the sheep could stay on the lower slopes during winter. We would not have to cull as many."

His planning and clear thoughts put me to shame. I had been too inward-looking. I had retreated to Hawk's Roost even before King Harald Finehair had sent his men to take my land. I had been Dragonheart's heir, but I had not even begun to replace him. I now realised that it had been Ylva who had led the people and when she had sacrificed herself then the Land of the Wolf was without a leader. I found myself fingering the wolf I wore around my neck. My great grandfather had given it to me.

The next morning the crew who would sail were assembled on the dock. Harald of Dyroy was an old man but he had a sharp eye. He walked along the warriors who would row and was not shy about prodding, poking and squeezing their muscles. He first pointed to Ebbe and Bear Tooth, "You two know the drekar and I know your strengths. You have grown from youths to men and you two shall have the first oars. Ebbe to steerboard and Bear Tooth to larboard." The two clambered aboard and, after placing their chests down as a seat, chose an oar. The ones at the fore would have the best oars. He then went down the line until every oar was manned. The ones who were left looked disappointed. He then went down and placed a second warrior next to the first. When that was done there were still warriors left. "The rest of you, and that includes Lord Sámr, will take over when the rowers flag. Fótr will make that decision for at sea he is the master! You will also hoist and lower the sail when commanded." The man was not afraid of upsetting me and I nodded. He pointed to Erik Black Toe, "You will have to learn to steer and to navigate when Fótr sleeps. I know that you can be taught for your skill when we made the map was clear to me." He turned to me, "I offered to come for you will need skilled men but Fótr said I should stay here."

"And that is right, Harald of Dyroy. You are correct, we do lack experience but so did you before you set off across the Great Sea."

"Aye, lord, you have the right of it!"

We had no shields for we were not going to war and getting over the gunwale was easy although carrying the chest aboard was not. I was the last on the drekar and I placed my chest by the mast fish. Halfgrimr and Farbjorn were at the oars behind Ebbe and Bear Tooth. The front oarsmen would be the ones who set the pace. We all had much to learn. Fótr patted the gunwale and said, "Lord Sámr, join me here for I need your knowledge about the men you brought."

Guilt filled my head for I barely knew the men I had brought. Dragonheart would have known every warrior. Despite my misgivings, I nodded. He pointed to two of the men who had not been allocated an oar and stood near to the mastfish. Fótr had told me that had been the place the women had sat during the long voyage. There was more room than on any other drekar I had seen. "What are your names?"

"Rolf Red Hair, Captain."

"Buthar Faramirson, Captain."

"You two get back on the dock. You will untie the ropes and, after pushing the drekar, jump aboard." He smiled at me, "We normally have ship's boys for such tasks. Here we will use men." He nodded to them, "When we reach an anchorage or a port your task is to jump either into the water or on to the dock to tie us up."

The two clambered over the side and awaited his command.

Fótr shouted, "We will not need the sail today. That lesson is for tomorrow. By the end of this day your hands will bleed, and you will curse me." He laughed, "That is good for tomorrow will be worse. Now oars up!" The oars came up and I saw Harald of Dyroy frown; it had been a ragged cast off! The two men from Cyninges-tūn gave a mighty push and leapt. The drekar began to move with the tide and there was soon a gap. "Larboard oars out and push us from the dock. Steerboard oars at the ready."

I saw the wisdom of Ebbe and Bear Tooth being at the front oars, the ones behind could simply follow what they did. It might be a heartbeat later, but they had a model.

Once we had clear water, I watched Fótr push the steering board over, noting that Erik's eyes had never left Fótr. "Row!"

It was laughable. The front four oars on each side bit almost at the same time but the rest did not and, even worse some oars fouled the others. It did not bode well.

Fótr merely nodded and shouted, "Keep on rowing until you are in time with your fellows." He nodded to Erik who began to sing. It was the saga he had composed when my great grandfather and Haaken One Eye had died. I had never heard it sung on a drekar.

The Dragonheart was truly named
With a sword and spirit rightly famed.
All enemies knew his heart was true
Each foe was dealt what he was due.
The land he made is a land which is strong
Filled with warriors who there belong
You have not died, you are just at rest
Of all the warriors you were the best
When the land has need you will return
With a sword from Odin, all will burn
We mourn you and we curse the Dane

30

But were ever the Danish Bane
Dragon heart who was the Viking Brave
Born to lead and taken as a Viking Slave
Dragon heart who was the Viking Brave
Born to lead and taken as a Viking Slave

Ebbe and Bear Tooth had never heard the song, but they began to sweep their oars in time to the saga. I knew then that Fótr and Erik had discussed this. The beat was one for a long voyage and not when attacking. It was good. I began to remember it and joined in. Some of those who were rowing had heard it and sang the parts they knew. Erik and I kept singing and more and more joined in. Even Ebbe and Bear Tooth who had never heard it began to sing. Its effect was nothing short of miraculous. Within eight renditions of the song, the oars all dipped at the same time. We were far smoother. The smile on Fótr's face told me that he was happy.

It was when he said, "Lord Sámr, where is the land?" that I realised the true result of the song. I looked astern and the Land of the Wolf was a thin line to the east.

We rowed for an hour. I saw that Fótr had an hourglass and he kept glancing at it. He shouted, "Replacement rowers start to change from the front. Lord Sámr next to Bear Tooth!"

I had to stand next to the gunwale and wait to be able to slip onto the chest. It was so many years since I had rowed that I was nervous. Ráðulfr Ráðgeirsson slid out and I slid in and grasped the smooth oar. The wood was not one I knew. I began to row, and it was only when I did so that I remembered it was better to row without a sword strapped to your waist. It was too late to do anything about that. I heard cracks as some oars smacked into others but soon, we had the rhythm again. At first, I found it easy but then my hands began to chafe. I had an easier life now and the only exercise and hard use I put my body to was practising with the sword. Not only my hands hurt but my back complained, and my arms burned. By the time the next hour was up I was weary beyond words, but my ordeal was not over. We had stopped singing when we had changed rowers, but the beat was still in our heads.

I saw that Erik held the steering board and Fótr pointed to the men we had replaced, "Take over from the rowers who have not rested!"

This was easier to do for Bear Tooth was next to the centre of the boat and Ráðulfr Ráðgeirsson simply slid in and helped me to row. There was a barrel of ale by the mast fish and I saw those who had rowed for two hours join Ebbe and Bear Tooth to drink some ale. The

31

hands of the men I had brought were bleeding. I knew that mine would be too. When they had drunk, I saw Ebbe and Bear Tooth apply salve to the hands of their fellow rowers and then take pieces of hide from a chest to wrap around their hands. They could have done so before we started but I knew why they had not. We had to realise what we had to do and experience the pain. There would be worse hardships on our way east.

By the time the next hour was over, I was looking forward to the relief of not rowing. Fótr shouted, "Up oars!" I wondered why and then I glanced over the side and I saw that the dock was just twenty feet from our side. "Rolf Red Hair and Buthar Faramirson, tie us up!" My two men leapt over the side and, despite their bleeding hands tied us up. "Put your oars on the mast fish and go ashore! There is food waiting!"

After I had done as I was asked, I went to the steering board. Bear Tooth had some salve there. He grinned, "You did well for an old man, Lord Sámr, but this will help. The witch of the clan, Gytha, after whom this ship is named made up this salve on Bear Island. What we will do when it is all used, I know not but it works. Rub it on your hands and then bind them with this deer hide. We hunted these deer when we were close to my home. It will help when we row again this afternoon!"

I groaned inside for I had hoped we had done enough for the day. I realised that I was being foolish and resigned myself to the pain. By the time it was late afternoon and we had finished for the day we had all rowed what seemed like the distance from Whale Island to Dyflin and back! That evening as we ate, I could barely keep my eyes open. Bear Tooth was right, I was an old man. Fótr and Erik were in good spirits.

"The crew did far better than I might have hoped, Lord Sámr. We may be able to leave the day after tomorrow if they handle the sails as well as the oars."

I held up my hands, "With hands like these?"

"The salt air of the open sea will help, and we should not need to row for as long. I wanted a three-hour row in case we hit adverse winds on our voyage and have to row to flee a foe."

I saw now that despite his lack of years Fótr knew his business. "You say that your brother was the navigator?"

Fótr nodded, "He taught me, but he was without a single flaw. He was younger than I was when he took us west and found the Land of Ice and Fire. He did not seem to have to work at it. It was as though Njörðr himself had sired him. He knew what to do by instinct. I have to think about what I do the whole time."

The men were quiet and that, I think, was down to exhaustion. They would soon recover but it created a nagging doubt in my mind that they might not be ready for this. Did I dare risk them, Fótr and the drekar? Was my family worth it? I did not sleep well that night despite my weariness.

The next day we only had to row until we were out of sight of land. This would be a lesson for Erik Black Toe for he would need to learn to use the compass. Erik Fótrsson also came with us for, although he would not come to Norway, Fótr wished his son to learn to be a ship's boy and he shinned up the mast to sit on the cross tree as a lookout. I smiled as I watched his mother's face. Aethelflaed would have been the same. She was terrified. Ebbe and Bear Tooth were the ones who showed us how to raise and lower the sail. They taught us how to adjust the fore and backstays as well as the bowline, buntline and shrouds. I knew the names and their function, but my young crew did not. The Clan of the Wolf had long ago ceased to go a-Viking and those that had were long dead. It was hard work but different from the previous day and the crew would find that different muscles ached.

"Ship to the west!" Erik Fótrsson's voice made every head turn. Worryingly for me none, save Ebbe, Bear Tooth Erik Black Toe and myself reached for a weapon. Even my oathsworn seemed transfixed. A few moments late and Ebbe shouted, "It is *'Hibernian'*!"

Fótr shouted, "Reef the sail!" and the crew did as I had hoped they would do and leapt to obey. Ebbe and Bear Tooth had already identified the crew who had the most aptitude for sail work and Fótr would adjust the oars accordingly.

We hove to and the Captain, Padraig, and Fótr spoke to each other across the dark sea. I listened. The words I heard were worrying, "Captain, return to port, there is danger."

Fótr knew his people well and he merely said, "Do we need to travel together?"

"No, for the danger is not immediate but concerns the drekar!"

This would be a foreshortened day but Fótr was right to return to his home. We needed to discover the news. We reached there first for the Hibernian ship seemed like a pregnant cow in comparison to the drekar. The crew now knew that there were many tasks to be completed before they could go ashore and leaving Erik Black Toe to supervise, I went with Fótr, Ebbe and Bear Tooth to await Padraig.

"What can the danger be, Fótr?"

"It could be anything, Ebbe. He has just sailed to the islands and Dyflin. It could be news of Finehair or from Dyflin. Worrying about it will help no one. What will be will be."

I nodded, for one so young Fótr was wise, "It is the sisters, Ebbe, and they are spinning still. Fótr, is the spell on the sail yet?"

He shook his head, "I had intended to do it tonight! Perhaps I should not have delayed."

"I made a blót and that does not appear to have been heard. You are right. The Norns have spun."

The lumbering ship used sails rather than oars and we had the best berth for we reached there first. Eventually, she tied up just along from us and I saw a good crew at work. The ships' boys had her tied up so quickly that it was like a blur.

The two Hibernians were the first from the cargo ship. I had not seen them since I had met them when they first arrived, but they had not changed. It was Padraig who spoke, "Fótr, Lord Sámr, the men of Man know what you intend. They have ships watching the sea between here and Hibernia."

"They mean to take us?"

"No, Fótr, they intend to wait until you have sailed and then raid the stad. With the warriors gone they will enslave the people and take our treasures."

"You are certain?"

"We have friends there as well as family and they spoke truly. There is more. We have heard that there are men in your land who seek to take the Land of the Wolf from Dragonheart's heir. They were just rumours and we had no names, but we thought we should let you know that there is treachery abroad in the Land of the Wolf."

I looked at Fótr whose face had fallen. This had not been in our plans!

Chapter 4

"How did you learn of this?"

It was Aed who spoke. "We have made many friends in Dyflin through our trade. We are Hibernians as well as being of the Clan of the Wolf. We were told by one we trust. Word reached them almost a week since that Lord Sámr was going to take men across the seas. They did not know where you were going, lord, but they knew that the drekar would need many men. I fear that King Harald may well have heard the news and he would know your destination!" I nodded.

Ebbe asked, "Then, Fótr, what do we do to save our families? Do we take the drekar and seek them? Bring them to battle on the seas?"

Fótr shook his head, "We do not know where they are, and we have old men and young men. Neither is well suited to a sea battle. Would you agree, Lord Sámr?"

I was distracted for I had been thinking. I nodded, absent-mindedly, "What we could do is sail the drekar away and let them attack."

Padraig shook his head, "No, for we have women who are with child and cannot risk them."

I smiled, "There would be no risk for we would send the women and the children in the drekar. Fótr, how many men would it take to row the drekar?"

"*'Gytha'* is very forgiving. When we sailed east, we managed with just ten men. Why do you ask?"

"Padraig is right, pregnant women, the old and the very young cannot be risked. Suppose we made a show of loading the drekar but just crewed her with ten of your men who are too old to fight and under the command of Harald of Dyroy. If she sailed north with shields along the side, then they would assume we were leaving to raid. They would attack at night and we would be waiting."

Bear Tooth grinned and gave a yelp of joy, "That is good. I like that, Fótr, it would work."

Fótr looked at Ebbe who said, "Some of the women could take an oar too. They did when we came east, and the men of Man would not suspect anything. I like the plan too."

I looked at each of them and they all nodded. Fótr said, "Then I will speak with Harald and Æimundr Loud Voice. I will let Æimundr make the choice of who will go and who will stay," he smiled, "he is not a man to be crossed!"

I went to see our men. We would need some of them on board and I knew that they would be unhappy. They were but they accepted my command albeit with ill grace. My weapons needed no sharpening, but I told those who would be fighting to sharpen theirs. That night I sat with Æimundr Loud Voice, Fótr and the others who knew the stad well. We discussed our plans. I had to admire this small clan for they had built their settlement carefully and made it defensible when they had been building. There had once been a fishing community who lived here but they had been raided and enslaved so many times that they had left. Fótr, Ada and Æimundr Loud Voice had known what they wanted and created a community which appeared to live apart, but their homes were built so that each one was a separate fort. Fótr's, as the largest and most important, had a good ditch and a bridge which could be drawn in front of the door. It made it secure but to make it a place from which to attack they had put arrow slits in the top of the wall. Those wind holes acted to move the smoke up into the roof and kill vermin. It was clever. The other dwellings, while apart from each other were like a maze and when they had their door bridges up an enemy would be channelled through the settlement allowing ambushes at each house. We had all day to plan them. The men of Man would not come close until dark. If they did not come the first night, it was not a problem as the drekar had enough food aboard for two days. The snekke would bring news when it was safe for them to return.

I saw, the next day, that Fótr's people were far closer than mine were. Even though we were doing something so different from anything they had done before the whole of the settlement worked as one. There were smiles and there was cooperation. We had lost that when the Norwegians had come. The people who would be sailing in 'Gytha' were the ones who lived by the sea. Those who lived a half a mile away or more would stay in their homes and their men would join us for the fight. Shields were arrayed along the side of the ship and when the tide was at its height Harald of Dyroy set sail. Not all the women had gone. Reginleif, Ada, Anya and Helga had remained with their children. It was Ada who pointed out that the men of Man would be suspicious if they saw neither women nor children and the women would spin spells to confuse the enemy. They had swords and if it became necessary then they could fight. I did not think they would need to do so. When darkness fell, they would be safe in Fótr's hall. It was my men who had the harder task as they had to remain hidden close by the dock and the beach. Aed and Padraig took their snekke to fish, but they stayed less than a mile from the coast. I had Hrólfr Haakensson and Ketil Arneson climb the slopes to the small flock of sheep which grazed there above the stad. Without mail and helmets, they would be taken for shepherds and would act as sentries.

Fótr and I would have to stay hidden for we might be recognised and so we stayed inside Fótr's hall. He told me, as the long day passed, the full story of their flight from Orkneyjar, Larswick and the Land of Fire and Ice. It explained the resilience of his people and the fact that they were stoic about their fate. The blood of the Clan of the Wolf would be better for their presence. Already some of my younger warriors were casting admiring glances at some of the maids who had come from the west. Many of the girls had skin which was much darker than the maidens of Cyninges-tūn. As Fótr told me, the sun burned hotter in the west.

It was noon when Ebbe came to speak with us. "Hrólfr Haakensson came to warn us. He saw a drekar come from the west and then sail down the coast. He could not identify it but from his description, I think it was a threttanessa from Man. We will have confirmation when Aed and Padraig return."

After he had left Fótr said, "So they nibble at the bait. Will they take it?"

"We need them to. If they do not, then we cannot leave. From what you told me this is as it was at Bear Island. We have to hurt these warriors so much that they never again return." He nodded for he understood. "When The Dragonheart ruled this land, we had ships sent from Whale Island. They ensured that no pirate of Man, Hibernian slaver or Saxon ship would dare to attack us. For all Finehair's dreams of an Empire, all that he did was to destroy our drekar and then squat behind his walls. When I have my family back then we start again to build drekar. I will repair Bolli's shipyard at Úlfarrston and we will make ships. The men who I have brought with me will be the heart of the wolf which will defend our land. I will do as The Dragonheart did and make those who have the skill into hersir. They will captain their own ships. We do not need huge ships like *'Dragon's Breath'*. A well-handled threttanessa can be just as effective."

He said, quietly, "You may lose men this night which we need for the rescue. Have you thought of that?"

I shrugged, "The Norns spin and we are helpless to affect what they do but the sail now has the spell upon it, and I hope that Ylva's spirit will help us still."

I saw him smile, "I still feel her within me and although I do not wield the sword which was touched by the gods, when I use my own sword I feel more powerful than I did."

"I know what you mean." I patted the sword which Bacgsecg had made for me after we had ousted the last of the Norse from our land. "When Bacgsecg made this blade I still had a wound and we used the blood from my injury to temper it. Then he used water from the Water to seal it and I know that the spirit of Erika, Dragonheart's wife and my grandam, gave it power. We named it Viking Killer, but it has yet to taste blood. Tonight, we will test it."

"May I see?"

I slid it from the scabbard. The scabbard had been decorated by the women from Kara's Hall and it had spells woven into it. The sword itself was a copy of the lightning scorched blade my great grandfather had wielded. It was a one handed weapon with a short guard. The difference was that Bacgsecg had put a channel on both sides of the blade. I had asked him its purpose and he had told me that it made the blade lighter without taking away from its strength.

Fótr spun the sword and nodded, "It has a good balance and yet it is light. It is a little longer than the sword of Dragonheart."

I nodded, "Just a thumb but that can make a difference. Like my great grandfather's it has a sharpened tip. It was one of his blows he taught me. A strike at a mail link, if well struck by a good blade, can rip open the mail and end the fight. Most warriors fight with the edge which soon becomes blunted and then it is like fighting with an iron bar."

We spent a pleasant hour or so distracted from the worry of the battle as we talked of weapons. I had a pair of shorter weapons which I kept inside my sealskin boots. One was an old seax. It was a good slashing weapon and the other was a long dagger with a very narrow blade. I had fought men wearing face masks and the blade was perfect for ramming into an eye. I called them the Gutter and Eye Taker. It was important to name a weapon for when the weaponsmith gave it life then it needed to be named.

We watched the light from the arrow slits fade as the afternoon wore on. Aed and Padraig entered the hall along with the women who had been gutting fish at the fish hut. It was beginning.

Padraig said, "They have taken the bait. One ship came from the west and one from the south. The one from the south sailed up the coast but they could not have seen *'Gytha'* for Harald would have had her in the estuary at Ulf's Stad. They were threttanessa. They did not come close to us and when they had seen all that they wished they headed west."

Fótr nodded, "They want us to think they were from Dyflin and the people there are our friends. Were there any markings on the ships?"

Padraig shook his head, "No and the shields at their sides all had covers over them."

That alone told me that all that we had heard was true. When a Viking sailed, he wanted those he met to know who he was. His shield was a unique thing. No two were alike and they identified the warrior. The Dragonheart's red wolf had drawn enemies to him in battle. I had one which was almost identical but instead of a red wolf, I had a black one with red eyes and yellow teeth. The women in Kara's Hall had painted the leather before we had attached it to the shield and they had made the wolf look as though it was about to pounce. The black wolf was on a red background and so echoed my great grandfather's. My enemies had not seen it yet for it was new, but they would. The shield itself had a spell inside the grip and the double set of willow boards were glued in such a way that their grain went in two directions. With a metal rim and studded with metal from the arrowheads we had collected at Hawk's Roost after my rescue, it would blunt an enemy's weapons.

I stood, "We had better prepare for war!"

I had learned much when I had followed my great grandfather, not least the importance of preparing for war. The hall was crowded but I found space so that I was alone. I first donned the padded kyrtle which would help to spread the weight of the byrnie. Them, before I did anything else, I applied the red cochineal to my eyes and chin. The face mask on my helmet, a copy of The Dragonheart's, would cover the rest of my face. The red cochineal sometimes intimidated a younger warrior. Dragonheart and Haaken One Eye had taught me to take every advantage that I could. I then donned my padded arming cap. Many warriors did not bother with one but I found it made a tighter fit and absorbed blows to the head. Dragonheart had worn one! Then I donned the mail hood which covered the arming cap and my shoulders. Finally, I put on the mail byrnie. This was a new one. My own had been taken when I was captured. I missed my old one but the new one was well made by Bacgsecg and each mail link was attached to five others! It was strong. I attached my sword to my belt and slid one leather strap over my shoulder. I had found that it was easier to carry that way as some of the weight was supported by my upper body. I would not be using a spear and so I picked up my helmet and went to join the others. Darkness had fallen. My shield was behind the hall with the rest of the shields. They were hidden from view. Without speaking to the others, I went to pick up my shield. I hung it from my back so that my arms were unencumbered. When I needed to, I could easily swing it around.

The men I would be leading gravitated to me. My two oathsworn flanked me; they would not leave my side until they were dead, or we had won. Fótr and Æimundr Loud Voice would lead two-thirds of the men: those from the stad and half of my men. They would ambush the raiders in the stad. I would wait with my men, one-third of all of the warriors available, and we would sneak to the dock and attack them in the rear. First, we would take their drekar. I went around them checking their equipment. Some had leather straps on their helmets, but, in their eagerness to fight, they had failed to fasten them. I told them to do so. An unfastened helmet was a danger to all. We had all practised with shields and the swords we would use but some of the younger men were trying to appear casual and they had not fastened the leather strap around their back. Perhaps they thought to emulate me. My shield was over my back and would remain there unless we had to make a shield wall. I told them to fasten every strap. We had left Ketil Arneson on the fell slope. He had a lighted pot and it was hidden from view by a cloak. When the ships appeared, he would flash it towards us three times. Hrolf Haakensson was watching the slopes. We would see the light, but a convenient rock hid it from the sea.

There was the usual nervous banter. Even the Ulfheonar had not been silent before a fight. "The light, lord, they come!"

I nodded to Fótr, "May the Allfather be with you!"

"And with you."

Æimundr Loud Voice growled, "And let none of these slavers live! Let those at home wonder what happened to their menfolk."

I led my men towards the beach and when we reached it waited until I could see the ships. There were two threttanessa and they were edging, under oars, towards the dock. The men who crewed them knew what they were doing. They had made rolls of material which hung down the sides. They would stop the hulls from banging against the wood. The tide was low, and I led my men along the rocks which made an approach to the beach dangerous for a ship. The water came up to our knees, but the rocks masked our approach. I watched the men of Man as they flooded along the dock. I had done this before and knew that they would leave guards. There would be the ships' boys and men to defend the two ships against the likes of us. As we neared the dock, I waved the six men without mail who would swim along the sides of the drekar and climb aboard. I still had more than enough men to do the job. We waited, crouched against the fish hut which lay at the end of the dock. During the day it was the noisiest place in the stad as the women and children chattered while they gutted the fish which would be salted or brined in vinegar. Now it just stank of fish and afforded us cover. I slipped my seax from my boot. I would use Viking Killer and Gutter. This would be close in work and fighting in the dark needed two weapons.

40

I heard the first shout and then the roar as Fótr and Æimundr Loud Voice led the men to fall upon raiders who thought they had found a village full of sleeping women, old men and children. I raised my sword and we ran along the dock. We did not shout but we were not silent. Sealskin boots thudded on the wooden dock. The six sentries shouted the alarm, but their shouts were wasted. In the heat of the battle of the stad none would hear a word! The men left on guard wore no mail, but the ships' boys had bows. I ran hard and although I was almost twice the age of some of those who followed me, I reached the first two guards before they did. I slashed Viking Killer in an arc but did not slow and I rammed Gutter up under the arm of the man to my left. One spear clattered off my helmet, but it was securely fastened. The first raider dropped his spear for my seax had ripped through his armpit and tendons had been severed. My weight and Viking Killer had knocked the other to the ground and it was a simple act to slash Viking Killer across his unprotected throat. As arrows slammed into the shields of some of my men my six ship climbers had clambered up the sides of the drekar and the ships' boys were killed. There was no place for mercy! I was tempted to race towards the other guards, but I held back. I needed to see my men in action. Halfgrimr and Farbjorn, annoyed no doubt by my speed, had shields protecting me and I watched Haaken Ráðgeirsson lead Danr Danrsson, Ulf Olafsson, Gandálfr Eriksson and Qlmóðr the Quiet to dispatch the other four guards with consummate ease. Admittedly the men had no mail, but they had weapons and now were dead.

Asbjorn Ulfsson had led the ship climbers and he ran to me, "There are none left alive."

"You six guard the boat. The rest of you, follow me. We will see if you can remember how to make a wedge!" As I rapped out the command, I sheathed Gutter and swung my shield around. We needed shields if we were to use the wedge!

I knew this was risky as some of those who should be in the third and fourth ranks were not with us. This would be a test of their ability to think. I did not have to do anything. I stood there and my oathsworn stood behind me. We did not have the luxury of time for the attack by Fótr and Æimundr Loud Voice had been so ferocious and unexpected that the men from Man fled to return to their ships. Our plan had worked too well. We had had a handful of men blocking the dock to try to stop a drekar and a half of warriors. The sisters were spinning, and I knew that this was a test. I heard a horn and knew that it was a signal to the men of Man. They would fall back. They were not here for a glory raid to fight other warriors and go back with the treasure of weapons,

41

mail and honour. This was a slave raid and a robbery. Robbers and slavers do not stand and fight; they cut and run!

We stopped at the end of the dock where the trail from the stad met the wooden structure. The first of those who had fled emerged from the darkness between Aed and Padraig's homes. These were the ones who had no mail and could run faster. They stopped just ten paces from us. While there was no moon the shields, helmets and swords told the men of Man that they had been trapped. There was no way on to the dock except through us or if they wished to risk it, through the sea on the snekke side of the dock. I cursed myself. I should have had Haaken Ráðgeirsson put two men there. If the snekke was stolen, then it would be my responsibility. I put that from my mind as the first of the warriors formed their own hurriedly improvised wedge and ran at us.

I held my wolf shield before me and blocked the blow from the sword easily. Halfgrimr and Farbjorn jabbed their swords forward as I brought Viking Killer down from on high. The warrior tried to block with his shield. He partly stopped the strike, but such was the power of my blow that his shield cracked, and he cried out. I had hurt his arm. I had a metal boss on my shield and when I pulled it back and smashed it into his nose he fell backwards stunned.

"Forward!" Halfgrimr and Farbjorn had slain their men and as we stepped forward, I stabbed down at the stunned man below my feet. We moved off the dock and I said, "Shield wall!"

The effect was to prevent any more from entering the sea. I had seen at least four of them step into the water to try to get to the snekke. The flight from Fótr's stad was now a rout and that was always dangerous as we would have to stem a mighty tide. It was then that the man leading the men of Man in their rout went berserk. I had seen it before and I was not intimidated but I knew that the men around me, and that included my oathsworn would be. The powerfully built warrior bit on the edge of his shield and then hurled it towards us. This was a leader, perhaps even the one who had led the raid. Sometimes going berserk was the last resort and often resulted in victory. Aiden the galdramenn had once told me that men could make themselves go berserk by taking a potion. Some warriors painted the potion around the edge of their shields so that they could take the potion even in battle. I saw that Fótr and the rest of our men were hacking into the rear of the band which had stopped. No one interfered with a berserker. He licked the blood from the axe he held and yelling, "Odin!" raced at me for I was in the centre of the line or perhaps he recognised me.

I felt the rest of my men take a step back. I did not blame them, and, in many ways, it helped me as I now had room to swing Viking Killer.

This would be a test of my shield. He ran and leapt high in the air, screaming, bringing the axe over his head as he did so. Every instinct in me said to run but I knew that if I did, I would die, and the heart would go from my men. I braced my shield and began to swing my sword. His axe hit my shield a mighty blow, but I had swayed my body to the right and as the blow hit, I angled my shield. The axe caught on the boss as it slid down the side of the dragon shield. Before his body could hit me, Viking Killer had hacked into his left arm. He was still in the air and the blow not only cut flesh but also knocked him to the side. He crashed into the ground and I shouted, "Attack them!" to stir my shocked warriors into action. The berserker began to rise despite the fact that I had cut his left arm to the bone. The potion meant the man felt no pain. Even a fit man finds it hard to leap to his feet and I rammed my sword at his left shoulder while he rose. This time the sword went almost all the way through. I twisted to make the wound larger and the blood flow faster. He would have to use the axe one handed but the wild eyes I saw told me that he would happily do so. He hit a half-hearted blow at my shield. He had not waited for a good swing. As he pulled back for a more forceful strike, I swung Viking Killer in a wide arc. His axe shuddered on my shield as Viking Killer sliced through his neck and took his head. Still, with wild eyes, the dead head flew into the air to land in the shallows.

My men had obeyed me and, isolated, I was barely in time to block the sword blow from the mailed warrior with the full-face helmet and long sword who ran to avenge the berserker. I swung the edge of my shield towards him. My counter blow had opened him up and the edge of the shield caught him unawares below the chin. His mail and helmet took some of the sting from the blow, but he reeled, and I lunged at his mail. Bacgsecg had done a good job and the tip slid into the mail link and tore it open. I kept pushing and the links around it popped open allowing Viking Killer to rip open the padded kyrtle. Even as I pushed, I saw his eyes register that a sword was about to gut him, and he could do nothing about it. I used my legs and shoulder to push the blade into his body. Once it was through the padded kyrtle I angled it up to slice through as many organs in his body as I could. When my hand touched his mail, I saw Viking Killer pop out of his shoulder. I ripped it out and the dead man fell to the floor. I whirled around to face my next foe and saw that the enemy were all dead. It had been a ferocious fight but short in duration.

Fótr the Wolf raised his sword and shouted, "Mighty Lord Sámr, Berserker Killer!"

Men began banging their shields with the pommels of their swords. I whipped my head around and saw that the snekke had not been taken and Haaken Ráðgeirsson and my other men had slain those who had attempted to take it. We had won. Now we had to count the cost!

It was not as high as it might have been. Three of the men I had brought from Hawk's Roost were dead and four were too badly wounded to be of any use on the raid. They would recover but it would take weeks rather than days. Æimundr Loud Voice was a hard man and he had every one of the raiders decapitated and their heads placed on a spear. They adorned the dock as a grisly reminder of the price of failure. At dawn Aed took the snekke to fetch back *'Gytha'* and we examined the two threttanessa. They were not particularly well-made ships and none of us even considered taking them instead of Fótr's drekar but if we returned then we could take them and make our own raids on Man. All of us were determined to make the pirates of Man pay the price for their treacherous act.

Despite the victory, my men were not as elated as they should have been. Halfgrimr and the ones who had been with me on the dock felt that when they had stepped back they had somehow let me down. They had shown fear. Fótr was close by when I spoke to them. I do not think that he had ever witnessed an attack by a berserker.

I had washed the blood from me and taken off my mail. I was too old now to sweat beneath that weight. I told him what I knew of berserkers. "A berserker is the most dangerous enemy you will ever face except, perhaps, a she-wolf protecting her young. A berserker does not fear death and he feels no pain. He is not like a warrior you can wear down with blows which make him bleed. A berserker will not stop until you or he is dead! I could have taken his arm and he would have tried to fight on. Had he got close to me he would have tried to bite out my throat. I took his head and ended it. Had you tried to help me, Halfgrimr, then you might have got in the way. If a man fights a berserker then let him do so alone. If he dies, then another can try. Many warbands have men who volunteer to become berserkers. Licking his shield probably allowed him to take the potion. Others choose to take a potion before a battle. This was a test and we passed. We have three dead warriors who are the price of the lesson. We honour them by learning from it." They nodded. "Now collect the treasure from the dead and burn the bodies before the women and children return.

As they went to obey my orders Fótr and Æimundr Loud Voice came over to me. The grizzled old warrior clasped my arm, "Lord Sámr, you have the blood of The Dragonheart in your veins. You took the berserker and then their best warrior." He shook his head, "I am not sure I would have survived either encounter."

I smiled, "Had I not seen a berserker before then I too might have been frozen to the ground. Olaf Leather Neck was a killer of berserkers and he had an interesting technique; he would swing his Danish axe and take their heads. He told me that so long as a warrior wore mail then he had a good chance of defeating such a reckless man."

He nodded and Fótr said, "Do you need seven of the men from my stad to come with us to replace your losses?"

"You do not wish that and nor do I. The Norns spin. We have lost men, but the rest have endured their first battle and it was against a hard foe. I have no Ylva to help me, but I believe that we have enough men. To rescue my family, we need cunning rather than numbers. They do not know that Erik Black Toe knows the layout of their stronghold. I do not believe that they will be expecting us. By the time we reach Norway, it may well be Gormánuður and the nights will be longer than the days. It is the time when warriors sit in their mead halls and drink. They do not expect madmen to risk their ships on the sea. Our greatest battle is likely to be the one with Njörðr, but I think he favours you, Fótr, for when he took one drekar and almost took a snekke, he left you alive."

Æimundr Loud Voice nodded and put a huge paw around Fótr's shoulders, "Aye Fótr. They called your father unlucky. I think that to make up for his lack of luck they made you and Erik their chosen ones. I believe that you will return and with Lord Sámr's family." He suddenly laughed, "Perhaps now that I have fought my last battle, I can become a seer and predict the future!"

Fótr shook his head, "No, Æimundr Loud Voice, I am happy that while I am in the east you will be guarding my family for I know that they will be safe."

Chapter 5

The mail and helmets we recovered from the men of Man enabled us to equip another fifteen warriors with mail. They were the ones who had slain enemies in the battle. Spare weapons and shields were stored under the deck of the drekar. Not all of my men had managed to kill a raider such had been the shock of our attack. The ones who had yet to be blooded were keen to join their shield brothers and become warriors who had killed. We left two days later, and I feared we had left it too late to leave for the weather was squally. Although it meant we did not have to row it made for an uncomfortable journey, especially once we had cleared Hibernia and we felt the full force of the gale which hit us. I stood with Fótr the Wolf and Erik Black Toe at the steering board. Fótr was remarkably calm and philosophical about it.

"We would have been glad for this strong wind when we left Bear Island and *'Gytha'* does not mind it for it comes from the land where she was born. Now a wind from the east might upset us but this is a warm wind and it takes us where we wish to go." He nodded to the charts which were hidden in his chest. "When it is noon and we take a sun sight we can work out a rough position with the compass. You need lessons, Erik. We will then find an island, hopefully without people, where we can camp."

"You have such a route planned?"

Although we had discussed the journey Fótr was the Navigator and he would be the one who decided which passages we took. "We will make this a long day for the lands to the north of the Land of the Wolf have enemies and I intend to land at Sandaigh which has no one who lives upon it. It looks like an upturned spoon. We did not visit it when we came south, but Erik marked it on the map because my uncle, Snorri, had it marked as a safe haven. Then we will head north to Hí passing the island of Suðreyjar. It is eighty or more miles but *'Gytha'* can cover that in a day and it will allow us time to find a deserted beach or island. I would have us spend a night ashore while we can. There will come a time when either Erik or I will need to keep a night watch but that will be after Orkneyjar. We will have a similar length voyage to Skíð and the next day to Ljoðhús."

I shook my head, "How is it that the distances are the same? It is as though the gods placed the islands there for us."

He nodded, "My father and uncle believed that. The islands are now ruled by warriors such as we. Those who were there first, the old people, did not have ships such as we have nor did they have good weapons. They were easy to kill and explained why King Harald Finehair was so successful when he made his kingdom of the isles. He simply used the warriors of the islands who did not flee his arrival!"

Erik asked, "And after Ljoðhús?"

"That will be a long hard day for it is over one hundred and ten sea miles. We struggled when we came west from Orkneyjar as the winds were against us, but we may be lucky as those same winds may move us east. I know the island a little better as I spent a year or two there with my family and it was on a beach on that island where we built the snekke. I would spend a day or two there to repair any damage to the drekar and to fill both the water barrels and the barrels for food." He made a slight adjustment of the steering board as the sail flapped a little, the wind had shifted and said, "After Orkneyjar we have more than three hundred and sixty miles of ocean to cross. There will be little sun and we will need to avoid all other ships. I want *'Gytha'* perfect when we make the voyage."

I left them and went to the mast fish to speak with my men and to calm them. They were excited and they were nervous. I had sailed as far as Miklagård, but I was also sailing waters I did not know and I knew that their minds needed to be at peace when we faced harsher challenges! As we continued north, I wondered at the enormity of the task I had undertaken. The sun, had we been able to see it behind the bank of black and grey rain-filled clouds, would have been dipping in the west when we left the shelter of Hibernia. *'Gytha'* heeled to steerboard but Fótr, Ebbe and Bear Tooth appeared to be unconcerned. Some of the younger warriors clutched at their hammers of Thor or the gunwale. They would be in for far worse once we left Orkneyjar! I smiled when I saw Fótr hand over the steering board to Erik. Ebbe and Bear Tooth lounged nearby, and I knew that the three of them would spring into action if Erik could not handle the mighty ship. He looked nervous and although I did not notice any change in the handling of the ship, a short time after he had handed over the board, I saw Fótr tap his shoulder and point to the pennant on the masthead. Erik put the steering board over and we ploughed on more smoothly.

Sandaigh looked exactly as Fótr had described it. He took over the steering board and we sailed around the lump that was the inverted spoon into a large bay which looked north towards the mainland.

"Rowers, to your oars!"

Some of the young warriors looked blankly at me and I said, "You have been passengers long enough and you will need to row us to shore!"

"Prepare to reef the sail!" This time the designated warriors raced to their positions.

Fótr kept us heading north around the edge of the island. When he saw that the rowers were in position and the sail could be reefed, he shouted, "Oars out! Prepare to come about!" As soon as he turned the steering board over it was as though the drekar had hit a wall. "Reef the sail!"

Ebbe shouted, "Row!"

I had taught the crew more of the chants my great grandfather had used and Ebbe used an easy one which would take us swiftly to the beach. We had changed just a couple of words.

Push your arms
Row the boat
Use your back
Gytha will fly

Clan of the Wolf
Are real men
Teeth like iron
Arms like trees

Push your arms
Row the boat
Use your back
Gytha will fly

I pointed to the warriors who would jump ashore with the ropes. I shouted, "Take the hammer and a stake. There are no trees here." I did not assign the other two men who went to the side of the drekar and that showed that they were thinking. We had assigned two men to take the ropes and moor us, but the hammers and the stakes needed to be driven in by others.

Fótr was in total command, "Larboard oars in! Jumpers, over the side! Steerboard oars, slowly does it."

As the four men jumped into the chest-deep water and the larboard oars were raised so that they were vertical the steerboard oars pushed us close to the sand and shingle. Fótr judged it well and shouted, "Steerboard oars up!" as we slid along the sand. We had survived our first day at sea! "Stack your oars at the mastfish." I heard the stakes being hammered in to hold us safely close to the shore.

I saw Ebbe and Bear Tooth with slung bows jump over the side and they sprinted off up the beach towards the round-topped dome of a hill. I went to Fótr and cocked a questioning head. He smiled, "We take nothing for granted, Lord Sámr. The island looks deserted and there is no smoke but Bear Tooth and Ebbe will climb the hill and make certain. They take their bows to hunt." He waved a hand around the bay, "Have the men search for shellfish. We will eat well tonight, and we can sleep without a sentry. This will be a rare night!"

I felt like a novice and yet Fótr was far younger than I was. We could not make this voyage without him. I set half of the men to search the shore for shellfish while the rest collected wood and made fires. Fótr was right. The mainland looked uninhabited. Even if there were Vikings on the mainland, by the time they reported the fires and sent a ship to investigate, we would be gone.

Fótr was a real leader who needed to check on everything himself and he walked the drekar with Erik to check ropes, sheets and stays. While I went ashore, I saw them walk around the hull. It was only when they were satisfied that they joined us. It was dark but I watched the two of them examining the chart they had begun to make. They were recording the journey. Bear Tooth and Ebbe rejoined us much later after it was dark. They had hunted some of the birds on the island. After they had plucked and gutted them, they were added to the shellfish stew which bubbled away. We had the bread we had brought. The voyage and sea air had made it soft but Ebbe showed the young warriors how to place it on the stones around the fire to crisp it up slightly. I was learning as much as my young warriors.

As we ate the stew, which was delicious, and picked the meat from the lobsters and crabs, Bear Tooth spoke, "Lord Sámr, I am the scout. I need to train some of your warriors to help me. It is all very well for just Ebbe and me to scout here on Sandaigh but when we reach the land of Finehair there will need to be more of us. You know your men better than I do. Who do you think will be suitable?"

I had an idea already, but I gave the question due diligence. "Buthar Faramirson and Fámr Ulfsson lived in Lang's Dale and were hunters. Would they do?"

He nodded, "Hunters are perfect, but we need at least four."

"Then Ulf Olafsson and Gandálfr Eriksson are also hunters."

"Good, send them to me for I can begin their teaching this night."

The next morning, we left before the sun had broken through the ragged clouds in the east. The day promised the occasional flash of sunlight. We had to row for we needed to head north and west until we cleared the mainland. Fótr had to sail for many miles with the wind from our larboard quarter before we could turn north and pass Suðreyjar to steerboard. It was noon before we were able to rest the oarsmen and take full advantage of the wind. We flew.

This time we reached the island well before dark. Fótr told me that there was a monastery on the eastern side of the island. We landed on a beach in the west. It was not as tranquil as our first camp and I could tell that Fótr was nervous about camping there. "We can light fires but, Lord Sámr, we will need sentries this night and Erik and I will sleep aboard."

I nodded, "That is good, Fótr, for the crew need to learn these skills."

I allocated the sentries and I woke myself in the middle of the night to ensure that they had not fallen asleep. They had not and I was happy. Once again, we left before dawn had truly broken and headed north. Ljoðhús was not going to be such an easy camp. This time it was me who had the knowledge. "There are many Vikings on Ljoðhús and if we are seen then they would investigate."

Fótr nodded. Erik was steering and my navigator could give me his full attention, "Then we sail until we see no sign of smoke and an empty beach. When I went with my brother to seek a passage home to the Land of Ice and Fire, we found many rocks and islands which had no people on them. Our water barrels are full. All we need is somewhere we can moor. If we have to then we can try to push on to Orkneyjar. Erik has shown me that he has real skill."

Erik beamed, "I think I must have picked up those skills when I sailed on the knarr."

As we neared the island there was an alarming number of smoke trails climbing into the air. We could not see the settlements, but smoke and fire meant people and in this part of the world that meant Vikings. We were about to try to sail on, through the night, when Bear Tooth, who had the best vision of any of us, shouted, "I see a rock where we can land!" We had already passed bare lumps of rocks, but they had not offered any sort of anchorage. Fótr put the steering board over and the rock suddenly became not just one island but two. There appeared to be calm water between the two and under sails reefed to the bare minimum and with Ebbe and Bear Tooth hanging over the prow, we edged our way in. It was perfect. While there was neither vegetation nor animals it was sheltered. This time we had to get close enough to allow our jumpers to leap not into the sea but upon the slippery rocks. They managed it and they were thrown two metal spikes which they hammered into crevasses in the rocks. By pulling us close, against the prevailing wind, men were able to leap on to the land. Although we were in sight of the main island we were safe from investigation and I allowed the men to light a fire and cook shellfish, the fish we had caught with trailing lines and some pieces of the salted ham. Hot food is always better than cold, and we might have a week of cold meals. The more we could eat ashore, the better. Fótr and Erik slept aboard the drekar but the rest of us slept ashore until we were awakened by a shower in the middle of the night. Then we all returned to the drekar and slept the rest of the night beneath an old sail.

The next voyage would take us to Fótr's former home. It was now part of Harald Finehair's kingdom and so we would find one of the deserted beaches away from others. We would need to collect water to top up the barrels and augment our supplies. There would be no chance to do so in Norway and that meant we had to ensure that we had food and water for at least three weeks.

Fótr was in charge and he headed for Hrólfsey. Although this would give us a longer journey, he was more comfortable travelling there. He told us that there had been few people on the island when he had lived there. Most had left with his father when they had sailed for Larswick. "There may still be sheep we can steal and cook." He was the navigator, and these were his decisions to make. The longer voyage meant that we would be arriving either at dusk or just after. Normally that might be dangerous but Fótr had his brother's maps and charts and some of those had come from his father, Lars. They were detailed enough to give me confidence that he would not tear the keel from his ship.

We kept to the west of the island chain as the wind which had helped us since leaving the Land of the Wolf continued to push us. We had reefed sails to help Fótr to navigate and I stood to watch the islands as we passed them. The islands looked flatter than the ones we had passed further south, and I saw more buildings. There were also many animals grazing. I saw people who were watching us. Raids were not uncommon, and we had our shields along the sides. They would wonder if we were raiders heading home or hungry wolves seeking victims. They would be vigilant! The last days had been cloud filled with occasional flashes of sunlight and this one was no exception. A bank of cloud suddenly extinguished the light from the sun as it neared the horizon and we went from dusk to night almost in a heartbeat. We had just spied Hrólfsey and Fótr ordered another reef, "There is a tiny island in the middle of the channel, Eyin-Helha; it is called the holy island for the Christian monk from Hibernia who lived there. None could remove him from the island. Each time warriors tried their ships were damaged. He died long before I was born but my mother, who was a Christian, told me that his spirit still haunted the island. We have to pass that to steerboard if we are to successfully navigate the channel. There are beaches to larboard. We seek one without people. I believe that I know one."

I suppose I understood Fótr. If we were heading south, I would want to be close to my home, the Land of the Wolf, but this seemed to me a dangerous course of action. The old jarl, Eystein Rognvaldson, must have been long dead but that did not mean his descendants would not be there. When he pushed over the steering board to take us east the motion of the drekar became easier. He pointed out the island of Eyin-Helha. Bear Tooth peered into the dark and he suddenly grabbed the totem he wore around his neck. He had been listening when Fótr had told us his story, "I see the spirit of the holy man! I see him moving on the rock. He is waving his arms!"

I peered into the dark, but I saw nothing. That was not a surprise for my eyes were old. I turned to Ebbe who had also been looking, "And you? Did you see anything?"

He, too, was clutching his hammer, "Perhaps but I see no reason to risk the wrath of the gods. If it is his spirit, then I would not bother him!"

Fótr said, quietly, "Do not worry, Ebbe, I have no intention of visiting there but Bear Tooth's words are a warning. The spirit of the monk may have been sent to alert us to danger. There is a beach to larboard. It is not as large as the one I sought but the sisters are spinning, and we will heed them. Man the oars and take in the sail!"

We had done this enough times now to make it look easy and we were tied to the shore in no time at all. Ebbe and Bear Tooth, along with Buthar Faramirson and Fámr Ulfsson, loped off to scout. The other two potential scouts would be given their lesson later. We prepared but did not light the fires. Fótr intended to spend two nights on this island and so men made themselves comfortable. The novice warriors were learning veteran skills! The four scouts were away so long that I began to fear that they had come to harm. Fótr and Erik had remained on board. This was in case we had to leave in a hurry. They would only land when the scouts returned and told us that it was safe. When they did return, they reported to me.

"It is safe, Lord Sámr. We took longer than we wished as we found a farm and wished to discover if it was occupied or not. It was empty! There are no people close by."

I nodded, "Then fetch Fótr and Erik." I cupped my hands, "Light the fires. It is safe!"

The fires were lit and seawater was beginning to bubble when Fótr and Erik joined us. Fótr's face, in the firelight, looked pensive, "From what the scouts told us, Lord Sámr, it was my family's home they found."

"And you wished to visit it. That is why you sailed here."

"I did not lie, Lord Sámr. This is the last landfall before Norway, and I do need to examine the drekar."

"Yet you were not truthful with me. Did you think that I would be angry? Now I am disappointed, and I will have to look for the messages hidden beneath your words. This is not good, Fótr the Wolf. We should be as one."

He took my arm and led me away from the others who busied themselves preparing food, "You are right Lord Sámr but the truth is that my elder brother, Arne, was a leader and if he had commanded this expedition he would have forbade me to do as I did."

I understood a little. Gruffyd had been the same and it had been his attitude which had led to the downfall of the Clan of the Wolf. "I am not Arne, Fótr; no more lies and no more secrets. Speak now while we are alone."

"When I have examined the drekar I would go, tomorrow, with Ebbe and Bear Tooth. I wish to visit my home. I do not know what I hope to find there but whatever I find or do not find will clear my head. I cannot sail east with doubts in my mind."

"Doubts?"

"My brother, Erik, was the one with the luck. Arne and my father were luckless. When I walk into the hall where I was born then I will know if I am like Erik or like Arne."

"How?"

He took hold of his amulet and said, "I will know."

Then it came to me; Fótr and Ylva had spent much time together. I did not think that he was a galdramenn but perhaps the spirits spoke to him. The spirit of Dragonheart had spoken to him. The anger I had felt now subsided. Ylva had planted this thought in his head. I nodded, "Do what you must, Fótr. I trust you and the spirits of the dead will guide you." I pointed towards the island we had passed, now hidden in the darkness, "Perhaps Bear Tooth saw not the holy man but a spirit of one of your ancestors."

"Perhaps!"

We kept a watch that night for although Bear Tooth had said no one was close Fótr knew that it was a large island. Those on watch kept the fire fed and topped up the stew which bubbled away. They would add salted meat during the night.

The next morning Bear Tooth asked Ulf Olafsson and Gandálfr Eriksson to go with Fótr and Ebbe. This would be their scouting lesson and, as they were hunters, they might find food. Fótr did not have to spend a long time examining the drekar. He and Erik waded around the hull and found it sound. The deck was lifted, and the hold was dry. Fótr had Erik change some of the ropes. Although not frayed they showed wear and we had time. It was a couple of hours before noon when Fótr's group left us and, after leaving half a dozen men to build a bread oven I took the rest to the shore to collect shellfish and gull's eggs. We would not hunt the gull for it had an oily and unpleasant taste. Those we were forced to kill would be used for bait when we sailed east.

I confess that I did little work. I found a rock and sat to watch the men work for I had things on my mind, and I needed to make plans. The voyage had gone well and all that we hoped to do we had done. The drekar was sound and the crew now knew what they would do. I was confident in Fótr's ability to sail across the sea to Norway. The question in my mind was how we would manage to rescue my family once we were there. Erik had told me that they were guarded. Would their guards have orders to kill them in the event of an attempted rescue? That would not be our way, but King Harald Finehair was a different sort of leader. He was ruthless. He had happily employed Skull Takers to guard me and Erik's description of Uddulfr the Sly led me to believe that he would be as ruthless. We needed a galdramenn or a witch and we had neither. I would need to be as sly and cunning as our enemies.

Perhaps that thought was planted by the spirits of the dead, I know not but as I looked south, across the sea, I saw a movement on the island of Eyin-Helha. It was not an animal and I saw that there was not just one man on the island but two. This was not the spirit of a Christian holy man. I stood and I waved. As I did so, for the island was less than a thousand paces from where I stood, I saw another four figures rise from the rocks and wave back at us. My men stopped working when they saw the movement.

"Half of you come with me. The rest, continue to gather food."

Halfgrimr asked as we hurried back to the drekar, "Who are they, lord? Are they wights?"

"They look to be men, but the Norns are spinning, Halfgrimr, and we cannot ignore them. We cross the sea on the morrow, and I would not abandon men whose spirits might hurt us. We will sail across the water and fetch them."

"But Fótr is not here!"

"If Erik and we cannot sail a thousand paces across calm water then he will never be a captain. This is a test."

Erik was quite happy to sail the short way across the channel, but he showed caution for he said, "I would not tear out the keel, lord. I need two men, at least, to watch for rocks and I will sail under oars."

"And I think that you are wise to do so."

We had just eight oars on each side and Halfgrimr and Farbjorn were with me at the bows, after they had loosed us from the land. We did not use a chant and edged slowly across the channel. I used hand signals to direct Erik to the tiny sliver of sand that was the beach. The six ragged skeletons made their way to the beach from where they had waved to us.

I held up my hand and shouted, "Back water!" when I saw the rocks just ten paces from the bows. Our slow speed and the command in my voice halted us. I turned to Halfgrimr and Farbjorn, "Fetch ropes." While they did so I cupped my hands, "You will have to swim!" One, I took him to be the leader, nodded and they began to wade into the water. I could now see that they were Vikings. The clothes they wore were torn and ragged, but each had a hammer of Thor around their necks. Two had the remnants of sealskin boots on their feet. The boots were a little worse for wear but marked them as Vikings. The rest were barefoot.

Erik had the oarsmen sculling to counter the current which wanted to take us on the beach. This was not only a test for Erik, it was a lesson in controlling a drekar. As the six men were hauled aboard, I watched him as he looked to the pennant and then over the side at the water and then back to the oarsmen. The rest of us did not exist and that was as it should be for, at this moment, Erik Black Toe was the captain of *'Gytha'* and he and the drekar were as one.

As soon as the last man was aboard, I raised my hand and shouted, "We can head back, Erik!"

"Back water!" When we were two hundred paces from the beach he shouted, "Now row!" He pushed the steering board over and there was an uncomfortable moment as we crested a small wave and then *'Gytha'* pirouetted around and almost before we knew it we were back at our mooring. The men tending the fires were ready to catch the mooring ropes and attach them to the stakes. The shellfish gatherers were returning.

So far we had not spoken to the six men and, as the gangplank was fitted to allow us to disembark, I said, "I am Sámr Ship Killer from the Land of the Wolf and this drekar is *'Gytha'*."

The leader nodded, "Had you said that you were Norse we would have thrown ourselves overboard, but we know that the warriors of the Clan of the Wolf are the enemies of King Harald Finehair, as are we. I am Egil Sorenson and this is my son, Egil Egilsson, my brother, Fámr Sorenson. These other three are men from our village, Piotr Larsson, Ketil Eriksson and Grimbold Gandálfrson."

I nodded, "There is a tale here, but I can see that you are hungry. Eat first, have some ale and then you can tell us your story."

He nodded as he stepped towards the gunwale and the gangplank, "We have drunk water, but raw shellfish does little to satisfy a need for real food."

I saw that the temporary bread oven had been built and knew that these men were in for a treat. We had brought a barrel of flour and would make enough bread to last us across the sea. It would become hard but dipped into ale and with fresh cheese and sliced salted meat it would make us think we had dined well!

The six of them stayed close together and sat on the logs we had placed around the fire. I did not feel cold but then I was dressed for the season. I saw them shivering and knew that the fire would be more than welcome. I nodded to Ráðulfr Ráðgeirsson and said, "Ale first!" Rolf Red Hair was stirring the stew and I asked, "Is it ready?"

He looked at the six shivering men and said, "Aye, lord and there is more just coming." He nodded towards the last of the foragers who were fetching baskets of shellfish. Rolf ladled steaming bowlfuls of shellfish and salted meat stew into the wooden bowls and I handed them to the six men. I noticed that Egil Sorenson made sure that all of his men had food before he took one himself. He was a leader!

By the time they had each finished the second bowl and had another horn of ale, they were ready to speak. "So, Egil Sorenson, what brought six Vikings to this rock in the channel and why do you hate Harald Finehair so much?"

"You know the reason for that, Sámr Ship Killer. He is a greedy man who wants the earth. He wants every Viking to bend the knee to him and destroys those who do not. We should have left this island when Lars the Luckless did so."

"*Wyrd!*"

His eyes narrowed as he asked, "You know the name?"

I nodded and pointed to the ship, "This ship was built by the sons of Lars the Luckless and Fótr, his youngest, is the captain. The people who sailed from here went west and found a new world. Fótr brought back the ones who wished to live here in the east and they are now members of the Clan of the Wolf!"

They all clutched at their amulets, "I can see you speak truly for how else would you know his son's names?" He put his arm around his son.

"You were not born when they left and had I gone with them then your mother and sisters might be alive."

The man he had said was his brother nodded, "Aye and all my family too!"

Egil said, "We stayed and thought that he would let us live for we were a small village who lived by hunting seals. His jarl, Rognvald Larsson, had other ideas. He demanded taxes for living on the island. We paid him thinking that was a price worth paying but each year the tax went up until we were giving more to him than we were keeping. Food was scarce and our people began to die. We decided to sail away. We remembered Lars the Luckless. A trader had told us, many years ago, that he had settled south of the Land of the Wolf in Mercia. We decided to leave but one of our people told Rognvald Larsson that we intended to flee. He pursued us in a drekar. We had a snekke and a drekar. He caught us to the west of here. We were out of sight of land and thought we had escaped. A storm came from the west and began to drive us east. It was then that we saw his drekar. *'Serpent's Tongue'* is well named and he came for our snekke. We were the crew of the snekke and in an attempt to save our families and the knarr we tried to block the drekar. He ran us down and we were thrown into the sea. We had to discard out helmets and weapons else we would have died. He then rammed the knarr. It was filled with women, children, my second son and the old. They stood no chance. The drekar circled them until they were all gone and then came back to finish us off. He might have succeeded had not the gods made the storm so violent that his sail was torn, and he was forced to head west. I thought that we would die too but the snekke had partially survived and we six clung on to it. There were four others, but they were torn from the wreckage and drowned. The storm drove us here where the snekke finally died on the rocks and we scrambled ashore. That was a month since. Had you not come we would have died. Each time we saw a ship coming from the west we tried to attract its attention. You were the only one who saw us."

I nodded. Just then I saw Fótr and the others returning. They had four sheep on spears. I pointed to them. "There is Fótr Larsson, now Fótr the Wolf, and he has been to his family home. Speak with him and then, later, you can tell us what you wish to do."

"Wish to do, lord? That is easy. Find Rognvald Larsson and cut out his heart."

I said, "I understand your desire for vengeance; indeed, we follow the vengeance trail ourselves, but you cannot do so in your present condition. Speak with Fótr and hear his tale and then I will speak with you."

Erik had come ashore, and he had heard part of the story. "It is as though the Allfather sent us here to find them."

"Perhaps but I feel the spell of the sisters here. We shall see what they decide. I do not mind taking them to their home, but I fear I would just be sending them to their death."

"What else could we do?"

I smiled, "They remind me of you when you returned to us, but they are in an even worse condition. Although we are heading into danger they would be fed and safe aboard *'Gytha'*. Even if we fail and all die, there will be some, Fótr and others, who will still be aboard the drekar and they could sail home. I think that Lars the Luckless would like the ship built by his sons to save the last of his people, don't you?"

"Aye, lord." He shook his head, "I feel so small when I think of the sisters' threads. Are we their toys?"

"It feels that way does it not? Yet, if they had not spun and The Dragonheart and his mother not been taken from the Dunum would I have been born? Would you have been saved? You cannot take away one thread without making the web different. We just have to deal with what they throw at us!"

My eyes were drawn to Fótr and Egil as the skeletons greeted him. This was a private moment. Ebbe and Bear Tooth, along with my scouts, came over to us. I explained what had happened. Ebbe said, "I had heard that people were left on Hrólfsey and some who did not sail with us to the Land of Ice and Fire had left Larswick to return to these islands. I had dismissed the stories thinking that the people who had remained were foolish. I was wrong. What will they do?"

"Whatever it is will be their decision. Now let us get the animals skinned. Some of the meat can be salted and some cooked."

Bear Tooth grinned, "I could eat a whole one of these. It is a pity we did not have one of their young. That meat is the sweetest I have ever eaten. My people would love to have tasted such meat."

Erik asked, "Do you miss your people?"

He nodded, "Sometimes but as my family died and I now have a wife and son here in the east the memory is not as painful. I close my eyes at night, and I speak with the spirits of my family. They are happy for me and this is meant to be." He grinned again, he was one of the happiest people I knew, "It is *wyrd*!"

It was no coincidence that the first bread was ready when Fótr and Egil came to speak with me. The smell of freshly cooked bread is one of the most comforting smells I know. We still had fresh cheese and butter and I was smearing both on the bread when they came over. "Bread?"

The faces of the two men broke into broad smiles, "Aye, lord."

We ate in silence for it was disrespectful to the food to do otherwise. Erik brought us ale and I said, "Well?"

Egil looked at Fótr who nodded, "You are right Sámr Ship Killer. If we returned to fight Rognvald Larsson we would lose and we would die. That would not bring our families back. Fótr has told us of your quest and it seems to me that we were sent here to help you. When you go ashore to wreak your revenge on your enemies, we can guard your ship. By the time we return here, we will be stronger, and we can land and have a better chance of killing our enemy." He paused, "If you will have us."

"We lost men and your help would be invaluable, but you cannot yet fight and you should know that the chances of us being successful are slim. You may just die further east."

He nodded, "But we would have hurt King Harald and that is important to us!"

"Then you shall join my crew. Fótr, take them aboard. Give them better clothes and weapons. We have no boots yet but we may get some for you at Moi."

I grabbed Fótr's arm as he turned to take our new crew aboard, "Well, did the spirits speak?"

He looked content as he nodded and said, "Aye, Sámr. I am like Erik and not Arne. You are not sailing under the command of the luckless!"

That night we celebrated our new crew and it was fitting that we did so. We would be leaving this land with hope for we had saved six men from certain death. They might yet die but, if they did so then it would be as Vikings, with a sword in their hand!

Chapter 6

We did not put the new men on the oars, but they were able to help with the sails which helped for they were seasoned sailors. As we left our mooring we were armed and ready in case the drekar which had sunk Egil's ships was at sea. The Allfather smiled on us and we were alone; the dark seas and stormy skies were probably the reason. As soon as we left the protection of the islands the seas became stormier. There was little rain, as yet, but the winds were whirling around making it hard for Fótr and we were not making the progress he would have wished. He asked for some crew to row and our progress improved. I stood at the steering board with Erik and Fótr.

"When we sailed east from the New World, we often had to row for many hours at a stretch. We found the best way was to keep rotating the oarsmen. Let us put the hourglass to good use."

We put the system into operation, and I took an oar too. Egil's men kept supplying the oarsmen with ale although I was aware that we might run out before we returned home to the Land of the Wolf. The day progressed with the wind blowing from the south and west while we headed due east. As Fótr pointed out, this was probably the most efficient method of sailing. I bowed to his superior knowledge. Sailing across the Great Sea had taught him more about sailing than I would ever learn in the time left to me. When darkness descended, we took in the oars and the sails were reefed just to keep way upon us. We edged our way east. The rains began and so we had rigged an old sail to keep us dry. We ate once that was done. Fótr had managed four hours sleep during the day and a very nervous Erik was pleased when Fótr awoke and he found that we were still on course. Of course, Ebbe had been with him and Ebbe had sailed with Erik too. He could have been a navigator. I do not think that Ebbe had decided then what he wished to be. I had also managed an hour or so of sleep and as we rose and fell through troughs and crests, I kept him company along with Bear Tooth. We were well out to sea and there were neither rocks nor islands between us and Norway. The only danger so far as I could see would be another warship like us. Since leaving Fótr's Stad we had all kept weapons in our belts. Helmets and mail were in sandy sacks inside our chests, but we all had a bladed weapon in case danger loomed up out of the dark.

As we sailed Bear Tooth told me about his land and his people. I began to understand why Erik the Navigator had stayed there. Fótr had told me that although he had thought his brother was dead there had been a dream when he had stayed with Ylva and he now believed that his brother and his Skraeling woman, Laughing Deer, were alive. The people sounded like our clan and with no king to rule them and plentiful game it sounded like a paradise. Fótr said, "Perhaps, but not all of the tribes were as welcoming as Bear Tooth's people. The Penobscot were fierce warriors." Fótr joined us and we continued the conversation.

"From what you say though, they do not wear mail or have metal. Surely they are easy to defeat."

Fótr shook his head, "Do not sail that course, Lord Sámr. My brother Arne believed that, and it ended the lives of many brave warriors. Arne and Siggi were powerful and for them to be killed shows the danger of underestimating the Skraeling."

Bear Tooth said, "Your people are great warriors and any one of you can kill ten or more of my people but that just makes them even more determined to fight. The berserker you slew is like a Penobscot. When they die, they will go to a heaven where they hunt and fight for all time if they die in battle."

And that sounded like our people too. Ebbe and I snatched some sleep as did Erik. Bear Tooth stayed with Fótr. We were all close and that boded well for our quest.

We continued east and the weather improved the next day. We did not need to row, and men dried out as they watched the sea birds crying above. It was said that the sea birds were the spirits of the men who had died at sea and their plaintive cry was to seek help. Perhaps that was why they were so unpleasant to eat. As we sailed towards Norway, we saw the effects of the storm and the wreckage through which we passed told us that there were more new spirits crying in the sky and that someone was watching over us for we had no damage at all.

Each day which passed saw an improvement in the condition of Egil and his five men. It was not just the food, ale and clothes which healed them, it was the companionship of my young warriors. Egil and his men had seen the worst of other Vikings. In the young warriors, they saw the best for they were heading east not for themselves but others. They were going to help my family and we all knew that some would die. That was noble. Three days into the voyage Egil and I spoke. We were at the prow and the carved figurehead of the witch was somehow comforting. Egil's wife was dead and I knew not what Aethelflaed's fate was. Gytha, from what Ebbe and Fótr had told us, was a powerful woman in both life and death. Had she not been strong then the Clan of the Fox might not have weathered even one winter on Bear Island.

"If you wish us to, Sámr, my men and I can fight alongside you."

"It is a generous offer, but I will have to decline. You were sent to us for a purpose. Had we not found you then I would have had to leave four men with Fótr to guard our ship. Now I can leave six men to help them and have more men for our rescue attempt."

"And how will you affect their rescue?"

"I know not yet. This Uddulfr the Sly may well know me and possibly Erik but not Ebbe nor Bear Tooth. They both have experience and, I hope, can scout out the stronghold. We need to gain entry to the stronghold. We cannot take it by a frontal attack. Erik told me that the walls are too strong. This needs cunning."

He nodded, "If we can help then just ask. You have given us life and we are now reborn. Until you return us to Hrólfsey we are yours to command."

The winds changed two days later and after an incredibly stormy night which saw the sail torn and needing repair, it swung around to blow from the north. We could still sail east but we were slowed, and we had to repair the sail. We had made some progress for a number of days, but we had one day when we sailed at the pace of a snail. I invoked the spirit of Ylva but, perhaps, we were too far from the cave or I did not use the right words but, whatever the reason, I was not answered.

We had finished the bread and were now reliant on the fish we caught from the lines we trailed or the salted meat and fish from the barrels. The fish we caught was good and gave us sustenance, but I preferred food which was cooked, and this was cold and salty food. We had enough salt from the sea! We also had to ration the ale. I allowed the men one horn in the morning and one in the evening. Thanks to the rain we had plenty of water but we all preferred ale.

Fótr said as we watched the new moon appear, "If you can, Lord Sámr, you should try to steal a barrel of ale when you are ashore!"

I laughed, "Just one? If you are going to have me steal beer, why not four or five barrels?"

He laughed and pointed up at the moon, "The moon tonight tells me that we are almost at Norway. That means that Njörðr favours us. Let us ask for ale too, eh?"

I nodded, "Family first, then beer!"

I knew what he meant. There was no comparison between a family and barrel of ale but if we succeeded and rescued my family then why not take ale? Once I had taken that first step then the rest of the fantastic plan I conjured seemed easy. If the step after recovering my family was to take ale then I thought, why not take the treasures which Uddulfr the Sly would have in his stronghold? That wild thought then made me think that we could destroy Moi and all the ships which lay in the harbour. Looking back the idea seems almost absurd, but Erik had told me that they had the crews of just one drekar to guard the stronghold. Remembering the attack by the men of Man I realised that had we not been forewarned then they might easily have succeeded. If my band of avenging warriors could appear inside the fortress, then we had the chance to take it and with that in our hands, Moi would be ours. I did not tell anyone my plans and that was twofold. Firstly, because I was not sure that it was possible and secondly, because since Baldr's death and Ylva's entombment I had been alone. Fótr was a friend but not yet a shield brother.

It took ten days to cross the sea. The weather and the inexperienced crew both contributed but it did not matter as it had made our crew as one. The new men from Hrólfsey were only temporary but they were every bit a part of the crew. I had learned, as had Fótr, that a well-made drekar is a living thing and a crew, whilst made up of different men also becomes a single living being. We had endured harsh weather and fierce seas and emerged without loss. As the coast of Norway hove into view and the thin smudge of grey on the horizon became a black and jagged line of mountains and fjords, we all knew that we had served our apprenticeship and now we would face our sternest test. We were now in a land ruled by our enemy. King Harald Finehair was the enemy of all of us. That was not to say that all those we met would be our enemies. Many of the Norse resented the fact that they now had a king and would not necessarily fight us. What they would do, if we were seen, would be to tell someone that they had seen an unknown drekar. *'Gytha'* was unique; her lines, her figurehead and her wood all marked her as foreign. Of course, that very strangeness would hide the fact that it was Dragonheart's heir who was aboard.

"The first thing we need to do, Lord Sámr, is to find out where exactly we are. Erik did not use a compass when he was in these waters. We have an approximate idea of where we are, but Moi could be twenty or thirty miles north or south of our position. I intend to head inshore once the sun sets."

"We are that close?"

Erik spoke. The closer to Norway we were the quieter he had become. I knew that he had much on his mind. Everything depended upon him finding Moi once more, "I travelled over the mountains from Flekkefjord, but the stronghold lies at the head of a fjord with a very narrow entrance. I had not sailed down that fjord, lord, and I do not know what we might find. However, if we find that fjord, we know that we are close to the stronghold and you can make your plans accordingly."

"Then head inshore and I will have the crew arm themselves. If we are discovered, then I intend to fight."

I went to my chest and took out the metal-studded leather byrnie. I would not wear my mail until we were ashore. Halfgrimr and Farbjorn armed themselves too. They would not leave my side now until we had succeeded, or they lay dead! The sun was fading behind us and the seas, because we were closer to the shore, had become a little less violent when Bear Tooth whistled. He was at the prow and he pointed north. There were four fishing boats with lowered sails; they were working. Three of them appeared to be using a large net and rowing torwards the fourth. Had they not been doing so then they might have fled but a net was valuable, and they would not simply abandon it. As Fótr had the crew reef the sail we used the current to drift closer to them until we were in hailing distance. Our slow approach reassured them for had we intended harm we would simply have sailed through them. I kept to the shadows and I allowed Fótr and Erik to do the speaking.

One of the captains aboard the fishing ship spoke before Fótr could ask anything, "Are you lost, friend? You are sailing the waters of King Harald and you are dressed for war."

Fótr's voice sounded reassuring and friendly, "No, friend. We come from Hrólfsey. The ship of Jarl Rognvald Larsson, *'Serpent's Tongue'* was damaged in a storm and he asked us to come to tell the King. Is he at Stavanger or Hafrsfjord?" I saw Fótr point north.

This was a crucial moment and Fótr had shown that he was a clever man. If the captain pointed out that Stavanger was south, we would have our position. It also allayed any fears the fishermen might have for it was a plausible story.

I saw the captain point south, "The King spends the winter at Oddernes. Do you know it?"

Erik spoke, "I have sailed these waters a little. It is on the south-west coast, is it not?"

"Aye, friend, but I would not try to sail it at night unless you know these waters well. Head north for Hafrsfjord is not far from here, just three hours sailing."

"Thank you, we will heed your advice." Fótr turned and cupped his hands. "Take to the oars!"

The crew took the oars and we headed first west and then Fótr turned us north. As soon as we were out of sight of the four ships, he turned us in a circle so that we headed south, once more. Erik said, "I know where we are. The mouth of Moisanafjord is close."

Both of them looked at me and Fótr said, "Do we risk finding somewhere to hide under cover of darkness? When the fishermen return to their port and find that we are not there then they will be suspicious. It was good that we found our position, but the Norns have been spinning and it is they who have turned the supernatural hourglass."

He was right, "Erik, you say we are close; how close?"

"Two hours with the sail or perhaps an hour and a half if we use oars as well. There is a small island at the mouth of the fjord."

"Then have the men man the oars and we will cast the bones. The Norns sent the fishermen for a reason and we have come this far, let us see if it gives us a way into the stronghold."

We could not use a chant as we did not want the fishermen to hear us but the crew, knowing we were close, needed no chant and they were as one. Ebbe and Bear Tooth, on the front oars, kept a steady pace as we sailed due south through the darkness. I was at the steering board and saw Fótr's skill as we gradually edged further east until we saw the white flecks of the sea as it broke on the shore. Erik's time in the knarr paid off and it was he spied the island at the southern side of the mouth of the fjord. Fótr used hand signals to have us reef the sail and then he entered the narrow mouth of the fjord. It was just sixty paces wide! I prayed that it would widen. He was close enough to Bear Tooth and Ebbe to speak to them, "Slow down the oars. Lord Sámr, it would be useful to have experienced eyes on our course. Could you go to the prow and direct us?"

Erik said, "Moi is on the eastern side at the head of the fjord. If we can find a branch off the fjord then we can hide!"

I nodded and went with my two oathsworn to the prow. This would not be easy as there was no moon and the waters were dark. We could not risk this in daylight when we might be seen and Fótr was right; we had to try it in the dark! I hoped that the fjord would widen soon. Erik had told us that close to Moi it was as wide as The Water but here, at its mouth, it felt as though I could touch the sides. I could tell that the fjord went, at this point, southwest to northeast. Erik had said that close to Moi it ran north to south. I was not sure how that helped except that we needed to hide before the fjord turned north! I kept my hand up in the air to indicate that we could keep going straight. I glanced along the side and saw that the oars, which steadily dipped and rose, were in no danger of fouling the side. "Halfgrimr, let me know if we get too close on the larboard side."

"Aye, lord, but there is plenty of room, at the moment!"

The rocky sides of the fjord rose sharply and there would be little opportunity for us to land. The oarsmen were having to work as the current was fighting us. I knew that Fótr would keep changing the oarsmen to maintain a steady pace. After an hour or so the fjord had become a little wider and I felt a little more relaxed. I could not smell wood smoke and that meant no houses. It was now Gormánuður and there was a chill in the air; if there were people living close by then there would be fires. My sealskin cape kept out the cold and the damp. Egil and his men deeply regretted the fact that their own sealskin capes and boots had been lost when they had been attacked. Warriors did not need gold; weapons, mail and warm clothes were all far more important. I kept glancing down the drekar's side, and it was as I did so that I saw the channel on the steerboard side. I ran back down the

66

drekar. As I ran, I saw that the channel was as wide as the fjord had been at its mouth. Seeing me hurrying to him Fótr ordered the oarsmen to slow. The current meant that we were almost stationary.

I pointed, "There is a channel there. How far do you think we have travelled?"

"Perhaps eleven miles."

I looked at Erik who shrugged, "I did not travel the fjord, but I think it was seventeen miles to the sea."

Fótr was the navigator and he took the decision, "We will try it. Ebbe, Bear Tooth, back the larboard oars and forward with the steerboard."

The lithe drekar turned in her own length and I ran back down the ship to the prow. I saw, immediately, that the sides of this tributary were no longer as steep as they had been although we did not need to go ashore for we just needed somewhere to hide. I kept my hand in the air as we headed south. We had travelled less than five hundred paces when I saw a wall of stone ahead. We had reached the end of this branch of the fjord. I waved both of my arms to stop the drekar. There was no horrible grinding sound and we stopped with water beneath our keel.

Fótr came up and nodded, "There is room to turn around and trees to disguise us. We will step the mast and rest here. There may be somewhere closer but let us use Bear Tooth and our scouts to find it."

I shook my head, "This is too important. I will go with Bear Tooth and we will take Erik with us. He is the one who will know when we have reached Moi!"

Once more we turned but this time it was quite difficult as the branch was not as wide as the fjord had been. Eventually, we tied up to the north bank. Some of the younger warriors leapt ashore to tie us to the trees. Before we could even think of sleep, we had to step the mast and Bear Tooth, Ebbe, Buthar Faramirson and Fámr Ulfsson, went ashore to scout out the land. Dawn was not far off by the time we had the mast stepped and we had disguised the prow of the drekar with foliage hacked from the trees and shrubs. If we were spied by a ship coming down the fjord it would just look like storm-damaged trees had made a dam. Our four scouts returned at the same time and reported that there was no one within at least a mile of us. I did not risk a fire, but we did set sentries. We ate and I slept for an hour. I did not think I needed the sleep, but Bear Tooth would. I had decided that just three of us would scout in daylight. I wanted to remain hidden and the more men I took the more chance there was of being spotted!

When I woke it was to a shower; whilst not heavy it was chilling to the bones. We wore cloaks and sealskin hats rather than helmets. I took my Saami bow as well as Viking Killer. I saw Bear Tooth looking with interest at the weapon. "That looks to be a good bow."

"It is and can send an arrow further than any other that I have used."

Bear Tooth strung his bow, "When time allows I would like to try it!"

I turned to Fótr, "We will be back tonight, but it may well be after dark. Keep a watch for us. If there is danger, then save the drekar. Head back out to sea if you must but do not get caught."

"Fear not we will not risk the ship. She is too important to Ebbe and me."

I spoke to the crew. I wanted no misunderstandings, "Until I return then Fótr the Wolf commands. Obey him as you would me!" I saw my oathsworn looking less than happy at the prospect of me wandering around Norway alone but, like the others, they nodded.

I let Bear Tooth lead and kept Erik between the two of us. I had strung my bow and I carried an arrow next to it. Bear Tooth had his bow, but it looked nothing like ours. Fótr said that the Skraeling was comfortable with it. I saw he wore strange footwear. Fótr had said they were called mockasin. I saw the imprints left by Erik's sealskin boots but not the mockasin and it appeared to be useful footwear for a scout. He moved silently too, almost as though he was part of the land even though he had been born far to the west. There was neither game nor man-made trail to follow but Bear Tooth seemed to have the ability to choose the easiest path through the heavily forested land for us all. I had the impression that if Erik and I had not slowed him down he could have run through the forest without leaving a mark!

The land rose and fell. We passed water but they were tarns and not connected to the fjord or if they were connected then the stream was too shallow for our drekar. Suddenly the trees ahead ended, and we emerged above a broader piece of water. It looked to be wider than the fjord at its mouth, in fact it looked to be as big as The Water close to Hawk's Roost. Bear Tooth held up his hand and sniffed the air. Seemingly satisfied he led us down to the water. It looked to be a river and it joined our fjord. Even better was the fact that we could make our way along it. We followed it for about two miles, and I would have been happy to turn back and tell Fótr that we had found a better place to hide but Bear Tooth kept going. The river narrowed to less than forty paces and I was going to tell Bear Tooth to turn back when suddenly we found ourselves looking at a vast expanse of water. It was as wide as the fjord and headed north. It widened to at least five hundred paces and looked perfect. The trees came all the way down to the water and we saw no sign of any habitation. It was as though this was virgin forest. We stopped and ate some food.

Bear Tooth tasted the water when we had eaten, "This is good water, Lord Sámr, but even if the trees were cleared it could not be farmed and I have seen no sign of any game."

I nodded, "My great grandfather told me that it was a harsh land and the men who lived here were tough. You can see why they come to our land to try to take it."

We backtracked until we came to the great fjord and then headed back to the newly found anchorage, "Does anything look familiar, Erik?"

"This water seems to be the one I passed along. It was frozen then and I had to travel its whole length before I found the road which headed across the mountains to Moi. The journey took me five days, but I saw no one. I do not think there are people here. When I was on the road, I passed farms, but they were well to the north of where we are."

"Then we can use this to hide the drekar. The only drawback which I can see is that if it was found it would be relatively easy to trap our ship here."

"When I was in Moi, I saw just two drekar. One was Uddulfr the Sly's boat, *'Loki's Revenge'*."

"Loki? Is the man a fool tempting that god?"

Erik shrugged, "I do not think he sails very often. He is renowned as a cunning warrior rather than a sailor. Those I spoke to did not question his skill with weapons, but they all felt that he had no honour and would do anything to win."

"And the other drekar?"

"All that I know is that it had a figurehead like a wyrme or a snake! It was well painted, and the ship looked to be neat and tidy."

Bear Tooth looked up at the sun, "We had better leave, lord. I can make my way through that forest in the dark but…"

"But you think an old man might fall! You may be right. Let us make quick time for I would anchor here and, perhaps, give the men some hot food." There were places along the side of the larger piece of water where we could light fires. We were getting close to my family and I wanted men with full bellies who would be able to tear through Moi and Uddulfr the Sly and his warriors. I had not given much thought to getting out of the fjord and it came to me that the narrow fjord up which we had travelled was not the place to meet another.

It was Erik who made the noise as we approached the drekar and we were spotted. I was pleased for the guard. His life would have been made a misery by his oar brothers if we had just appeared.

"You have found somewhere for us to shelter?"

"Aye, Fótr, and it is not far away. We do not have to sail far, and we have found a large piece of water where we can hide. There is one very narrow section, but the water is deep enough and wide enough for *'Gytha'* and her oars"

We manned the oars and Fótr had Erik at his side. I stood with Bear Tooth at the prow. With every oar manned and no mast to slow us, we moved very swiftly. I waved when I saw the narrow entrance and the turn was so quick that I knew Erik had anticipated the move. It seemed much narrower as we rowed towards the place I thought of as The Haven and I wondered if I had miscalculated. Then I remembered that I had had Erik with me; he knew the dimensions of the ship better than me. When we burst through the narrow entrance, I almost gave a cheer. Fótr took us to the west bank and found a sort of beach although it had no sand. It was just a patch of earth without trees. The crew assigned to moor us were spoiled for choice as there were almost too many trees for them to choose which one would tether us to the land. I decided to risk a fire and an oven for we had seen no signs of habitation. We still had some flour and a meal with bread always made it feel much more normal.

The bread oven would not be ready until the next day, but I intended to scout again with Bear Tooth and Erik. The difference this time would be that I would take my oathsworn with me for I would find Moi. They sat with Fótr, Ebbe, Erik and me. "We will not wear helmets, but we will take swords. I intend to spy out Moi. From what Erik has said we do not have far to travel. Now go and prepare." When my oathsworn had gone I addressed my words to Fótr. "If all goes well then the day after tomorrow, we will rescue my family. You have the men of Hrólfsey, and the current will be with you. I will send a message to you to tell you either of our success or failure."

"And I will just wait here with Ebbe and the men of Hrólfsey."

"If things go wrong for us then you may be the only way that we escape. Thus far it has gone well but I am not a fool, Fótr. The sisters could have twists and turns planned for us and you do not take on a man like Uddulfr the Sly without expecting trouble."

He nodded, "From what I have seen of this land, beautiful though it is, I can understand why so many men choose to go a-Viking and then take their families to settle the land. Even the Land of Ice and Fire has more to offer than this!"

He was right and I now knew why my great grandfather had fought so hard to keep the Land of the Wolf safe.

Chapter 7

We left before dawn and headed due east. When we had made the turn, the night before, Bear Tooth was convinced that he saw lights in the distance. We marched through the forest for what I took to be three miles. A warrior learned to estimate distances. The forest became lighter when we neared the fjord, the fjord of Uddulfr, and Bear Tooth stopped us thirty paces from the water which we could see, dark blue and glisteningly chilly. He disappeared and when he reappeared, he took us all by surprise. "There is a road, lord and, just a short way up the fjord is a large town. I see a wooden wall. I think that it is Moi."

I patted Erik on the back, "Well done, Erik! My great grandfather would be proud." Turning to Bear Tooth I said, "Do we risk the road?"

"No, Lord Sámr, most definitely no. Boats travelling up and down would see us. If we travel through the forest it will not add much time and we will be hidden." He turned and pointed south-east, "Our camp is just two or three miles in that direction. I am catching the faint smell of our fires." He saw the shocked look on my face and shook his head, "Can you not smell it, the smoke?" I shook my head. "I was given this nose for a purpose."

I was glad that we had the Skraeling with us, "Then lead on, Bear Tooth!"

We loped off behind Bear Tooth. Erik was still between us, but I had my oathsworn behind me. Bear Tooth might not be a Viking, but he seemed to know the land and he was proved correct within half a mile of our journey. A knarr was rowing upstream. We all stopped to watch it and I could see that it was laden. It was late in the season, but the protection afforded by the fjords meant that ships like the knarr could hug the coast and use the fingers of water to escape the wrath of the sea when storms blew up. We carried on towards the town and even I could detect the woodsmoke. As we ran, I saw that the trail next to the fjord was not well used. If we made this journey after dark, then we might well be able to use it. The trees prevented us from having a good view ahead and I knew that we had to be patient. Erik had said that he had entered Moi from the north and that there were farms there. That made sense. I could see no reason for any to farm this long, narrow and rocky steep-sided fjord. We had sailed up Uddulfr's fjord and turned up to moor in The Haven. There was no bridge. The only way people could travel would be by boat. We were safe, so long as they did not come to look for us.

We had been travelling for almost two hours when Bear Tooth stopped us. Erik pointed and said simply, "Moi." As I made my way to pass him and view the town, I was thinking of how long it would take us with captives. My son was hamstrung, and my wife was a lady. It could take twice as long and if we were pursued, we would be caught. I looked between the trees and my heart sank. Getting my family to safety without pursuit was the least of our worries. There was not just one drekar in port but two and equally disappointing, there were two snekke moored there too. They had doubled the garrison.

I had been taught by my great grandfather to be positive and to look at a problem from every angle. Even when Aiden had told him that he had a worm-eating him from within he did not panic and he had found a solution, even though it was a dramatic one. Bear Tooth and Erik were both examining the town too and it was Erik who pointed and said, "Over there, Lord, on the other side of the fjord. There is a fire and men are watching."

I turned and looked. He was right. Five men were perched above the fjord and were obviously there to watch for ships heading up the fjord. I nodded, "They know we are coming. The men of Man, it seems, were not the only ones who had the word of our quest. We have a land to scour when we return home."

"Lord, have you seen enough?"

I shook my head, "No, Bear Tooth, we need to get as close as we can without being seen."

"It is risky, Lord Sámr."

"Erik, it is riskier to bring my men here and not know all of the problems we might find. I would like to see where the crews of these ships are to be found." I had already worked out that the crews of the four boats could not all fit inside the stronghold. Besides, they would need to keep crews on the boats in case we appeared up the fjord. It was a question of numbers.

It was Erik who led as he knew the layout of the town. We stopped, not close to the fjord, but up the slope where we were afforded a good view down into the town. We could see the four ships and they had more than just a deck watch. There were at least six men on each of the two drekar and two on each of the snekke. The five men who were watching on the slope above the fjord were not the only watchers, two hundred paces below us was another fire and four men were sat around it watching the other side of the fjord. Had we walked up the trail we would have been seen. The presence of the sentries meant we could not speak. I looked at the palisade and the stronghold. There were two wooden towers at the end of the wall and the gatehouse was well made

73

and had arrow slits. I counted fourteen men walking the walls. I could not see much beyond the walls except for the Great Hall and it looked large enough to accommodate at least a hundred men. I did not think that there would be that many within, but the situation had changed since Erik had been here. We had brought just one drekar and men because we thought there was one crew guarding the prisoners. Now it was clear that there were at least two crews and more. We could dismiss the snekke crews but not the ships. They would be fast and, compared to *'Gytha'*, greyhounds who would run us down if we fled. The plan I had conjured on the drekar was now in tatters and I would need to make a better one. I saw that there were also four knarr in the harbour. Two were unloading while the other two rode high in the water and were awaiting either cargo or the right conditions to put to sea again.

I had seen enough, and I tapped my men on the shoulder and stood. The Norns were spinning or, perhaps, Farbjorn was careless. As he stood a stone skittered down the slope. It was a steep slope and the ground beneath the trees was covered in more stones. It had to be the sisters for the first stone found an unlikely path between the trees and gathered others to make a small rockfall. The watchers turned and saw movement. They gave the alarm. Bear Tooth had his bow ready and his arrow flew into the chest of one man. If they examined the arrow it would confuse them for his feathers and the wood were from his land across the sea.

Erik turned to run back in the direction we had taken but I said, "We do not want to lead them to our ship. Head north as you did when you left the last time. Bear Tooth, when we lose these men find us a way home. Now go!"

I nocked an arrow and stood between two pines. Farbjorn and Halfgrimr flanked me. I drew back with the Saami bow and when I saw the face one hundred paces from me, I let fly. The arrow smacked into the warrior's head and threw him down the slope. That left just two men who were following, and they took cover.

"Run!"

It was not Farbjorn's day; the sisters are like that. We were running up and across the slope and he slipped but this time it was not a small stone he dislodged but a large one and, as he was holding his sword, he lost his balance to tumble down through the trees. The two men who had hidden from us ran along the slope. I nocked another arrow. Halfgrimr went to descend the slope, "Stay!" I had no clear sight of the two warriors and when Farbjorn's head cracked off the bole of a tree and he lay still I knew that his fate was sealed. I sent my arrow into the side of one warrior who raised his sword to end Farbjorn's life but the other hacked through his neck. "Run! Farbjorn is in Valhalla!"

We hurtled up through the trees and I hoped that I would find Erik and Bear Tooth. I had no need to worry. Two hundred paces later I saw him, but he had an arrow aimed at my chest. He shouted, "Both of you, down!"

As we did so the arrow flew, and I heard a cry. As I turned, I saw that the last of the sentries was dead. Bear Tooth gestured to the right and I saw that an old avalanche had sent man-sized rocks through the trees. Bear Tooth was hiding our tracks. I put my feet where he said and Halfgrimr followed. After eight paces I saw Erik waiting in the trees and he pointed for us to turn right. We would be paralleling our earlier escape route, but we would be a good one hundred paces higher. Bear Tooth soon overtook me, and he began to lead us back to our ship. I could hear the shouts from below as the five bodies were discovered. If we had been in position, then this would have been the perfect time to rescue my family because I knew that they would have most of the warriors searching the fjord side for us. We ran for our lives. Uddulfr had known we were coming and now he knew we were here. He would have every man looking for us and would be on the alert. What had been difficult before might now be almost impossible!

Bear Tooth stopped every half a mile or so and listened. The noises we heard for the first mile soon faded. They had continued to follow our northward path and our eastward course had fooled them. We stopped when we reached The Haven. I could not see the drekar, but I would have been surprised if I had. Fótr would know better than to expose our ship.

Halfgrimr was despondent, "We let you down, Lord. Had Farbjorn not been with us then he would not have kicked the stone and the enemy would not know we were here. You would be better off without oathsworn. We are cursed."

"No more of that. Are you a man? Behave like a warrior. Farbjorn made a mistake and he paid for it with his life. He is now in Valhalla and we can forget him. Yes, Uddulfr knows that we are here but he knows not where. He will tighten his defences and be vigilant and that is the only change which I can see. I had one plan and now I will start again and make another. Thank you, Bear Tooth, you saved our lives."

He shrugged, "Perhaps you should have brought scouts, Lord Sámr. You needed no bodyguards here. Farbjorn and Halfgrimr are the men you need when you stand and fight shoulder to shoulder. When you are skipping over rocks and stones then it is surefooted men who are of more use." He put his hand on Halfgrimr's shoulder, "I am sorry, Halfgrimr, but a warrior must speak the truth."

"And you are right." There was a change in Halfgrimr from that day. I believe that Farbjorn's death made him a better warrior and it certainly changed his thinking.

"Right, Bear Tooth, lead us home."

We reached the campsite just before dark. I could smell the bread oven and I knew we would have to douse that fire. Eventually, a search by our enemies would find us. I did not wish to help them any more than I had to.

When just four of us returned the others knew that disaster had struck but none spoke of Farbjorn. Halfgrimr would be the one who told them of his shield brother's death. Fótr and Ebbe looked at each other. Ebbe asked, "Are we in danger yet?"

I shook my head, "I do not think so but we must make our attempt in the next two days and I believe that our task is now much harder. I am sorry that you have had to risk the drekar for I fear this will not end well."

Ebbe smiled, "When we fought the storm in the Great Sea, as we headed east, I was sure that we would all die but Fótr just kept fighting. When dawn came and we saw neither of our consorts then I feared the worst, but we found the snekke and even rescued some of those from *'Njörðr'*. The Allfather smiles on those who never give up. You have lost one man and whilst that is sad it is not a disaster. Eat for we have freshly caught and cooked fish and the bread was baked using ale!"

I forced a smile, "Then there is hope!"

None could help me for I had to devise a plan. Four ships instead of one was an obstacle I could not have foreseen and I wrestled with the problem until exhaustion took me. When I slept, I dreamed, and it was a dream where I walked and talked. I could smell and I could taste. I had had such dreams before but only after Kara and Aiden had given me a potion and we had spent time in the steam hut.

All was dark and I smelled smoke. I heard cries and the sound of feet running on a wooden dock. I saw the two snekke were afire and men were rushing from the stronghold to prevent it from spreading to the drekar. All went black and I saw the face of Dragonheart and Ylva. They were with an older woman I did not recognise. Although they said nothing, their eyes and mouths were smiling. As darkness came again, I heard Aiden's voice and he said one word, 'Troy'! and I woke for I knew the answer.

It was still dark, but I dressed and began to run towards Uddulfr's fjord. The two sentries turned with swords ready to strike but when they saw me, they lowered them. "There is nothing amiss and I will return."

I ran down the narrow entrance to The Haven until I reached Uddulfr's fjord. Looking towards where I knew Moi lay, I breathed a sigh of relief. I could not see it and therefore they could not see me. It had not taken me long to run the short way from our camp. I knelt and put my hand in the fjord and, as I had expected it was bone-chillingly cold. I broke off a pine branch from a nearby tree and threw it into the fjord. It headed slowly towards the sea. I had the start of a plan, but it needed refinement. I headed back to the camp. The two sentries had woken Fótr and he, Ebbe and Bear Tooth were waiting for me.

I smiled as Ebbe handed me a horn of ale, "I have a plan and it is both wild and incredibly risky, but I believe we can make it work. Who is the strongest swimmer?"

The three of them looked blankly at me and it was Fótr who pointed out the obvious, "Lord Sámr, apart from us three the rest are your men. Who do you think is the best swimmer and why do you need to know?" I smiled and explained my plan to them. I told them of my dream and even Bear Tooth understood the significance of that. None of them understood Aiden's words and I had to tell them the story which I had heard in Miklagård.

Fótr nodded and said, "It is a risk, but I have seen both you and Bear Tooth send an arrow. That part may well work and then the rest depends upon timing."

When the camp awoke, I gathered them around me. "I have a question to ask and I want an honest answer. I have a plan to rescue my family, but it needs someone who can swim in an icy fjord." Hands were raised and I shook my head. "That is not the answer I wished to hear. If the warrior is not a skilled swimmer and he fails, then the whole plan fails and this drekar and its crew will all be in jeopardy. We have no time for a trial. If this is going to work, then by noon I need someone to be in the fjord!" I glared at them and then said, "Who can do what I ask? Who can lie in the icy fjord for, perhaps, half an hour and still have the ability to fight?"

None raised their hands until Halfgrimr did so. "I am a good swimmer, Lord Sámr. At Hawk's Roost Farbjorn and I would swim across to Cyninges-tūn and back. The fjord will be colder, but I can do this." I looked beyond his eyes into his mind and he nodded, "I speak the truth, Lord Sámr."

"Good."

When we had first found the entrance to this haven, we had cleared away the small dam of logs and brushwood which had gathered at the mouth. I had the crew use it to make a natural looking raft. Bear Tooth and I had our bows. Halfgrimr lay on the improvised raft with was secured to a tree by a rope and, with my crew hidden in the trees we waited. We allowed one knarr to head downstream to the sea and I feared that we might have to wait another day for one travelling upstream when we were rewarded by a whistle from Gandálfr Eriksson who was across the other side of the mouth of our fjord. He had seen a knarr heading upstream.

"Ready, Halfgrimr?"

"Aye, lord." His sword was hidden beneath his body. Whilst not entirely immersed in the fjord he would be chilled to the bone and there was always a risk that the raft would disintegrate.

We let out the rope and the current drifted the raft with what appeared to be a body upon it, across the fjord. We saw the knarr which was using oars to row up the fjord. It was laden and they were not moving quickly. We stopped the rope when the raft was sixty paces from the shore. Any closer to the bank and the knarr might have ignored Halfgrimr and any closer to the middle would have meant a smaller chance of success. The knarr's captain pushed over the steering board. He was alone at the stern for the other four of his crew were rowing. As they neared the raft I heard him shout to his men to keep the knarr steady. As he stood to help Halfgrimr, Bear Tooth and I stood with nocked arrows aimed at him.

"Captain, bring your knarr over here!" He turned to race back to the steering board. My arrow slammed into it. "My friend here is even more accurate than I am. Do as I say, and I swear that none of you will be hurt."

I saw him nod and he said to his crew, "Do as these pirates command, Lord Uddulfr will have their heads on pikes before the week is out!"

I felt better about my action for I now knew that these were part of Uddulfr's warband. "Pull Halfgrimr back in."

We attached ropes to the knarr, and my crew and I hauled it to The Haven. I had already told Egil and his men that they would be the guardians of the knarr crew when I had explained my plan to them, for now, speed was all-important. The five men were bound and taken aboard *'Gytha'*. The rest of us prepared for war. Halfgrimr and Erik would lead six of my men to crew the knarr and sail towards Moi. We would have to time it so that we reached there at dusk. We needed confusion and darkness to make the plan work. As I donned my mail Erik said, "Lord, explain to me again about this Troy."

I smiled, "When we were in Miklagård Aiden was told a story about some Greeks who were trying to get into a place called Troy. The walls were too high and so they built a horse and filled it with men. They left the horse outside the gates of Troy and it was taken inside. You and Halfgrimr will be our wooden horse. They will just see a knarr bringing more goods. By the time you have unloaded the vessel, it will be dark. We will have slain the sentries who guard the slopes and you will set fire to the snekke and the drekar. Once that is done you will leave the mooring and anchor in the fjord. The knarr will be the way I rescue my family."

He looked at the ground, "Then the success of this depends upon me."

"And those who sail with you." I put my arm around his shoulder. "I trust you, Erik, and I trust the others! This plan came from the spirits and I trust in their judgement!"

Chapter 8

Bear Tooth took his scouts and went ahead. I knew that Uddulfr would have increased those watching the fjord but Bear Tooth's skill with a bow and the fact that he knew how to kill left me in no doubt that we would reach Moi without our enemies knowing. Getting out successfully was another matter altogether. I led the rest. Erik and Halfgrimr would travel as slowly as they could up the fjord to arrive just when the sun was beginning to set. In the hold they had all the dried material we could find, and they had a burning pot to begin the fires faster. They had four smaller pots filled with kindling to accelerate the fires in all of the vessels. We would be in position well before dark so that we could gauge the opposition. When we reached Bear Tooth and the dead sentries, I saw the skill of the Skraeling. There were six warriors and three had died with arrows in them. I wondered how the Skraeling and his scouts had managed to kill them so silently for we were just a hundred paces behind them and we had heard nothing. Certainly, as we peered down into Moi it looked peaceful enough. The Norwegians were being vigilant but there was no sign of urgent activity. Once my fire starters had done their work and the gates opened, we would race inside the stronghold. Only Erik and two others would man the knarr and they would be standing by to take off my family. We had to kill as many as we could and hope that, in the confusion, we were not noticed until it was too late. It would be dark and men, I hoped, would be fighting the fires. This was where I missed the Ulfheonar. Bear Tooth was the nearest we had to one but even he could not hide in plain sight. Had we had the likes of Bjorn the Scout, the Shape Shifter, Haaken One Eye, and the others then they could have slipped inside and guaranteed the safety of my family. If Ylva or Aiden had been with us, then we could have used magic. We had neither and would have to use courage, cunning and as much luck as we could muster!

Darkness had almost fallen, and I feared that Erik had left it too late. He had not and I saw the knarr nudge gently into a space close by *'Serpent's Tongue'* which was the end vessel. We were more than two hundred paces from them, in the trees, and could not hear a word but it was soon clear that there was no suspicion. The two guards who had approached them to ask their business soon returned to the main gate. We watched as some of the sentries from the ships trooped back into the stronghold. It was time for food and the daytime sentries would be replaced by the smaller night watch. Guards would change after the meal, but they would not be as fresh. They would have drunk ale with their food and might not be as vigilant as those on duty during the day. Only two of our men were unloading the official cargo from the knarr. Erik, Halfgrimr and the other four were stacking the kindling close to the four ships. Once the fire pots were hurled on board then the kindling would follow. There was one man for each ship and one fire pot for each ship. We had one spare. Halfgrimr and Erik would use their swords to prevent the handful of guards who remained from interfering. My two men who were ostensibly moving the cargo were ready with their swords. I watched Bear Tooth nock an arrow; he was ready too. The guards who remained on the drekar helped us. The two ships were stern to stern for the steering boards had been removed and the four guards were chatting. No doubt they were bemoaning their fate and the fact that they had to do a duty. There was just a single man on each of the snekke and the two sentries at the gate were lounging against the palisade. The sunset had been a glorious one. The clouds of the day had scudded away, and it was a red fiery sunset. It might not last long but the sentries on the walls and the guards at the gate were looking at it. The light hung for a moment and then it was if a candle had been extinguished as the sun set behind the rocky walls of the fjord. Dusk became night in an instant.

I saw the flaring of the four pots as their tops were uncovered. I raised my sword and led my men down towards the walls. We left the forest and passed houses where the people were inside and eating. We padded like ghosts towards the palisade and I heard the first cry. It was a question. "What are you...?" The speaker got no further and then, suddenly, one of the drekar, *'Serpent's Tongue'* burst into flames. There were more cries but these were of pain. I heard the whoosh of an arrow and saw, silhouetted against the flames, one of the sentries plunge over the side of his boat into the icy waters of Uddulfr's fjord. I held up my sword to stop my men and we waited in the shadows of the houses. There was a clash of steel which told me that some men were still fighting, and a bell began to toll from one of the towers. There were two more flashes of flame as fires took hold on more vessels and in the light, I saw the knarr, the one we had captured, edge away from the inferno. The last thing we needed was to lose my family's only means of escape. Three of the ships were now aflame and fire raced up the masts of the two drekar as well as one of the snekke. Then the second snekke began to burn. I hoped that my men were safe, but I could not worry about them. I had to time our attack perfectly.

I signalled with my sword and we moved towards the palisade as men poured out from the inside. They were not looking to us for the burning ships held their attention. I heard orders shouted; they intended to douse the flames with water. I waited until I estimated that forty or fifty men had left the stronghold. I could wait no longer for some would be returning to fetch water and I ran. My shield was on my back and I held Gutter and Viking Killer. The first two men I slew took us for men returning for water. One was hacked across his neck and the other had his throat torn out by Gutter. Bear Tooth was still using his bow and his arrows slew any who gave commands or looked like leaders. Of course, that told our enemies that they were under attack, but they could not tell the direction. They were still looking down the fiord and did not know that we were behind them. As soon as I was inside, I ran towards the Great Hall. Erik had said that when he had been in Moi the rumour was that my family were kept there. I knew that they would have left guards to watch them. We were black shadows running towards them, silent black shapes. I had briefed my men so that the oathsworn would come with me while the rest secured our retreat.

I did not look behind me as I ran. I had to believe that I had my men behind me. There were two sentries at the double door leading to the interiors and when Bear Tooth's arrow struck one in the chest, I knew that I had at least one man who had followed me. His companion shouted a warning and turned to run inside. I was racing to save my family and the Allfather gave me speed. I hit the doors as he was trying to close them from the inside and the force was so powerful that I knocked him to the ground. I did not hesitate but ripped Viking Killer across his throat. The hall was richly appointed and Uddulfr had curtains hanging from his walls; some were well decorated. Uddulfr the Sly liked his comfort. There were women in the hall, and I heard them scream. It was time to announce my arrival.

"Aethelflaed, Ragnar, Ylva; your father has come to rescue you. Where are you?"

I was answered not by the voices I wished to hear but the sudden arrival, mailed and armed, of ten warriors. I guessed by his mail, for it was well made, that the leader was Uddulfr the Sly. I shouted, "'*Gytha*' to me!" Even as I heard feet stamping behind me as men ran to form a wedge, I saw an arrow sprout from the shoulder of one of Uddulfr's oathsworn. Bear Tooth would not fight in my wedge. He would fight his own war, the deadly Skraeling way.

Then I heard a shout, "Sámr!" It was Aethelflaed and she had heard me although it sounded to be some way away.

It was when I heard Ráðulfr Ráðgeirson's voice behind me instead of Halfgrimr that I knew something had happened to my oathsworn and he had not made it to my side after the knarr had sailed. "You have men behind you, Lord Sámr. Let us end this and kill these men!"

I shouted, "Dragonheart!" and raised my sword as I stepped forward. The training I had done meant that my men moved as one and the enemy, who had obviously not trained as well as we had, rushed at us in a mob. Uddulfr the Sly lived up to his name and he allowed two of his men to move forward. One died when an arrow flew between Ráðulfr and me to smash into the nose and skull of one of them. As the blood and brains splattered over the second man, I brought my sword down with a backhand swing to hack diagonally into the right side of his neck. He wore no coif and Viking Killer tore through his flesh to break bones and then find an artery. Blood spurted and showered all of us.

The others who were trying to get at us did not learn the lessons of the first two deaths and they rushed at the wooden and steel wedge. We wore mail and had good helmets. They could not find a way through and their attacks were uncoordinated. Ráðulfr brought up his sword to slice under one warrior's arm as Gandálfr first punched a second in the face with his shield and then skewered him as he tried to regain his balance. They were losing.

I heard Aethelflaed call for me again. "Bear Tooth! Find my family!" I saw that Uddulfr now had no men left between him and me. His other warriors came at my men and that suited me, "Break wedge!"

Once again all of our training came to the fore and with a roar, the first noise they had made, my young warriors all unleashed a simultaneous attack on the enemy. Uddulfr had a hand axe and a sword. My sword was longer and I had my seax for I had my shield on my back.

"I have had your woman and she was a disappointment. Are all Saxons so limp and lacking a fight?" He was trying to anger me, but it would not work. I had long ago worked out that he and his men would have despoiled my wife and my daughter. I had not prevented that and when I got them home, I would have to heal them. If Uddulfr was trying to goad me then he thought he was going to lose. I could see his face but mine was hidden. The firelight accentuated my red eyes and my silence intimidated him. He blinked first which signalled his intentions and he launched a ferocious attack with axe and sword. I used my sword to make a horizontal block and I swung Gutter up and under his arm. Our byrnies do not offer much protection to our arms and the seax tore through his arm and ripped open tendons and muscle. I brought my head back and butted him as he screamed in pain. Remarkably he managed to keep hold of the sword, but he could not use it effectively. He reeled backwards and fell over the body of one of his men. As much as I wanted to make him suffer my outnumbered men were outside buying me this time and time was a luxury. I rammed Viking Killer through his screaming, open mouth.

I turned around and saw that the only ones left alive in the hall were my men. The women and others had fled. I heard a shout and, looking up saw Aethelflaed, my children and Bear Tooth as he brought them from the rear of the hall. They had all suffered for they were dirty, emaciated and gaunt. I saw that Ragnar dragged one leg. I felt anger and my natural reaction was to comfort them, but we did not have time; already we might be trapped here. "Bear Tooth go to the door and make sure none are close."

"I have but four arrows left, lord."

"Then use them wisely." After sheathing my seax I went to the fire burning in the middle of the hall. I picked up one of the logs by the end which was not burning. "Gandálfr, take these men and get my family to the knarr." I wanted to kiss and hold my wife but that would have to wait. "This darkness has not yet ended, my love and my family. The Allfather willing it soon will be. These men will guard you with their lives and we will lead these men away from you."

Aethelflaed, said, "Take care my love! These are evil men."

"I know and they will pay!" I threw one brand at one side of the hall's walls and then did the same with another burning brand on the other side. The flames licked up the curtains and tapestries which hung there. They would burn and set alight the walls and joists of this hall. The turf roof would not burn but the hall would be destroyed and, more importantly, the inferno would draw men to douse the flames. I reached the door and saw that although Bear Tooth had but one arrow left, for he put the other three to good use, there were no men nearby. The ground, however, between the hall and the knarr, which I could see just beyond the dock was filled with fighting men. It was a confused scene for some of Moi's men were still fighting a losing battle to save their ships. On the ships, there were other men trying to save equipment and chests. Wooden ships are like tinderboxes and oiled ropes burn!

"Come Bear Tooth. We will let these men of Moi know who has come amongst them. When we reach the door give a Skraeling scream!"

He opened his mouth and gave the cry which had sent shivers down my spine when I had first heard it at Hawk's Roost on the day I had been rescued. It had the same effect as the cry of the wolf the Ulfheonar used. It was like inspiration from the dead and I cupped my left hand and gave the wolf howl. Both cries seemed to freeze motion. I saw warriors cease fighting flames and men and look to the skies. Smoke from the fires was obscuring us.

I shouted, "I am Sámr, Dragonheart's Heir and I am here to end the poison that is Moi! *'Gytha'* to me!" Bear Tooth and I ran not towards the knarr but in the opposite direction, in the direction of the houses we had passed and the forest where we had sheltered. Ebbe and four men waited there with bows ready to help our escape when we had made our way to the gates. As I had expected my name drew men to me. I was not the warrior to be feared that my great grandfather had been, but I was a prize which their king had lost. Whoever killed me or took me captive would be richly rewarded. Their best warriors came at me and I had just Bear Tooth for protection for my oathsworn were watching over my family. His last arrow blossomed from the chest of a warrior who looked down at the feathers sticking from his chest. He wore mail and had thought he was protected. Bear Tooth slipped his bow over his shoulder and picking up the fallen Norse spear hurled it at those who ran at us. It made them falter and he drew his small axe and sword. I held Gutter and we did not break stride but ran at the enemy.

Two men charging twenty sounds like suicide, but it is not. We had space between us and the enemy who came at us were fighting each other to try to get close. Even without looking to the side, I knew that our reckless and wild charge had worked. We had drawn the warriors away from the knarr and Gandálfr would be able to safely deliver my family to Erik. Then, he and any others who had survived could come to our aid. I brought Viking Killer down on the shoulder of one warrior as my left hand flicked instinctively to my left, deflecting a sword which came at me. A spear slid along the side of my helmet, but it was securely fastened and did no harm. And then we were in the middle of the enemy. Their very numbers and their press made it hard for them to use their swords while Bear Tooth had his hand axe and I had Gutter. We did not need to swing them. We wore helmets and most of those we fought did not. Few had mail and we were encased in iron! I butted, slashed and stamped. I held Viking Killer horizontally and the press from those before us drove one Viking's neck into the edge of Viking Killer and Bagsecg's blade ended his life. Bear Tooth was a revelation. I had never fought next to him before and his arms were a blur. He used both his axe and short sword with such speed and force that none could stay close to him. Bloodied bodies seemed to fall all around him.

We might have begun to suffer wounds for an axe head, brought from before me hit my left shoulder and it hurt. Had I not had padding beneath the mail then I might have suffered a broken bone. Gandálfr led the survivors from our attack with a cry of, "Cyninges-tūn!" and smashed into the back of the enemy who surrounded us.

Now we had more space as men turned to face the new threat and I was able to use my two weapons more effectively. I blocked the blow from the sword with Viking Killer and then tore Gutter across the warrior's throat. He had had a shield, but he had held it too low. Two men before me each had a spear and a shield but neither helmet nor mail. Seeing this bloody apparition slay men with such contemptuous ease made them turn and flee to the north. I revolved and saw that Gandálfr and the others had despatched most of the others. Soon, however, we would have more men to contend with for those who had been fighting the fires would be giving up and seeking their own vengeance. One drekar and two snekke were already settling into the water and the last drekar, *'Serpent's Tongue'* would not be long in following!

"Fetch our wounded and get back to *'Gytha'*!" This time we would not be able to hide our trail. Darkness would aid us, but they would be able to follow. I stood with Bear Tooth who, in the light of the last fiery drekar looked to be covered from head to foot in gore and blood. He grinned in the dark. He did not like a full-face helmet and wore just a metal band around his head, "That was a good fight! A warrior could die and face his ancestors with head held high after that!"

"Do not do that my friend, live and tell the tale to your grandchildren!"

"Aye, Lord, you are right! Come for our friends are now gone and your family sails down the fjord. Erik has them!"

Bear Tooth's sharp eyes confirmed what I felt in my head. The spirits told me that they were safe. I saw the shadow drifting down Uddulfr's fjord. We ran towards the forest. Those in the houses had wisely stayed inside and not interfered. They would be the burghers who made money from Moi but would not shed blood to save it. They seemed to me to be like the people of Whale Island. I had a score to settle with them. Since Fótr's news and Erik's experience they had much been in my thoughts. We entered the wood and it seemed much cooler. Here we were forced to go at a slower pace. There was no real path and we had wounded men. We had left dead in Moi and their bodies would be despoiled but that could not be helped. They were in Valhalla now.

I heard a voice in the dark behind me. There was still someone to give commands, "Prince Uddulfr is dead! Let us avenge him. Follow me!"

They were coming. I shook my head. Uddulfr had delusions of grandeur. What was he the prince of? A cesspit in Norway. I knew then just what we had in the Land of the Wolf and why so many sought to take it from us. I had much to do when we returned home but first, we had to get there. The route we took led us up a steep slope and Bear Tooth and I, now with sheathed weapons, had to slow. At the top of the rise, we found Ebbe. "You survived, lord." He and his men were armed with bows and each one had an arrow nocked.

I nodded. "Aye, but there are men following."

"Then get to the ship and we will hold them."

I shook my head, "Bear Tooth take the left side and I will take this side."

We heard the men as they laboured up the slope. When a man runs up such a slope, especially at night, he looks down to watch his footing and then looks up to see where he should place his feet. Ebbe was no Bear Tooth but at the short range of twenty feet he could not miss and as the leading warrior lifted his head to see the direction of our trail the arrow slammed into it and threw him down the slope towards the others. Ebbe had chosen his ambush perfectly. He had time to nock another arrow for his bowmen slew the next five men who tried the same route.

I heard, from the dark, the voice which had commanded pursuit, "Spread out and flank them!"

"Aye, Jarl! We will get them and rip out their hearts!"

As those following all cheered the sentiment I said, quietly, "Now we move. Ebbe, find another ambush."

"Aye, lord, we have one in mind."

Bear Tooth and I stood in the shadows and waited. It was so dark that it was hard to see anything and in the black forest, a man who stood motionless looks just like the trunk of a tree. Those who followed us moved, they grunted, and they sucked in air. The first Viking to die knew nothing about his death for I swung Viking Killer sideways as he head appeared. He made not a sound, but his head flew through the air and I heard a cry as it landed near to one who was following. Bear Tooth must have also killed one.

A different voice from the first one shouted, "Jarl, they are waiting for us!"

"Go in pairs! I have a gold piece for the one who brings me Sámr's head!"

I tapped Bear Tooth on the shoulder, and we moved up the slope. I sheathed my sword. This would need Gutter. We did not follow Ebbe. I had thought of another way to slow them down. We found two huge trees and waited behind them. Below us, we saw the moving shadows as men paired up and followed Ebbe's trail. Two men appeared below us. They looked left and right before they moved on. I guessed that they were the extreme left side of the enemy line of beaters trying to drive

87

the game. I moved forward when they had passed, and Bear Tooth followed. I would take the warrior to the right. He had a sword and a shield. He was moving slowly and picking his path. Without waiting for Bear Tooth, I stepped behind him, pulled his head back and ripped Gutter across his throat. Bear Tooth's axe split the helmet and skull of the other warrior and we moved on. We were now behind the enemy line and they were only looking ahead.

I heard a cry from below me and a voice shouted, "Ambush!"

I put my mouth to Bear Tooth's ear and said, "We give a war cry and fall upon their flank. Let us make them think we bring the whole crew!"

He nodded and grinned. I drew Viking Killer and placed myself to Bear Tooth's right. Ebbe and his ambushers were slowing down the men of Moi and forcing them to try to outflank the ambush.

"Dragonheart!"

That and the Skraeling scream precipitated our wild charge down the slope. The shields of the men we hit were to their left and that gave them protection, but they could not use their swords effectively. My weight knocked a pair to the ground and as they became entangled in the trees I hacked and chopped at them. I heard cries of panic amongst our enemies who ran down the slope. The Jarl who commanded them shouted, "Stop! There cannot be many of them!" It was a cry in vain. They took the line of least resistance and ran down the hill. Even if they were rallied, they would have to struggle up the slope.

"Bear Tooth!" We headed towards where I expected Ebbe to be. When I found the first body with an arrow in it, I shouted, "Sámr and Bear Tooth!

"Come!"

"We can run back to the ship now. They will still pursue but it will take time for them to be rallied."

Bear Tooth led us, unerringly, through the trees. He came from the other side of the world but the Allfather had given him a natural ability which was terrifying. He could navigate where there were no paths. It would soon be dawn. As we descended the slope towards The Haven I wondered if Erik had successfully sailed the knarr.

As the first glimmer of dawn appeared in the east, I saw the knarr tied to a tree. He had made it. The camp was empty, and I saw faces lining the drekar. They had fitted the mast and crosspiece. The sail was in place, but the faces were looking anxiously for us. The knarr's crew were still bound close to the moored ship.

I sheathed my sword and said, "Get aboard, I have something to do." Bear Tooth and Ebbe led my men to the drekar. I shouted, "Prepare to leave."

As I headed towards the knarr and its bound crew I heard Aethelflaed's voice, "Do not kill them! They are not worth it!"

I had no intention of doing so. I stepped aboard the knarr and slashed the forestays, backstays, sheets and buntlines. I walked to the steering board and cut the steerboard withy. The knarr would sail again but not until we were well out to sea. I stepped aboard *'Gytha'*. "Fótr, take us home!"

We were not yet out of danger. There had been knarr in the harbour and if they sent one down the fjord then they might be able to block our escape. I saw Aethelflaed and my two grown-up children close to the mast fish. The crew who were without wounds were at their oars and Ebbe was tending to the wounded. We had all the oars manned but there were no replacements. I went to the steering board where Erik and Fótr waited for the oarsmen to be seated, "Row!"

Erik stood before the front oars and stamped his foot as he chanted.

Halfgrimr was a warrior brave
He gave his life for another to save
Oathsworn to the end with sword in hand
He was the best of Sámr's band
Faithless Vikings fell to his blade
Ten men were by him slayed
Warriors from Dragonheart's Land
Warriors forged in Sámr's warband
Warriors making one last stand
Warriors from Dragonheart's Land
Farbjorn's fate was spun in a cave
By the sisters who killed the warrior brave
They flicked a stone and made him fall
The oathsworn had no chance at all
Warriors from Dragonheart's Land
Warriors forged in Sámr's warband
Warriors making one last stand
Warriors from Dragonheart's Land
Warriors from Dragonheart's Land
Warriors forged in Sámr's warband
Warriors making one last stand
Warriors from Dragonheart's Land

By the time we reached the fjord and headed for the sea, Erik had finished the first singing of the saga of the raid on Uddulfr. He had composed it in his head when he had sailed the knarr down the fjord. He began again and men joined in the chorus. Fótr said, "Lord Sámr, we do not need you. Erik can watch. Your family needs you."

I saw that the three of them were like an island. They were alone and I could see, from their faces, that they had not yet realised they were free or, perhaps, their ordeal had been so bad that it had changed them. I nodded, "Call me if you spy trouble. I have a lifetime with my family!"

Fótr shook his head, "That is what my brother Arne thought! Life is for the moment. Live it."

He was far younger than I was and yet seemed so much wiser. Perhaps the New World changed a man.

I went to the mastfish and Aethelflaed and Ylva moved apart so that I could sit with them. I put my arms out and held closely the two women and my son. Aethelflaed and Ylva wept and sobbed. They were not tears of pain but of relief. I was aware, too, that Ragnar was silently crying. Neither of my offspring was a child. They were a man and woman grown but taken when they had barely seen fourteen summers. Their whole life had been turned upside down. They had been almost nobles in the Land of the Wolf. There were descended from The Dragonheart and accorded respect. Looking at their ragged and dirty clothes they looked like the poor of Lundenwic. I cursed myself. I should have had the foresight to bring clean clothes for them. The sun broke fully in the east before they ceased crying. By now Erik had stopped his singing as we had the current and the rowers had their rhythm. The boat was eerily silent. The men were thinking of the oar brothers they had left behind and some who had not lost friends, like Bear Tooth, would be reliving each blow that they struck in the Battle of Moi. When Erik heard all the stories then, like a witch's spell it would be added and spun into the saga to be sung in our halls on long winter nights when we remembered the dead and honoured them. I counted the crew and worked out who had died. In the maelstrom of the battle I had not noticed but now I could mourn them.

That was what I would normally be doing but I was trying to work out how to bring back my family from this pit of despair. My great grandfather had told me tales of descending into caves. I had been in the witch's cave beneath the sea at Syllingar and my great grandfather had rescued me. Dragonheart had fought a magical dragon to rescue Ylva, his granddaughter. Here there was no one to fight. I could not bring Uddulfr back and torture him. I would have to fight daemons I could not see. I missed Ylva and Kara for they would have known what to do.

90

My mother would have been perfect for she was the gentlest soul who ever walked the earth and oozed kindness and love. I had no one save myself. I closed my eyes and invoked the spirits of the dead, Erika, Ylva, Kara and Astrid.

Chapter 9

Once we hit the sea, we were able to use the sails. The wind was coming from the south and west, but we could still make progress albeit more slowly than when we had sailed east. Fótr was confident that we could make Føroyar where his brother had found seals, water and food. It might add a week to the voyage, but we had taken supplies from the knarr, ale and fish, and the alternative was to have exhausted men to row. As the crew came nervously towards the mast fish I said, "Let us go to the prow and speak there. Fótr told me that Gytha was a powerful witch and her figurehead was carved by her husband. I need her help."

Ebbe saw what we were doing, and he waved Bear Tooth and Erik to help him move the wounded to the mast fish. There the motion was less violent, and a sail could be rigged to give shelter to those wounded in the rescue. We said nothing as we passed but I saw the three of them look at Bear Tooth. He had worn mail when we had fought but he did not enjoy wearing it and had stripped it off. His dark-skinned body and angular features marked him as different. I saw my wife and children staring at him. It came to me that I had a way to tempt them from the cave of darkness in which they hid.

I sat with my back to the prow. Aethelflaed was on my right and a shivering Ylva to my left. Ragnar sat with his back to the steerboard side gunwale.

"Erik, fetch the sheepskins!"

Erik hurried down with the skins we had taken on Orkneyjar. He laid them over the three of them, "I am sorry that you had to endure your torture for so long. Forgive me." Aethelflaed looked at me and I smiled, "I have much to tell you, wife. First let me tell you the tale of this drekar, its captain, Fótr and the Skraeling, Bear Tooth. If you wish to sleep, I will not be offended."

Ragnar said, "I would like ale, father!"

It was almost as though Bear Tooth had read his mind for he brought four horns of ale. "This is Bear Tooth and he is not a Viking."

The Skraeling grinned, "And I am honoured to have helped you and slain so many men! If I was in my own land, I would have many signs of my victory to wear!"

Aethelflaed was ever mindful of being polite. It was the way she had been brought up, "Thank you Bear Tooth. I look forward to hearing your story!"

Ragnar quaffed the ale in one and I handed him my horn which he also finished. I then told them of Fótr and the New World. I spoke of

Ylva and her magic and then told them of my rescue. Aethelflaed said, "Then it is not only we three who have paid the price of a king's ambition."

"You three endured far worse for I am a warrior and when a warrior loses he expects to pay a price."

Ragnar wiped the froth from his mouth, "And I will never have the chance to become a warrior."

"Ragnar, you are too young to remember but there was an Ulfheonar who went to war with The Dragonheart. He was Karl Word Master. He was lamed but he was the captain of the guard at Cyninges-tūn. He trained the young warriors and he was a great warrior. Before he died in the last battle, he slew ten men. You do not need to be a warrior but if you wish it then it is more than possible. But you have to make the choice."

I then told them of my year of indolence and the return of Erik. I saw the three of them look at him with new eyes. They now understood his words.

Aethelflaed kissed my cheek, "You have no reason to reproach yourself for you were a prisoner when the worst abuses took place. Ylva and I were abused for the first year but when we stopped fighting them it became less enjoyable to them and they used others, fresh victims. We were lucky. Some of the other girls were used until they died or killed themselves."

My daughter snapped, angrily, "I do not feel lucky! I can never look at a man with anything other than fear. I can never have children for who would wish to have such a one as me bear his children?"

When Aethelflaed was silent then I knew they were her thoughts too. "I cannot undo the past and I dare not try for the threads of the Norns cannot be undone save by a witch. Ylva, you are beautiful and the soiled hands of the men who abused you will never touch you again. It took me a year to become Sámr once more. This will not be a swift journey for any of you but once we reach the Land of the Wolf and Hawk's Roost then we shall let the land and The Water heal you. The spirits of the dead are in The Water. Ylva's spirit is still in Myrddyn's cave. You are still scarred. Let the Land of the Wolf heal you."

I could see that my children were not convinced but Aethelflaed squeezed my arm, "Give them time, my husband. We are tired and although it is daytime, we will be able to sleep for the first time since our capture. When you expect pain, you do not sleep well. Hold us in your arms and the healing will begin."

My wife and daughter were asleep almost immediately, but Ragnar spoke to me quietly when he heard the heavy breathing of deep sleep.

"You cannot know what they endured. It was not just the abuse it was that it was done before others. Uddulfr the Sly enjoyed bringing them out when one of his friends came to visit. The cruellest was a jarl called Rognvald Larsson."

I looked up quickly, "I have heard of him. His ship was in Moi."

"He arrived a week ago."

Wyrd! The Norns were spinning.

"And you, my son, I know they hamstrung you, but I fear to ask what else they did to you."

"Then do not for I am ashamed. Let us say that if I see any of those enemies again then I will make them suffer." He looked east to the distant coastline. "You say Uddulfr is dead?"

"I killed him."

"Then there are others I will look for." He leaned into me and I saw the pain etched on his young face. "They will come for us. King Harald Finehair often visited and enjoyed mocking us. Our capture seemed to make him think he was Dragonheart. He seeks the sword."

"And that he will never have for it lies beneath The Water and is protected. We drove the last of his men from our land when Fótr's people came."

"I know for six months since he came and had the three of us whipped. It was not as bad as the other abuses we had endured but it showed his anger. I listened while I was a captive. If he had not had trouble in his islands, then he would have returned to the Land of the Wolf before now. I fear that our rescue will begin another attack."

"Let us get home first and worry about that when we have the walls of Hawk's Roost around us. I am proud of you, son, and I will do all that I can to keep you safe. Now sleep. Your mother is right. Sleep is the best medicine for you."

I did not sleep. My body was weary, but my mind was a maelstrom. I had not seen another warrior of Uddulfr's stature in the battle. Rognvald Larsson was still alive. I had not only rescued his king's captives I had destroyed his ships. King Harald would also come, and we had perilously few men to fight him. The ones we had were young and untried. I needed allies. I would not ask the Danes for they were too treacherous. That left the Vikings of Hibernia. Long ago they had been our staunchest allies. Now I was not so certain. They were, at least, not enemies. I also needed to scour Whale Island of the traitors who lived there, and I would need to be ruthless. What would my great grandfather have done? He had been a great warrior, but he had also been clever. He knew how to make friends and defeat enemies. A plan began to form but it would need sleep for when I slept then the dream dragon began to conjure and when I woke what had been unsubstantial smoke became a reality.

Erik came down to join me at noon. He brought food and more ale. He spoke quietly. "Their faces tell tales that no singer can ever make into songs."

"Aye, Erik. You might understand better than any. Ylva and Ragnar need love and understanding."

Erik nodded to Bear Tooth, "He is a wise one. I would like to meet more of his people if they are all like him. He said that he lost all, and it was the love he earned from the Clan of the Fox which healed him. Fótr said that Ragnar might like to wear his wolf fur. It is magical."

I nodded, "That is a good idea. Fetch it and lay it over him. It cannot hurt. Perhaps we will go on a wolf hunt to Úlfarrberg when we reach our home. By then it will be Mörsugur and the best time to hunt the wolf."

When he took away the platter, I thought of all the threads which bound us. We had begun the vengeance trail, but it was far from over. When a warrior stepped on to that trail he had to keep going to the end. If you stepped off too soon then the Norns would punish you. King Harald Finehair and Jarl Rognvald would not rest until they had their vengeance too. This time we had to fight until either they or we could no longer fight again. We could not do as the Clan of the Fox had done and flee west. If we did so, then Norway would have won. King Harald Finehair's ambition must be thwarted. I was no Dragonheart, but I was reborn. I had been through the fire and now that I had my family back, I would make my land a fortress.

I was forced to move when I needed to make water. As I did so men came down with sealskins to make a better shelter for my family. I made water over the side and then joined Fótr at the steering board. Ebbe, Erik and Bear Tooth were there, and I waved Egil over. I told them what Ragnar had told me.

"Egil, I can still take you home, but I think that our threads are now bound." He nodded. "If you would come to the Land of the Wolf then we can equip you as warriors and if Ragnar is right then your enemy will come to us. Better a death with a chance of victory than a wasted one alone."

"We had spoken of this when we waited at The Haven and would have asked to sail to your home. There is nothing for us now on Hrólfsey, but can you fight Finehair?"

"Thank you for your honesty." I nodded, "I have thought on this. His early victories were because he surprised people as they did not realise the scale of his ambition. The islands now fight him and if he finds

95

them hard to subdue then he might discover that, prepared, we would be a harder morsel for him to swallow. We have destroyed two of his drekar and killed many of his warriors. If he had power, then when I was rescued, he would have brought his full might down upon us. He did not and so he is not as powerful as he once was. The last time we lost because my family was divided, and he used cunning. We are no longer divided, and we can be as cunning as he. I know not how we will defeat him but our victory at Fótr's stad has shown me that our clan has the power! I just need to use it well."

We sailed into a cold grey afternoon on a lonely sea. There were troughs and crests, but we had endured worse. Fótr would sleep in the afternoon and Erik had taken the opportunity to sleep now. He was close to the prow. I wondered if he still felt guilty that he had not sought my family sooner. Fótr nodded at my family and said, "I do not envy you the task you have set yourself. Wounds of the body are easier to heal than those of the mind and I can see that they are all scarred."

"This time I will not flinch. I know, from The Dragonheart, that being a leader means having to look beyond a family. He lost two sons that way, Arturus, my grandfather, and Gruffydd. I will not make the same mistake. I do not want to endure the pain of the last couple of years." I looked at Fótr. "Of course, you know that they will come for you, too?"

He nodded, "All know of Bear Tooth the Skraeling and he does not fight quietly. Like you, we will have to make our home more like Larswick and I also know that we are isolated."

"There is an old Roman fort on the road from your home to Cyninges-tūn. If you built a beacon there and lit it, we could see the smoke from our land."

He nodded, "Lars Bennisson lives not far from there. His family suffered on Bear Island because they lived too far from help. He will understand better than any." He made a slight adjustment with the steering board. He was watching the sail, the sea and the prow all the time. He was a navigator. "It seems our people are doomed to fight for land and against greedy enemies. My family would happily still live on Orkneyjar but for Finehair. The Danes drove us from the Land of Fire and Ice."

"And Bear Island?"

"That one was of our own making. My brother, Arne, forgot the reason we had fled and sought power. He had a worm within him, a desire for power, and it consumed him. If he had not gone to war we would live there still, and we would be happy. It would have been interesting to see what we made of the land. We had not found iron and that was the only fault that I could find with the place. A man only needs gold if there are markets but iron is needed to make metal." He patted the gunwale, "Gytha wished to stay there and she wanted my brother Erik as jarl. The men chose Arne for he was a warrior." He shrugged and stood for Erik was walking down the centre of the drekar. "You cannot change the past and the future is an unknown country. A man makes definite plans at his peril." Erik changed places with him. "The course is still the same. We cannot take a compass reading which is accurate because of the clouds but I have left both within reach. Wake me if the wind shifts or you have need of me."

He went to join Ebbe and Bear Tooth who were sleeping close to their rowing benches and their chests. They had concocted a shelter. Travelling for as far as they had must have given them valuable lessons in sailing in comfort.

"If there is anything I can do for your family, Lord Sámr, then let me know." Erik was a kind man. The Dragonheart had known it and now I began to realise it too.

I nodded, "You are closer in age to my children than am I. Try to be their friend. I am their father and I know that Ragnar will try to be the man and hide his pain while Ylva is a woman and they have always been a mystery to me. I wish that Ylva the witch had not passed into the spirit world. She could have found a way to heal her namesake." It was clear that Erik had thoughts of his own and so I went back to my family to sleep. This would be a long voyage home.

When I awoke it was late and getting on to dark. As the men were rested Fótr asked for the oars to be manned and we rowed for two hours until dark and sailed due west. Navigators all know how to read the weather and are almost like galdramenn when it comes to predictions. He wanted to be further west than north when the winds changed. "When the winds change Lord Sámr, they will bring some clear skies and that means we can ascertain our position better."

I knew that Fótr would have a much better idea of our position than I did. All that I knew was that we were to the north-west of Moi and Stavanger. I doubted that word would even have reached Stavanger and the King would not hear of our attack for at least a week and perhaps more. A ship would not find us in the vast and empty sea, and he could not raise a fleet and an army in Gormánuður. Soon days would be a mere five or six hours long. He might wish to punish us or even make an attempt to conquer us but that would not be until Spring.

I ate with my family. Even though we ate cold fare with the bread we had made a couple of days ago, it was far better than the scraps they had been given. We finished our own ale and started on the barrel taken from the knarr. Ragnar enjoyed that even more than the food. When Erik came to sing him the saga of the last battle of The Dragonheart he actually smiled. It was a small step but a step, nonetheless. Ylva too managed a smile for Erik had a good voice and as well as the sagas had silly songs which he liked to sing. I thanked whoever had sent him for without him my family would still be prisoners and his presence seemed to make life easier for our family. I cuddled Aethelflaed.

"You know, husband, I wondered if I could ever bear a man's arms around me, again. When we lived in Uddulfr's hall I used to shake with fear when I heard and smelled the approach of a warrior. When first you embraced me, I kept my eyes open so that I knew it was you. I am sorry. You are a good man, but you will need patience."

"And you shall have all the time you like." I paused, "If you wish then you and Ylva can live for a while in Kara's hall. They are all widows and kind."

"You would do that?"

"Of course, for your pain and that of Ylva makes me angry, sad and helpless all at the same time. The sisters have spun, and we must deal with the consequences."

"You know I did not believe in the three sisters." I nodded. She was a Christian. "This experience has made me think again. God does test us, but this test seemed…" her hand went to her throat, but her cross had been taken from her, "somehow barbaric." She smiled as Bear Tooth approached, "They say he is a barbarian, but I doubt that his people would behave as Uddulfr and his folk did."

Bear Tooth was a gentle member of the clan unless he had a weapon in his hand. I had fought next to him and knew his power. Now he was just kind and thoughtful. "It is good to see you smiling, lady. My people believe that we should all look for what is good. When my family were taken from me, I was sad, but I knew that they would be happy in the Otherworld." He used our word for heaven. "It is too easy to live in a dark past. I would like to live in a bright future and that is the Land of the Wolf." I do not know if any asked him to speak but his words had a greater effect than mine and all three smiled and looked a little happier. *Wyrd*!

The next few days saw a continuation of the same routine and we edged closer to Orkneyjar. Knowing that the jarl whom Egil and the others hated was in Moi made it less likely that we would be in danger but Fótr was taking no chances. An icy two days of cloudless skies allowed Fótr to ascertain that we were less than a day and a half from Hrólfsey. We still had a long way to go but it would be island hopping and we would be able to land at night. Aethelflaed and Ylva had found it hard to hang over the prow to make water. The crew were tactful and looked astern but either Ragnar or I had to be there to hold on to them.

Fótr was correct the weather was due to change but none of us could have expected the storm which blew up overnight. We were lucky that it was Fótr who had the steering board. He and Erik worked for four hours at a stretch and Fótr had just come on duty. It was not Erik's fault that he had not seen the change in the seas for the white flecked water, at first, appear to have barely changed, but as soon as Fótr stood at the stern, so Erik told me later, our captain sniffed the air and told him to rouse the men. Of course, they did not wake me, but I was sensitive to noise at night. My daughter had murmured in her sleep on the second night at sea and I had tried to comfort her. I rose and, as the air was chill, I slipped my sealskin cape around my shoulders. As I made my way to the steering board, I saw that men were reefing the sails and we had changed course. For the last two days, we had been heading south and west towards Hrólfsey, but I saw that Fótr had moved the steering board to head due west into the open seas. Other men were manning the oars.

"What is it, Fótr?"

"There is a storm coming." He touched his head, "I feel it here. It is as though there is a great weight on my head. That means a storm and I do not wish to risk the rocks of the islands or the land of the Picts. The wind is coming from the northeast and so we will have to use the oars to keep us to the west of danger." He smiled in the dark, "This helps us as when the storm abates or daylight comes, we will have a faster passage south!"

It was a strange kind of optimism. I went forward to be with my family. I led this warband but at sea, I was probably the least useful of the crew. The three of them were not aware of any danger and they blissfully slept in their sheepskin lined nest. Erik and Bear Tooth had brought chests to make a kind of shelter and with the old sail above them, they were cosy. What would happen when the seas rose and the motion became violent I did not know. I slid another chest across their feet to complete the wall of wood which held them in and then I stared over the prow. I could sense nothing, and I wondered if Fótr's imagination was being overactive. I could feel nothing. Then oars bit into the sea and we moved a little faster. I could see whitecaps ahead but that was normal. Suddenly, I realised that the waves were a little stronger and soon the troughs became deeper. In the dark, there is little sense of time. The clouds obscured the moon and so I knew not how long it was until the bow hit the bottom of a trough so hard that the chests around my family moved and Ylva woke. The oarsmen were fighting the sea. The troughs and waves meant that not all of the oars struck the water and those that did not sometimes fouled another oar. I heard Erik shout something and then the crew began to sing. It was the new saga with an extra verse.

Halfgrimr was a warrior brave
He gave his life for another to save
Oathsworn to the end with sword in hand
He was the best of Sámr's band
Faithless Vikings fell to his blade
Ten men were by him slayed
Warriors from Dragonheart's Land
Warriors forged in Sámr's warband
Warriors making one last stand
Warriors from Dragonheart's Land
Farbjorn's fate was spun in a cave
By the sisters who killed the warrior brave
They flicked a stone and made him fall
The oathsworn had no chance at all
Warriors from Dragonheart's Land
Warriors forged in Sámr's warband
Warriors making one last stand
Warriors from Dragonheart's Land
Bear Tooth's cry filled the sky
All evil creatures away did fly
With Dragonheart's heir by his side
By their blades the enemies died
With cries of terror the Vikings fled
Leaving the fjord filled with the dead.
Warriors from Dragonheart's Land
Warriors forged in Sámr's warband
Warriors making one last stand
Warriors from Dragonheart's Land
Warriors from Dragonheart's Land
Warriors forged in Sámr's warband
Warriors making one last stand
Warriors from Dragonheart's Land

My family were awake now and huddled together. The men's voices drifted towards us at the same time that I noticed there was less cracking of oars. The steady saga was giving the men the time and rhythm. Erik walked down the centre of the drekar, not an easy feat as

100

sometimes he was climbing and sometimes trying to stop himself running. I had clambered over the chests to be a human rock for my family. I braced my boots against the thwarts and held them tightly.

Ragnar asked, "Are we going to die?"

I shook my head. I had to shout above the sound of the wind and the rain which had begun to cascade. Added to the seawater it meant that the men rowing would be soaked. The few who had sealskins would be the only ones who would have any protection from the wet. "Fótr, Ebbe and Bear Tooth endured much worse than this. He is confident we will survive."

Ylva pointed to Erik who still walked amongst the crew to give encouragement. "And how can Erik Black Toe do that? Why is he not clinging to something?"

"Erik became a sailor when he sought you. He has not sailed the Great Sea but he was in a knarr which had storms such as this. He walks amongst the crew for they are all young warriors and, like you, have never had to sail in conditions like this."

It was as though the scales had been lifted from her eyes, "These young men all came from Cyninges-tūn to rescue us." The words of the chant drifted over and her eyes widened, "Men died! Halfgrimr, Farbjorn, the others! They died and we did not get the chance to thank them."

My wife had already spoken of the sacrifice but Ragnar and Ylva were young and like most young people saw little beyond themselves. After the pain and suffering they had endured that was understandable but now realisation flooded their faces as they looked at each other.

Ragnar said, "I prayed for death when we were in Moi, but I am not sure that I was ready for it. Life is precious and I am happy that we clung on to life. I knew not the young men who died." He shook his head, "They died before me and yet I did not give it a thought. I was just glad that you had come for me." A look of horror came over his face. "I stepped over the body of a young warrior close to the door of Uddulfr's hall."

I nodded, "Rolf Red Hair. His mother farms close to Skelwith. When I reach the Land of the Wolf then I will need to visit her. She has other sons, daughters, and grandchildren but Rolf was her favourite."

Ylva asked, "How many died?"

"We lost fifteen warriors."

Aethelflaed made the sign of the cross and I saw her lips moving. She was praying for their souls. It was kind of her but unnecessary as they were all in Valhalla. They were seated at the table with The

101

Dragonheart and his Ulfheonar. They were telling the tale of the battle and Dragonheart was smiling.

Ylva was a thoughtful young woman. Her trials and tribulations had made her look inward and that showed in her next words, "They will never marry and never have children. The courage of those warriors will not be passed on to the next generation. Our rescue has made the clan weaker!"

Although the storm was at its peak none of them appeared to notice. It was as if the storm was irrelevant and they were forced to think of the cost of the rescue. My two children had been wallowing in self-pity and I understood that. Had the Allfather sent the storm to shake them free?

"Perhaps but the Clan of the Fox has now joined us and Egil Sorenson and his men have joined us. They are all hardy folk and their blood can only make the clan stronger. I had not seen this before my great grandfather died. Like you, I looked inward. The Dragonheart drew the brave to him like moths to a flame. Except that unlike a moth, they did not die but prospered. When I sat in my own pit of despair, I had forgotten that. When we reach our home, I will remedy that, and we can all put the past behind us." I saw Aethelflaed nod and she held Ragnar's right hand and Ylva's left. "We are all alive. The past is another land; a frightening one but we have left it behind. Before us lies the Land of the Wolf and a life which we will make." I pointed to Fótr, "Look at him, he has lost all of his kin and sailed the world. He chose to come to save you and leave his family behind. Each day from now on, think of the sacrifice that these men were willing to make for you."

Ylva's right hand grasped mine, "And I, for one, will. I have seen the worst of men and now, I have seen the best of men."

Just then Erik reached us. He was smiling, "The Navigator says the storm is abating and soon it will be easier." I saw that he was looking at Ylva, "I hope you were not afraid."

Ylva said, "I was but I no longer have fear. Thank you, Erik Black Toe."

He looked confused, "What for?"

"You set off on a quest to find us and you did. You put your own life at risk for others and I want you to know that I am grateful."

The look on his face was one of pure joy. The storm changed all of our worlds!

Chapter 10

Fótr was right and by dawn, the sea was just a little fresh. We had sea room and the oars were put on the mastfish, the sail billowed, and we had a wind from the north-west to take us to our home. We had suffered some damage and that first day was spent repairing. Ragnar helped and Aethelflaed and Ylva left their fortress at the prow and went to prepare food. I saw Fótr beaming and I joined him.

"The Allfather does nothing without a purpose, Lord Sámr. I see a different family this morning. They are not yet healed but the wounds are not as raw as they were." He nodded towards Erik who was helping Aethelflaed and Ylva. "Erik is smitten you know."

"What?"

"Ylva, he is in love with Ylva."

"How do you know?"

He laughed and I saw that he missed nothing, "I have eyes and I can see. Bear Tooth and Ebbe saw it too, however, Erik himself told me one night, on watch. He asked me if someone like him could ever hope to marry a lady like Ylva."

"I did not know."

"You are her father and he is in awe of you." He smiled, "You need do nothing, Lord Sámr. The Norns have spun, and their threads are now bound. Each day they will become closer as she comes from the place she is hiding. I saw it with my brother and the Skraeling. We have seven days before we see my stad and by then I believe that there will be a change; in Ylva at least."

"And galdramenn, reader of weather and people, what do you see for Ragnar?"

His face became sad, "His journey will be harder, and I confess that I know not. I would use Bear Tooth to get close to him. The Skraeling of his tribe, the Mi'kmaq, understood wounds to warriors. He will know a way."

As I looked astern, I felt a pang of guilt. Erik had said that there were other captives but we had seen none. What had happened to them? I had to get my family home first and then, when King Harald was no longer a threat I could consider seeking them.

On the way south we stopped at uninhabited islands again but not the same ones as when we had headed north. We were taking no risks. All the time Fótr was adding to his map. As we headed towards the channel between the Land of the Wolf and Hibernia I stood by Erik as he adjusted the sail. I had been thinking about all of my warriors on the way home and wondering about their future. Many of the younger ones would have rid themselves of the need to go a-Viking and would find a wife to start a family. There were others, like Ráðulfr Ráðgeirsson, Ulf Olafsson, Gandálfr Eriksson and Qlmóðr the Quiet who had asked if they could be my oathsworn. I had agreed. The only one I needed to speak with was Erik.

"Erik, what are your plans, when we reach my home?"

He shot me a guilty look and seeing no deception in the question smiled, "I have not given that any thought at all, Lord Sámr. The last few years have seen me on a quest to find and then rescue your family. That is now over, and I have a void in my life. I will need to fill it."

I nodded and tried to read the message beneath the words. Dragonheart had the ability to do that but I struggled. "Know that there is a place for you at Hawks' Roost. I have four oathsworn, but it is a large place. Baldr had his own hall and that is empty. While you make your decisions then stay there." I saw a question in his eyes as well as hope. "You will be helping me for Ylva seems calmer when you are around, and I believe that you help Ragnar too. Until my children have healed a little more stay with me." I smiled, "There must be more songs for you to compose."

He nodded and said, "But the one I wish to make, the story of the evil Uddulfr the Sly I cannot do for that would add hurt to your family. The world will never know of his evil."

"What we did do was destroy Moi. When we fled and I looked back I saw that his stronghold was burning fiercely and we both know that the dock was badly damaged. We killed the evil that was Uddulfr the Sly, but you are right, there will be survivors and the evil they did must be avenged."

"Then I will stay with you but only so long as I am of use. I would not be a burden to you and your family."

"Erik, you could never be that."

Bear Tooth had spent a great deal of time with Ragnar and as we approached the coast, our journey's end, he took me to one side. "Lord Sámr, I have spent time with Ragnar, and I believe that he is healing but I can see a problem which may not be obvious to your people." He lowered his voice and took me aside, "Your son has drunk ale heavily since his return. None other appears to have noticed and they see nothing amiss with the amount of ale he consumes. I am not of your people and while I like your mead and drink your beer, I do not need as much as the rest of our clan. Watch your son. Where other men drink one horn of ale, he drinks two or three. Where other men can sit and chat, he cannot do so without a horn of ale in his hand. I have begun to drag him from the darkness of the world of Uddulfr the Sly, but I fear he is in danger of falling into a different kind of pit. Since the ale has run out, he is an angrier young man."

I knew that Bear Tooth was too honest to make this up and I put my arm around his shoulder, "Thank you, Bear Tooth. I will heed your words. I believe you although I have not seen this. Perhaps I am too close to him."

As I went to the steering board I went back through the voyage and I realised that Bear Tooth was right. Fótr had told me that the barrel of beer we had taken from the knarr would see us safely home but two days ago we had run out and Ragnar had been in a bad mood since then. The fact that we were so close to home meant that men were not angry that their beer had run out. We had plenty of rainwater. Ragnar, however, had been low, and I now saw the reason. I had put it down to the fear of returning to the Land of the Wolf, but I now saw that I was wrong.

We reached Fótr's stad not long after the sun reached its zenith. The last four miles had seen a blue sky with the occasional cloud scudding by. Although Fótr offered to give us beds in his hall I was anxious to get my family safe inside my walls. It was almost Ýlir and we would soon have snow. The pass of Vreinihala was often closed and was named after Vreini who had lived here in my great grandfather's time. He and his family had died at the farm during a particularly hard winter. The pass had been renamed in his honour.

We had left the ponies with Fótr's people and they were well fed. Some of us would ride home. Egil and his folk chose to come with us. We divided the weapons we had taken from the dead but, in truth, we had little treasure. The treasure we had was in the form of three people. The partings were heartfelt. We knew how much we owed to Fótr, Ebbe and, perhaps most of all, Bear Tooth. Fótr and I just clasped arms for the long watches on *'Gytha'* had allowed us to speak openly and we had seen inside the heart of the other.

"We will take care of the two threttanessa we captured. You still wish to use them to raid?"

"As I said on the way home, we need allies and we need to make our waters safe before the Norwegians come."

"Then when you need them, they will be ready."

Erik asked to stay at the stad for a day or two. He and Fótr had become close and he wished to copy the charts they had made. I did not mind but I saw that Ylva was sad that Erik was not travelling home with us.

We made good time, but it was well after dark when we parted from the men who would return to Cyninges-tūn. The goodbyes were silent while the clasped arms were firm. Men who had fought together needed fewer words. Egil and his men, along with my oathsworn would return to Hawk's Roost. When the mighty gates slammed behind us Aethelflaed fell into my arms and wept. They were tears of joy. She was home. Soon she and Ylva, not to mention Ragnar, would wear clean clothes and sleep in their own beds. They were not the same ones in which they had slept when this had been their home. All remnants of the Skull Takers had been removed and burned but I had built a perfect replica. After eating and drinking well we retired. Bear Tooth was right, Ragnar drank more than any other and stayed up after we had retired. This was not the time for a confrontation and so Aethelflaed and I shared a bed again. We just lay in each other's arms in comfortable silence. She was healing. When I heard her steady breathing then I knew she was asleep. I stayed awake for a while longer. I had much upon my mind and plans to make. I had wasted time before, but those days were gone.

I woke early and slipped from the bed while it was still dark. This was the first day in my land and I did not want to waste a moment of it. Valborg had wept when we had returned for Aethelflaed and Ylva were still dressed in rags. I was not sure if either she or Uggi had slept for the hall looked immaculate. Uggi grinned, "I do not think we will see Ragnar early this day, lord. I helped him to bed just a short time ago."

I nodded. Today was the day when I would need to speak with my son. "We will need the steam hut today. My family will wish to be cleansed of the poison that was Moi. I will also use it. We have plenty of charcoal?"

"Aye, lord, I had the charcoal burners working in the forest by the Tarns and the Haughs."

"Good." I turned to Uggi's mother, "Valborg, Egil and his people will stay in the warrior hall with my oathsworn. Both they and my family will need clothes. We still have cloth we raided, do we not?"

"Aye, lord but none of it is suitable for Lady Aethelflaed and Lady Ylva."

You will find, in my chest, two fine garments. One is mine and one was The Dragonheart's. They are made from an expensive material and come from the Empire of the east. Make those two garments into dresses for the ladies."

Valborg looked shocked, "Cut up an heirloom from Dragonheart?"

I smiled, "Neither he nor I will ever wear them, and he would like it if it was worn by ladies in the family. He was never precious about what he wore. There is plenty of material but the women who work it will need skill."

"I will supervise them myself." She bobbed her head, "I will fetch you food, lord."

Uggi had returned with some small beer. "Uggi, do we have enough male thralls? Men who can labour."

"Aye, lord, there are four Danes and two Saxons."

"Then when you have lit the fire in the steam hut fetch them to me."

Valborg must have been ready for me to come down for she brought in freshly baked rye and oat bread along with some slices of salted ham which she had fried. On the top of each piece of ham was cracked a runny egg. Along with the slab of fresh butter and sheep's cheese, it was a breakfast fit for a king and, as I ate it, I felt like one. It was good to be home, but I chastised myself for entertaining thoughts of pleasure. I had grown used to such breakfasts and lingered longer over them than I ought. I wolfed it down and then donned Viking Killer. I was a warrior and gone were the days after my rescue when I wandered my land just appreciating its beauty. It was beautiful but too many people wanted it. The task for the lord of the Land of the Wolf was to protect it!

Uggi returned with the six thralls. The two Saxons had been with us for years, but the four Danes had been taken when we had scoured my land after the battle to retake our home. All six had the thrall's yoke about their necks and whilst they were well treated, they were locked in the thrall hut each night. The Saxons all looked resigned to their fate, but I still saw resentment on the faces of the four Danes. They were not Skull Takers. If they had been then I would have executed them. These four were mercenaries. I faced them with my hands on my hips. Their heads were down; thralls learned that pose early on.

My words shocked them and made them all snap up their heads to view my face and see if I had gone mad, "Would you like your freedom?" They did not know what to say but just nodded, the Danes somewhat suspiciously as though they expected a condition. There was, of course, a condition but it could be easily met. "Then here is my offer. I want you to work from now until Einmánuður on the defences of Hawk's Roost. We need more towers, deeper ditches and the area around the walls cleared. It will be winter work and hard. I am willing to take off your yokes if you swear not to run." I looked at each of them and they nodded, in turn. "When the work is done then you have two choices: I can give you land to farm or you can fight for me. Is that an agreeable offer?"

107

Scanlan the older of the two Saxons said, "It is many years since we fought, lord. If we had our freedom, then we would like to live in Cyninges-tūn. I have learned to smith while here and I would like to work for a weaponsmith."

"Good. That is easy to arrange."

"And you four Danes?"

"You would have us fight for you?"

I laughed, "When does a mercenary question his paymaster? I have enemies and I am happy to have you fight for me."

"Would you trust us?"

"Haldr, you will swear an oath. The breaking of an oath stops a man from going to Valhalla. It is your choice." He looked at his companions who nodded and I took out my sword and held it before me. "You Danes swear on this blade that you will not try to escape and that you will fight for me." They put their hands nervously on the sword. It was sharp and they would not grip it too tightly, but I knew that they felt the power which Bacgsecg had created in the blade.

"We so swear." They pulled their hands back as though burned.

I held the sword in my hand so that the pommel and hilt made a cross. "I know that you are Christians. Swear before this cross and then make the sign of the cross. Swear by this sign of your White Christ!"

"We swear by the cross that we will not run and we will serve the clan!"

"Uggi, remove their yokes and then wait close to the main gate."

"Aye, lord."

The relief on their faces when the yokes were removed was a joy to see and I felt guilty about making them endure them for so long.

I headed for the warrior hall. As I had expected the men were all up, dressed and had breakfasted. Valborg knew how to feed hungry men. I stood and addressed them, Egil and his men and my oathsworn. "Today we begin to make Hawk's Roost impregnable. I have just freed six slaves to help us begin the work. We need the forest moving back by forty paces. The wood we will need for palisades and a tower. When that is done there will be other jobs, but I do not think we will be ready for them until we have endured the snow. I will show you where we keep tools and weapons." I paused and said, "Four of the men are Danish mercenaries who have sworn they will fight for me. The oath was a sword oath but watch them, eh?"

I took them to fetch the tools and then led them to where they would begin work. There were just four axes but enough hand axes and saws to enable them to make the trees into usable timber. I was not shirking when I set them to work and I fully intended to join them, but I had other things to do first. I went to the tower which faced Cyninges-tūn and attached the banner, the standard of the clan, we had brought back from *'Gytha'*. We had not needed to fly it, but it would now serve to signal my stad and let them know I was home. Haaken Ráðgeirsson, Ráðulfr's grandfather, would no doubt come to see me. The returning warriors would have told him of my predictions. I would find time to visit with Bjorn and the other leaders in my land. I had walked the vengeance trail, but they would be affected by it! By the time I returned to my hall my wife and daughter had risen. Valborg fussed around them even more than she had me.

"I have had the steam hut lit. I think it would do you both good to use it. When Ragnar awakes then I will enjoy the pleasures of the steam hut and The Water with him." I saw a look of fear on my daughter's face. "I will have Uggi guard the hut. You will be safe, and the spirits of The Water can help to heal you within." I hesitated, "I still have some of Aiden's dream potion…"

Aethelflaed smiled and shook her head, "Perhaps another time but I think it would be good to clean ourselves from within and without. Valborg has some clothes for us. We can burn these rags!" The Skull Takers had destroyed, before my eyes, the clothes and precious things my wife and children had. This was like being reborn.

My wife was on the road to recovery, but I was not sure about Ylva. I needed Erik. I put on my old clothes and took one of the Danish war axes from the armoury. It was, in many ways, too good to use to hew timber but I needed to build up the strength of my body and the double-headed axe would do that. The weaponsmith could put a good edge upon it when I had spoiled it.

I heard the sound of axes hitting trees and even the crack as one tumbled to the earth. All Vikings know how to use an axe and how to fell a tree. When I reached the men, I saw that the Saxons and the Danes had been relegated to hauling away the timber, cutting off the smaller branches with hand axes and then sawing them into identical lengths. I saw that there were three trees down already. By the time we had finished, by Mörsugur, we would have more than one hundred trees which would have been felled. They did not know it but this was the easy task. The harder one would begin the next day when we began to dig up the roots of the pine trees to chop up and cook in the pine tar ovens we would build. We would need to seal the hulls of the two threttanessa.

I managed to cut down four trees before it was time for food and when the servants brought it Seara said, "Lord, Ragnar is awake."

I nodded. I ate a hunk of cheese and bread, washed it down with ale and then said, "Egil, take charge here. I need to see my son."

I had said nothing to any of the men, but they had been on the drekar with me. Their eyes told me that they understood. Ragnar was in the hall and had a horn of ale in his hand. An uneaten platter of food was on the table. I walked up to him and took the horn of ale from him. I placed it in its holder. "Come, we will use the steam hut!" I took his arm and propelled him towards the door. "Uggi, fetch some cleansing cloths and drying cloaks to the steam hut."

Uggi had been waiting nearby and shouted, "Aye, Lord Sámr."

Ragnar shook his head, "But I do not want to go to the hut. I want to drink some ale and doze before the fire. Other men in Cyninges-tūn will be doing the same."

I squeezed harder and pulled, "This is not Cyninges-tūn and you are the son of the Lord of the Land of the Wolf. You have Dragonheart's blood in your veins. This is not a request, this is a command."

Aethelflaed appeared in the doorway. She looked beautiful after the bathing and the cleansing; her hair positively glowed like a bright sun. Seeing her Ragnar said, "Mother, you are beautiful again!"

It was not the most tactful thing to say but Aethelflaed was his mother and knew her own son better than any, including me. She shook her head and folded her arms, "Your father is right. Your behaviour has become unseemly. We do not keep the servants up until first cock just so that we can drink even more ale! Go with your father, let the steam hut purge the poison from your body and your mind!"

He had no choice and I could not help but notice, as we passed them, that both Uggi and his mother were trying to hide a smile. The steam hut was by the water but outside the gate. It would not have done to give an enemy a means to set fire to our walls. After my wife and daughter had finished Uggi had added more coals. I stripped off and slipped the cloak around me. It was for the cold and not for modesty. Ragnar seemed unwilling to undress. I thought I knew the reason.

"If you are embarrassed about the wound do not be. I have seen terrible wounds before and, besides, I would like to see it so that when our enemies come if we capture some then we can inflict the same wound on them. Now undress."

Unbeknown to Ragnar I had already put a jug of ale in the steam hut, but I had laced it with Aiden's dream potion. I opened the curtain for him to enter and saw the jagged wound. It had not been inflicted cleanly and more fuel was added to my fire of vengeance. Once inside we sat on the two mat covered rocks and I poured a little water on the stones to make them steam.

"Ragnar, I would have spoken to you on the drekar, but we had no privacy. Here we do and I can speak openly and honestly. Know, first and foremost, that you are my only son and I love you dearly. All that I say comes from that." His head was down, and I sighed. I could feel all the dirt and sweat beginning to ooze from my body. If this took time it did not matter for my body would be healthier. "Let me tell you of a story about my grandfather, the first son of The Dragonheart. I did not hear this story from my father but The Dragonheart himself and so I know it to be true for he never lied." Ragnar's head came up for he loved stories of his great, great, grandfather. "Arturus was known as Wolf Killer for he killed a wolf when he was young. He became an Ulfheonar and was destined to become a great warrior. He and his father, Dragonheart drifted apart. At the time Dragonheart did not know the reason but he later deduced that Arturus, Wolf Killer, was envious. He moved apart and he and my uncle were murdered before The Dragonheart and his son could be reconciled."

I saw that he did not understand the point of the story.

I sighed, "We drifted apart because of King Harald but, unlike The Dragonheart and Wolf Killer, we have a chance to build a bridge."

"We need no bridge because I can never be a warrior."

"Forget being a warrior although I believe that you can be one. You are drowning in the bottom of a barrel of ale."

His guilty look told me that my barb had hit the mark, "I was not given ale in Moi. I was forced to drink the dregs they left."

"And since we have found you, you have made up for that. It is not just me who has noticed. It will kill you!"

He shrugged, "There are worse ways to die. I cannot go to Valhalla so…"

I was becoming angry but knew that would not help. "Here," I offered him the horn of ale, "drink this and then have no more for one day. What say you?"

I saw him lick his lips and when his eyes flickered up at me, they were full of lies, "I will drink this and abjure drink for the rest of the day."

That was when I knew that he was being consumed from within by a daemon! He drank the whole horn down and grinned, "That was good ale. I shall have some more of that tomorrow. I do not have a problem, father. I can stop whenever I wish."

I nodded, "Come we will plunge into The Water to clear away the soil from our bodies and then return." This was all part of Aiden's path to the dream world. When we plunged beneath the water then the spirits, somehow and I do not know how, entered our minds. The potion

111

helped us to sleep and to dream. I would not sleep but watch my son. He understood the need to plunge into the icy water. He had done this once before when we lived in peace at Hawk's Roost and Baldr and I would enjoy the steam hut. Even though I had not taken any of the potion as soon as I jumped into the icy water the shock made me almost freeze, I saw faces. I had seen many before even though I did not know them. Dragonheart's mother, Myfanwy, often came but she was not there. Erika, his first wife, was as well as Kara and Aiden. They appeared and then they were gone. I came up and saw that Ragnar was still below the surface. I reached down and pulled him up by his hair. He came up spluttering and coughing.

"What happened?"

"I saw The Dragonheart and he looked angry!"

I smiled, "Come, let us go back inside the hut. You may need sleep."

He leaned on me as I led him in and he nodded, "You are right. I feel as though I cannot keep my eyes open."

I laid his drying towel on the rock and he almost collapsed upon it. I did not think I had given him too much potion, but I could have made a mistake. I stroked his hair as he slept. I knew when he was in the dream world. His eyes fluttered like a butterfly and he began to mumble. At one point he thrashed about and then, suddenly, he went stiff and remained still. The dream was over. It did not do to wake a dreamer and was better to let them come to themselves. I put more coals on the fire and then took the strigil I had bought in Miklagård. I began to scrape the dirt and sweat which lay on my skin. I flicked it on to the coals and they hissed. It seemed an age, but he began to stir. He sat up and wrapped his cloak around his body.

"You gave me a potion."

"You dreamed?"

He nodded, "It is a terrifying world for you cannot move. You have been there?"

"I have been there. Tell me about your dream. I may not understand it but just speaking of it may help you."

"I saw Dragonheart and his granddaughter Ylva. She never spoke but she held my hand. We flew through the air and went to Whale Island. There I saw an egg and from that egg came a serpent. It kept growing until it became a dragon and then it wrapped its body around the walls of the stronghold and burned it. It was terrible to behold and I saw people burning." He shook his head. "I do not want to see that again."

"And then?"

112

"And then we flew to the top of Old Olaf and The Dragonheart pointed his arm at the lands to the south of us. He told me that I had a duty to be your heir and to rule the Land of the Wolf. I tried to tell him that I was lame, but the words would not come out. He told me that unless I changed then I would never have a good night's sleep and all ale would taste sour to me!" His wild eyes looked terrified. "He cannot do that can he?"

I stood, "Come, we will bathe once more and then head back to the hall." As we washed the sweat from our bodies I said, "The spirit world is most powerful here. We are protected to an extent but the land between Old Olaf and Hawk's Roost is ruled by the spirits. The further you travel away, the less power they have. Do you wish to move away?"

He shook his head, "This is my home and I would live here forever."

"Then the answer to your question is that he can do all that he promised and remember he sees inside your heart and head. You may be able to lie to me but not to yourself and certainly not to Dragonheart!"

It was a sober, in every sense of the word, Ragnar, who came back into the hall. I do not say he changed overnight but when we ate in my hall, that first night, with the oathsworn and Egil's people I noticed that my son was quiet and when he sipped his ale he wrinkled his nose. He listened more and barely touched his ale. Each time he did he quickly put down his horn.

His silence might have been his interest in the conversations of the others for Egil and the others spoke of the hewing of the trees. They had begun to get to know the six thralls who, seeing freedom on the horizon, chatted more than before. It was the Danes who became a mine of information. They were less than happy with King Harald for he had promised them money. When they had been taken the money, which could have been used to buy them back, was not forthcoming from the Norwegians. It was from the Danes that I learned of the Man connection. They served King Harald but did so in secret. As soon as I realised that they were his secret allies then much made sense. The attack on Fótr's stad was an example of the King's strategy. We would hurt them. I had already planned on doing so and when spring began, I would attempt to ally with Dyflin.

Ylva was quiet but I knew what was on her mind when she asked me when Erik was returning. I hid the smile and decided not to tease her, "As soon as he has copied the maps he will return here."

"Here? He will live here?"

113

"If he wishes to. He has served our family and the clan well. He can live wherever he chooses."

She brightened, "But he will want to live here, surely."

"Perhaps." My wife squeezed my leg below the table. The sisters had spun and we both saw a chance for Ylva and, I hoped, Ragnar.

Chapter 11

The men I had left to watch my land while I rescued my family came to see me in the first week of Ýlir. My messengers had taken a couple of days to reach them all. Their visit coincided with the return of Erik. I had wondered why Haaken had not come earlier but as he told me he and the other leaders had been doing as I had asked and scouring the land for traitors. I had a fine line to balance and, not for the first time I had to admire my great grandfather who had done so with consummate ease. How had he done it alone? Their words filled me with concern. There was unrest in Whale Island. The Northumbrians were becoming more aggressive in the land managed by the heirs of Ketil and there were signs of scouts and spies close to the place where my grandfather had died, Elfridaby.

Ragnar had changed a little. He still had to fight the need for ale but only Aethelflaed and I saw that fight. He sat with me when the old warriors who had fought alongside me told me their news. Erik also joined us for he had returned home with news from Fótr. Each individual morsel was not particularly worrying but when they were all put together then they were alarming. I saw that in their faces.

When they had finished Bjorn Asbjornson shook his head, "I had not worried about the spies and the scouts coming from the east for I believed that the rest of the land was safe. I thought to send men out in spring."

Haaken Ráðgeirsson sighed as he drank his ale. "It is the same with Whale Island. We thought that their treatment of Erik here was just bad manners but now I can see that it is more sinister."

"Explain."

"The hersir, as you know, is Pasgen Sigtryggson. He has made many new rules and taxes. The people feel that they would be better off under King Harald."

"What new rules and taxes?"

"That is it, Sámr, he said that they were your commands."

Each word hit me like a hammer blow. What a fool I had been. After we had ousted King Harald's men I had appointed someone whose family I knew to rule each stad. I had left them to act for me and I trusted all of them. I looked at the four men who were before me. Bjorn, Haaken, Ketil and Olaf represented the four who protected the east, the west, the northeast and the north-west. The one who was missing was Pasgen who protected the south.

"Then I will deal with Pasgen Sigtryggson and do so before the turning of the year. He may think he is safe in the depths of winter, but I will end his poison sooner rather than later." I looked at each of them in turn, "It is my fault that we are threatened. I have been asleep and the only one who deserved sleep is The Dragonheart for when he ruled this land was safe. We must aggressively prosecute those who threaten our land." Only Olaf Ulfsson had given me any good news. His land was safe for the men of Strathclyde were busy fighting amongst themselves. "Olaf, you have a drekar?" He nodded. "Then use it, even over the winter to patrol the seas as far as Fótr's stad. I will ask Fótr to do the same from his stad to Whale Island. Ketil Sigibhertson and Bjorn Asbjornson, have your men go beyond our borders and question any who are not known to us. They need a purpose to be in the Land of the Wolf."

Ketil, who looked like his great grandfather Windar Ketilsson, asked, "And if they can give no good reason?"

"Then either bring them to me for judgement or give summary judgement yourself."

"Kill them?"

"Kill them! We have too many enemies these days to allow ourselves the luxury of mercy. The last time we did that it cost me my father, the freedom of my family and my imprisonment. We should have done this after the last battle and for that I am sorry. I was not The Dragonheart's Heir but now I shall be!"

We spent the rest of the day while I explained my plans. These were the men I could trust and while I spoke to them I saw a different Ragnar. He looked focussed and interested in my ideas. This was the first time I had spoken to him of what I had planned, and I could see that he wished to be part of it. My warrior leaders stayed the night for the warrior hall was barely occupied.

Valborg and Aethelflaed ensured that we ate well. We had fish from The Water as well as deer which had been brought by Haaken who loved venison. My oathsworn joined us and Haaken sat with his grandson who led my oathsworn. Erik, unsurprisingly, sat with Ylva and their two heads bobbed up and down as they ate. Ylva's laughter drifted across to me and made me smile. She was healing. Aethelflaed played the lady and kept Ketil and Ulf amused while I spoke with Bjorn and Ragnar who flanked me.

"What are your plans for me, father?"

Bjorn had a son and I knew that I could speak openly before both of them, "That is your choice, Ragnar. Are you ready to take the reins of this horse?"

He looked confused, "This horse?"

"Hawk's Roost. You must know from my words that I will be away more than I shall be here. I need to leave someone who can rule the land in my absence. I need someone who can protect our family and our people. Are you ready?"

He looked at the horn of ale in his hand. He had not drunk as much as the others had and it was half full. He put it in its stand and nodded, "I know not what to do yet but thus far I have done little for the Land of the Wolf and it is time that I showed I have the blood of The Dragonheart in my veins. I cannot let this lame leg stop me!"

Bjorn clapped an arm around his shoulders, "That proves you have his blood! You know how to wield a sword?"

"Of course, but I have not done so since I was taken."

"Pah, that is nothing. You never forget. I have a one-armed warrior, Einar Five Fingers. A Danish axe took his other hand. He fights as fiercely as any. With a shield strapped to his stump he has made his right arm so strong that none can best him. You have two arms and can be stronger than any man."

"But my leg makes it hard for me to move."

Bjorn laughed, "Then why move your legs at all? Your upper body is young and supple. You use that and if your arms are strong then you wear down an enemy."

Ragnar looked at me and I nodded, "I am older now and I do not move my legs as much as I used to. In the last battle I fought Dragonheart stood on the walls of Cyninges-tūn with Haaken One Eye and two old men with aching joints and old bones held off every attack from their enemies. I do not ask you to join the shield wall but to defend Hawk's Roost. Make this yours!"

Our words persuaded him, and it was a vastly different Ragnar who went to bed that night than the one we had picked up in Moi.

The next morning, he joined me and my men working on the defences. Erik was there as well. As I used the Danish axe to fell more of the trees, I thought back to Dragonheart. He had not had to hew trees, at least not since he had come to Cyninges-tūn. I knew that he had done so when they lived on Man. How had he managed to rule such a vast land so easily? It was as I looked at Erik and Ragnar who were using hand axes to trim the trees that I realised the answer. Dragonheart had not been alone. He had had Aiden at his side as well as Haaken One Eye and the Ulfheonar. I had taken a burden upon my shoulders and tried to do it all alone. Dragonheart had never done it alone. He had been the figurehead but Kara, Ylva, even Karl the Lame had all played their part in making the Land of the Wolf the fortress that it was. I had

117

Ragnar and Erik. I had to trust my judgement and them and then there was Fótr. Only recently come into our lives I knew that he was a rock upon which our enemies would fall. I needed to use him. There is nothing like hard, monotonous labour to help a man to think. Your arms swing and before you know it a tree is felled, and you move on to the next one. You did not need to think. It was during the chilly day in Ýlir that I came up with my plan.

That evening I told Ragnar, Erik and Aethelflaed what I intended. As I expected it upset Ylva, but I could do nothing about that. I sent Ráðulfr Ráðgeirsson to see the men of Cyninges-tūn who had been on the rescue quest for I would need those. The next day we rose before dawn and I led my oathsworn and Erik to ride around The Water to Cyninges-tūn. Ragnar would command Egil and the freed thralls. He would continue the construction of our defences and we would ride to Whale Island to remove the poison which infected that land. That Ylva wept did not make me sad. It showed that she was recovering for the reason she shed tears was because Erik was leaving and that meant that her heart had not died when she was a prisoner. She could love and there was no gentler a man than Erik.

We reached Cyninges-tūn not long after the sun had risen in the east and bathed The Water in a chill, blue light. Ráðulfr Ráðgeirsson had not been idle and the thirty men we would take were already risen and armed. This time we would all ride on ponies. We had Ráðulfr's father, Ráðgeir, with us and four older warriors. They were vital for they knew Whale Island better than any. We headed down The Water and, for me, this was the first time I had ridden the road since the battle to retake it. That reminded me that I had been remiss. As we rode, I told the men I led what we had planned. Six months since I would have thought our actions reckless but the raid on Moi had shown me that I led men with steel for backbone. With them behind me then I could face any challenge.

Ráðgeir Haakensson said, "This is risky, Lord Sámr. You and just five men will enter the hall of a man you suspect is a traitor. Is that not dangerous?"

"It would be if it were not the place my father built, the place where Dragonheart's wolf came to our aid and where the spirit of my mother rests. I have to trust that Pasgen Sigtryggsson and the ones around him are the ones who do not have the blood of the wolf in their veins. If nothing else my fight in Moi showed me that I still have the skill and with these weapons, mail and men, I believe we will succeed. Besides, the alternative is to ride into the stronghold with all of these men and then we shall have a bloodbath. You are vital to this plan, Ráðgeir, for

118

you fought alongside Leif Siggison and it was he who told your father of the ill-feeling. Do you think that the men of Úlfarrston will support Pasgen Sigtryggson?"

He shook his head, "Leif still has the best interests of the Land of the Wolf close to his heart. The loss of his hand and eye in the last battle might have made him less of a warrior but he is a leader still." He nodded, "You are right, this is the best plan!"

We parted at the crossroads. Ráðgeir took the road which led past what had been the shipyard built by Bolli Bollison where Erik Short Toe had lived. I saw Erik look wistfully at the road. He had lived with my sea captain and I knew that he mourned his death still. "Do not worry, the spirit of Erik Short Toe still remains. One day we will begin to build drekar again and we will use his old home. That is for the future. We have many small steps to take and each one will make us stronger."

"But who will make the ships?"

I smiled, "The Allfather sent Fótr the Navigator to us. He did not stay here because of Pasgen. I hope that when we have made our land secure, I might persuade him to make his home here. You have sailed with him, he has saltwater in his veins."

"Aye, you are right and if he came here, he could leave Ebbe and Bear Tooth to lead his clan. Ebbe is ready for he is to be married."

"Married?"

"Aye, when we returned from the raid, he asked Æimundr Loud Voice for the hand of his eldest daughter, Gefn. They are to be wed at the Winter Solstice."

"Good. We need our young warriors to marry and to produce more warriors for the clan."

He looked up quickly, "And some of us may wish for children but…"

I said, quietly, "Erik, be patient."

"You know?"

"I am not blind. You are good for Ylva, but she is like a frightened deer. You will need patience. We will talk of this when our land is safe." I saw the walls of Whale Island ahead and I raised my voice, "And now we smile and play a part. We are here to tell them of our victory in Moi and to celebrate. Watch me and my actions. We ride armed because of the attack at Fótr's stad; understood?"

"Aye, Lord Sámr!"

Although we were mailed our helmets hung from our saddles and our shields were also hanging over our legs. The gates, I saw, were manned and closed. This was the first test for if they remained closed and I was denied entry then the subversion would be over and it would be open rebellion I faced. I did not want that for it would be a civil war and would cost us men we could ill afford to lose. Thankfully, the gates swung open and I rode through the stronghold where I had lived until I left to serve my great grandfather. I still remembered my mother's tears on the day I left. We rode between the houses to the hall. There were some smiles but not many and that was unusual. Whenever Dragonheart's heir rode into a stad there were usually cheers if only in memory of Dragonheart. Here I was not welcome and had I not spoken with Haaken then I might not have known the reason; now I did.

I did not know Pasgen Sigtryggson. After the last battle, I had appointed him the hersir of Whale Island. His father, Sigtrygg Raibeartson, had died in the fighting. We had lost many good men and Pasgen appeared to be like his father. Now I realised I took the physical appearance as an indicator of character and I was wrong. I might have had my doubts but the sullen looks of the folk of Whale Island confirmed my suspicions.

He smiled broadly at me as I dismounted from the horse I rode. "Lord Sámr, this is an unexpected visit. We did not expect you."

I knew how to play these games. I had been to Miklagård and seen the false smiles of courtiers. "I came for I thought you must be ill. I sent a messenger to ask for you to attend a meeting at Hawk's Roost; when you were the only one absent, I feared that you were dying."

"I received no message." He turned to his ten oathsworn, "None arrived with a message from Lord Sámr did they?" His oathsworn all nodded.

The messenger had been Hrólfr Haakensson. Like Erik, he had told me of his cold welcome, and I knew that he had delivered the message. Hrólfr Haakensson was at Úlfarrston with the rest of my men. It was another nail in the coffin of Pasgen. I smiled, "Then I will have to have a word with Hrólfr Haakensson when I return to Hawk's Roost. We would stay the night if it is convenient for we have much to tell you."

I could see that it was not convenient, but he could not refuse. I knew that we would not be able to sleep for fear of a blade in the night. My oathsworn and Erik led the horses to the stables. I wondered where we would be housed. There was a warrior hall and Pasgen had the quarters which were built by my father and designed by my mother. He revealed his intention when he said, "Your oathsworn can stay in the warrior hall. There is a chamber for you in your father's old hall." I knew then that he intended me harm and was separating me from my guards.

"Thank you but when we dine, I will need my men with me." I shrugged, "I am getting old and having them with me will help me to remember all that has happened since the summer."

"Of course."

He led me into his hall, and he introduced me to his wife and children. I did not like her from the moment I met her. She was a beauty, but she had dead eyes and her smile was false. "This is my wife, Halgerd."

She bowed, "Had we known you were coming, my lord, we could have prepared better quarters."

"I am used to hardship and besides, this is where I grew up. Any chamber will suit."

Halgerd was Danish; her name and her looks confirmed that. Few of my men had married Danes. There were Saxons, Norse, Hibernians, women from Strathclyde and even a few Franks but Danish women were rare. We did not raid for slaves and the Danish warriors did not bring them for war. The Norse sometimes did. Their children also showed the Danish ancestry. As I was led to the chamber, I let them think that they had me fooled. While I was freshening up for the meal, they would be plotting my death. The only thing which might save me was my knowledge of the hall. I wondered if I had been too confident. Pasgen and his wife were ambitious. I had seen that from their clothes. The rest of my hersir wore plain and simple dress. We all had fine clothes for special occasions but Pasgen and Halgerd had not only fine and expensive clothes but many rings on their fingers and their heads were crowned by coronets. They had delusions of power and that was not something I had foreseen. I had assumed he was working for someone else in the hopes of crumbs from their table. Now I saw that he wanted the whole table! Padraig's warning from Dyflin now came back to haunt me.

It did not escape my notice that the two warriors who escorted me to my chamber were huge warriors with battle bands, tattoos, and scars. Pasgen was trying to intimidate me. It would take more than two such as this to manage to do that. It was instructive as it showed that he considered these two his best men. If it came to a fight, I would have to take them out first. They opened the door to the chamber, and one said, "We will wait outside until you are ready to leave for the feast, Lord Sámr." They were at least polite but they were telling me that I did not have the freedom to move around as I ought. Had I wished to I could have slipped out without them knowing. After killers had been sent to Whale Island to murder us my father had built secret doors which led from the chamber. There was one just behind the bed. It was cunningly concealed, but I knew where it was. We must have been seen approaching the port for there was a jug of water and a cloth for me to refresh myself. I did so and then lay on the bed. This room had been reserved for two of my father's oathsworn: Benni and Folki. They had died with my father and Gruffydd. When I went to Valhalla there would be many warriors I would see again. Would they be as they were the day that they died? My great grandfather had died and gone to the doors of Valhalla. He had even peered inside and seen Odin and his dead shield brothers, but he never told me if they were as the day they died. I should have asked him but, like many other things we put off important questions to ask those which mean nothing. At the time I remembered that I was just glad that he had not died.

I stood and went to the door. As soon as I opened it, I was face to face with the two men. "You have rested enough, Lord Sámr?"

"I am anxious to discover if the ale is as good as when I lived here. The alewife, Anya, knew how to brew dark ale and golden mead."

The two men had neither wit nor intelligence. "The alewife is called Helga, Lord Sámr."

I shook my head and walked past them towards the hall. When I had lived there the better chambers were further away from the Great Hall. My mother liked peace and quiet and when men celebrated a victory, they were loud. If Pasgen had taken another room then it was not as well-appointed, and I could not see him doing that.

I was not surprised when I saw Erik and my oathsworn in the Great Hall. They knew the danger we were in and would have been anxious for my safety. They had horns of ale and mead in their hands, but I knew, even before I reached them that they would have barely touched them. None of Pasgen's men, save the two guards, had reached the hall and so we could speak. "I like not that we have been housed in the warrior hall."

"And I am unhappy, too, Gandálfr Eriksson, but for the moment we will have to live with it. Erik, I intend to use you to start the first confrontation. Ulf Olafsson and Gandálfr Eriksson, when we have eaten, I would have the two of you go to the main gate. It will be closed. If you are stopped then say you are on the way to the stables to check on my horse. I want you on the walls to watch for the rest of our men. You know what you have to do?"

"Aye, Lord Sámr, silence the guards, open the gate and guard until they are inside."

"Good. Qlmóðr the Quiet and Ráðulfr Ráðgeirsson, you have one task; watch our backs. Those two hulking brutes are the ones that Pasgen thinks are the best men he has got."

Ráðulfr snorted, "They are all chest and no brain. I have seen the type before. As my father likes to say, the bigger they are the harder they fall and a clever little'un can beat a stupid big 'un any day of the week."

Our conversation was ended when Pasgen and Halgerd entered like a king and queen. That is not to say that they were regal, but they entered with coronets on their heads and were preceded by six oathsworn and followed by six women who had painted lips and wore posies of flowers in their hair. I wondered if he was trying to impress me or the others who followed him, the great and the good from Whale Island. I was not surprised that I knew none of them. From what I had heard Pasgen had rid himself of all those loyal to me and replaced them with those who sought favour with the new hersir. I was annoyed with myself. Had I visited more often then I would have seen the dangers.

Even the way the two of them spoke told me that they had been seduced by power, "Lord Sámr, you are rested?"

"Of course."

"We have invited some of those who live here close to the sea so that you may meet more of the people. We see so little of you."

I nodded, "And that is my fault. I am here to clear up matters which, from what I have been told, have caused confusion."

I saw the first hint of disquiet and it was from Halgerd. She was the cleverer of the two. "Then let us sit and we can serve the food."

As we headed to the seats, I saw that the sun was setting. The men from Úlfarrston would be stealthily approaching and they would wait in the dark until Ulf Olafsson and Gandálfr Eriksson signalled them. I would bide my time. As Lord of the Land of the Wolf, I was accorded the honour of sitting first. None of my other leaders would have bothered and it just made me suspicious. They had seated Erik and my oathsworn as far away from me as possible but as I was seated between Pasgen and his would-be queen I was not intimidated; any killers would not risk hurting those two. I allowed the food to be served as well as the wine and ale before I unleashed my first shock.

"Pasgen, do you not recognise yonder warrior I brought?" I pointed to Erik who obligingly stood and smiled.

"No, I do not."

"Strange. His name is Erik Black Toe and he was The Dragonheart's standard-bearer. He came here, starving and with neither weapon nor sword. You and your people sent him hence without offering him either food or shelter. Is that the way of the Clan of the Wolf?" I said it mildly, but it caused a ripple of shock to race around the hall and I saw

123

everyone staring at Erik. Guilt filled the face of Pasgen. Erik had told me that it was he who had sent him away as a beggar.

He narrowed his eyes and shook his head, "I do not remember him, but we send away any who we think are a threat to the safety of the Land of the Wolf."

"Ah, I see." I addressed Erik, "So you see Erik, you should not have posed such a threat to us. Tell me again, where had you been and what did you tell the hersir?"

"I had been to Norway to find your family and when I told the hersir he said I lied."

Pasgen was caught and he knew it, "We have many people who tell lies. I am sorry, Erik, er, Black Toe. I have been busy, and this is a difficult place to manage."

"Is that why you charge high taxes which you do not send to me?" I smiled, "Not that I demand taxes from my people."

I saw a reaction from those invited by Pasgen. Their smiles turned to frowns for they thought it had been my decision. I nodded to Ulf Olafsson and Gandálfr Eriksson who rose and left while everyone's attention was on Pasgen and his wife.

It was Halgerd who defended her husband, "We need taxes for this is the most vulnerable part of the Land of the Wolf. We have soldiers to pay and defences to maintain."

"And coronets to buy not to mention linens which are as fine as those in Miklagård. The defences are the same as when I lived here and if you have paid for the men I have seen thus far then you have been robbed."

Pasgen stood, "I will not be insulted in my own hall. Why have you come here, Sámr Ship Killer?"

"To confirm what I was told that you and your wife desire power and you are making the people here and at Úlfarrston fear and hate me. You seek to ferment rebellion and unrest. You are conspiring with our enemies and your time is over!"

I had seen the two men who had guarded me rise but they were slow and witless. They lumbered towards me and made the mistake of standing behind me. Putting my feet against the table I kicked backwards. The heavy chair and the weight of me in my mail knocked them to the ground.

All pretence was gone when Pasgen shouted, "Kill him!" I rolled away from the sword of the third of his oathsworn which smashed into the table. Halgerd had been knocked to the ground and the fourth warrior who came to get me tripped over her. Viking Killer was out, and I had no compunction in hacking into the necks of the two men I had felled. I drew Gutter and slashed it across the face of the third man before ramming the pommel of my sword into the gut of the fourth man who came at my back. His sword slid along my mail links. The hall was in an uproar. Erik, Qlmóðr the Quiet and Ráðulfr Ráðgeirsson had raced across the hall knocking any who looked like he would draw a sword to the ground. Before the treacherous Pasgen could do anything, my sword was at his throat and his oathsworn either slain or disarmed.

Halgerd rose to her feet, "There are just four of them! Kill them! I will reward you!"

I whirled my left arm and had Gutter close to her eye before she even realised. "I have yet to kill a woman, but I have slain a witch and you seem to me to be the latter. One more word and you will die!"

The hall was frozen. The main doors burst open and there stood Ulf Olafsson, Gandálfr Eriksson, the men I had brought and the warriors from Úlfarrston. I pointed to Hrólfr Haakensson, "Hrólfr, Pasgen the hersir says that you did not bring a message inviting him to a meeting. What say you?"

Hrólfr was a huge warrior and he already had his sword drawn, "No man calls me a liar and lives. Give him a sword, lord so that he can defend himself."

I smiled, "Pasgen, would you like a sword?

He was shaking with fear even before Hrólfr Haakensson had crossed the room, "No, I beg of you. The message did come!"

I raised my voice for I was aware that the audience he had invited would be our potential allies, "And what of the taxes?"

"They were for us!"

I nodded, "Bind the two of them! We will take his oathsworn and execute them!" My men obeyed me instantly.

I saw that the real power lay with Halgerd for she said nothing but Pasgen pleaded, "And what of us?"

"You will die but the manner of your death will be determined by the answers to the questions we ask. If we do not like them then you shall be given the blood eagle and your wife burned alive! That is the usual punishment for a witch!"

That brought a reaction and a bony finger pointed in my direction, "I cur…" She got no further for Ráðulfr Ráðgeirsson hit her so hard that she fell unconscious. The curse died on her lips.

We took the oathsworn into the courtyard close to the gates. There the men brought to aid us made a square. The townsfolk gathered around. The oathsworn of Pasgen were resigned to their fate. I allowed them to hold their weapons, but men had nocked arrows pointed at them in case they decided to try to take my executioners with them. They

125

died well holding their swords in two hands as the axes took their heads. "Put their heads on the walls to be a lesson for others who choose to follow such snakes." While the square of men remained, I addressed those who were gathered there. "This town is now, once more, part of the Land of the Wolf. The time of Pasgen is passed. Erik Black Toe will, for a while, rule it for me." We had discussed this as we had headed south. It would not be a permanent arrangement and would certainly displease Ylva but it was the only solution. "Any who do not like this new arrangement may leave but the rest, the ones who remain, will swear an oath to be loyal to the Land of the Wolf. Pasgen demanded taxes that were for him. I will not tax you. I will ask that every man and boy over the age of ten will be ready to fight when I ask. All must be furnished with a weapon. Erik Black Toe will command this garrison and Leif Siggison will rule Úlfarrston. Both are loyal and brave. Now return to your homes."

Pasgen had watched the executions with increasing fear and trepidation. I nodded to Ulf who dragged him inside. Halgerd had awoken. If she lived long enough then she would have a black and bruised face.

"You will answer my questions and if, witch, you attempt to curse me then you shall have your throat slit." She stared at me with hate-filled eyes, but she nodded. She was not used to pain. She held her husband's hand. "Pasgen, who is your master?"

"I have no master and I answer to no one."

I shook my head, "Even now you try to lie your way out of this. Have you ever seen the blood eagle?" He shook his head. "A cut is made in your body and your ribs broken back to resemble an eagle's wings, then..."

I saw the horror on his face, "Enough! King Harald Finehair pays us to ensure that you are undermined and when he comes again, we will open our gates to his men."

"And how is this communicated to you?"

"The men of Man are his allies. In return for his leaving Man alone, they raid the channels twixt Man and Hibernia and the Land of the Wolf. The only ships allowed through bring messages from the King."

We asked more questions, but we had all of the information which we needed. I felt sorry for the two of them for they had been seduced by power. Power was a wicked mistress. I made their end quick. When I had all that I needed from them I nodded to Ulf and Gandálfr whose swords ended their lives in a heartbeat.

When the bodies had been cleared, we sat in the empty hall. My oathsworn and Leif's were all that remained. The rest were either on watch or in the warrior hall. We drank ale and mead and I said, "So, Erik, the ship which brought you was one of Finehair's."

He nodded, "And that makes sense. The captain did not fear to sail past Man and yet I knew that more ships were attacked than were not." He shook his head. "It is fortunate that they did not know who I was or else they might have simply hurled me overboard."

"That changes now. I will leave you ten young warriors from Cyninges-tūn to act as your oathsworn until I can appoint another to rule. This time I will use better judgement." I looked at Ráðulfr Ráðgeirsson, "It is yours for the asking."

He grinned, "No, lord, I swore an oath to you, and I am happy in what we do."

I nodded, "Erik, every ship which arrives unmolested is a suspect. We cannot allow word to reach Finehair that his puppet is dead. Not yet anyway. It is winter and there should not be many boats. I will go to Dyflin and speak with the warriors there. They were once our allies and with their help, we can scour Man of Finehair's influence. That will bring the wrath of the Norse upon us."

Ráðgeir Haakensson asked, "And are we ready to take them on?"

"In all truth, I know not. The sisters have spun, and I am no Dragonheart. I do not have witches and galdramenn to advise me. All I know is that we either fight and win or do nothing and die. The next time Finehair comes he will be ruthless. He will not simply hold me prisoner. He will kill every warrior in the Land of the Wolf. The battle we will fight will be for this land."

Ráðgeir finished his ale, "Then we fight!"

Chapter 12

I did not rest. When I left Erik, we did not follow Ráðgeir and his men to Cyninges-tūn, I took my oathsworn directly to Fótr's stad. It was now Mörsugur and almost the time of the solstice when our clan celebrated. As well as our rituals the followers of the White Christ would be preparing their own celebrations, but I needed to visit Dyflin. I spent an afternoon with Fótr, Bear Tooth and Ebbe. They needed to know my plans and I needed their snekke. When I had finished each was lost in their own thoughts.

Fótr was a clever man. I could see why his clan had followed him. "I always thought of my brother as the navigator but having sailed the seas I know that it is in my blood. My son will be a navigator too. Ebbe, you are ready to lead the people. When you are married it will be the right time for you to take over. Bear Tooth will be the leader of the warriors, but you are wise. Ada is now the matriarch of the clan and you do not need me."

"What will you do?" I could see from his face that Ebbe was happy to be given the responsibility.

He nodded towards me, "Sámr would have me make ships and that appeals to me too. There is something deeply satisfying in constructing a ship which sails beyond the horizon. It was Long Fingers who carved the prow on *'Gytha'*. I would like to do as he did."

I nodded for I understood the connection with a drekar, "Fótr, I wish more of you than that. If you were to make ships, I would like you to be at Whale Island. Erik's heart lies with Ylva and we need our back door secure. Leif is a good man, but you are better. I would have you as the Jarl. I wish you to rule the lands to the south of my home."

"And I would be honoured." He smiled, "It is *wyrd* for that land is close to where we had our ill-fated home at Larswick. My father's spirit lies close by there. It feels right, like coming home.

Ebbe asked, "And what more do you wish of us?" Ebbe was already thinking like a leader.

"I need to visit with the Vikings of Dyflin and the surrounding lands. I intend to attack Man in the spring. We have just three ships and that is not enough."

"Then go on *'Hibernian'* for Aed planned to trade there in any case. Your oathsworn will be added protection in case they are attacked."

Bear Tooth nodded, "And I will be on board for I need to find a wedding gift for my friend; it is the custom of my tribe."

It seemed that everything came together as though it was planned. Fótr would have his dream, Ebbe his and the Land of the Wolf would be more secure.

Considering we were just trading we carried almost as many warriors as a drekar. It proved to be a wise decision. The drekar which headed towards us, with shields along the side, came from Man. I could see from the way she rode in the water that she was an undermanned threttanessa. She was looking for easy victims, knarr and fishing ships. We were lumbering across the water and the lithe longship was able to dance around us. I had my Saami bow and Bear Tooth had his weapon too. When they came slightly too close to us, we loosed our arrows. I am not sure if we hit any flesh but as the two arrows landed in the drekar they must have given them a shock. I said to my oathsworn, "Stand and hold your shields. Let us show them that we are too big for their bellies."

Everyone began banging their shield and, after inspecting us, the pirate turned and headed back. Next time there would be two of them!

I stood with Aed as the drekar sloped off back to the island. "Who is lord of Dyflin these days?" There had been a time when we had been close to Dyflin but that was before Finehair and before my family fell apart.

"Karljot Einarsson. He has no love for King Finehair as he and his family were driven from their island home by the Norwegian King. He is a good warrior for he defeated Lars Karlsson in single combat, and he rules with a fist of iron. Veisafjǫrðr is ruled by his brother Karle Einarsson. He keeps the Hibernians at bay."

"And how does he feel about the pirates of Man?"

"He is not bothered as much by them as his knarr are escorted by drekar and it is mainly slaves that he trades. The pirates of Man, as you saw do not relish combat. From what you have told us the reason why Whale Island and Úlfarrston have suffered as they have is because of treachery and a lack of drekar. You should take one of the ships we captured back to Whale Island. It might deter the pirates."

I nodded for he was right.

Aed and his brother were well known in Dyflin and we were all greeted warmly. We went ashore without mail but kept our swords. Bear Tooth and the men we had brought went to the markets while my oathsworn and myself went to the hall of the Lord of Dyflin. In The Dragonheart's time, Dyflin had been ruled by a jarl appointed by The Dragonheart. As my great grandfather had never interfered in the affairs of the colony except when we were asked for help, we had a good name there. That was shown when I was admitted straight away.

Karljot was a young man and he looked genuinely pleased to see me, "Lord Sámr, the men of the Clan of the Fox have told us of your mighty quest and we are all pleased that you rescued your family from the clutches of King Harald. The men of Dyflin hold the Clan of the Wolf in high regard and we share a common hatred of the King of Norway."

I nodded as thralls brought us wine. My oathsworn stood with those of Karljot. I saw them comparing weapons and, I did not doubt, stories of war. Karljot and I were alone. Like me, he had no adviser. "Did you know that the men of Man serve the Norwegians?"

His eyes narrowed, "I did not but now that you tell me it makes perfect sense."

I told him of Pasgen and his treachery. "When the Norwegians defeated us, they took our drekar. We intend to build more. King Harald will return to finish what he started."

"And you seek an ally?"

He was, as Aed had told me, clever, "Aye but more, I would have you join with me and rid Man of the pirates. The Dragonheart did so once before and I have no doubt that, if we do eradicate the threat, sometime in the future the pirates will rise again but I wish to hurt the King of Norway and to free the seaways for honest knarr."

"Lord Sámr, I know you are of the blood of The Dragonheart. I would speak with you as though you were he. I would have honesty between us. What say you?"

I nodded, "That is my way too. Speak freely and I will answer you as honestly as I am able."

"If we did free Man from these pirates would you object if I took over the island?"

Was I replacing one threat with an even more dangerous one? I used the mind trained by Aiden in long games of chess and the logic he had tried to teach me. Karljot hated the King of Norway. If he ruled the island, he would prevent the Norwegians from simply taking it over. They would have to defeat him and even if he did turn against us we would be no worse off than we were now. If nothing else I was buying time.

"I have no objection."

He smiled, "Together we will defeat this foe, I will have my brother fetch his drekar too. We have eight crews we can bring."

"And I have three drekar and *'Hibernian'*. That should be enough."

When you take a man's word, you clasp his arm as I did then and feel the grip. That tells you something of the character and then you try to see behind the smile. I saw into his eyes and saw no sign of treachery. I was close enough to the Land of the Wolf for the spirits to

130

let me know if they sensed danger and the peace in my mind was reassuring.

That decided, we spent the afternoon discussing plans. We knew that there were three main settlements on the island. There was one to the west, one in the south close to the Calf of Man and one in the east. The settlement my father had built on the north side of the island was now deserted. Even the men of Man feared the spirits there. It was there that The Dragonheart's sword had been touched by the gods and where his mother and some of his people were buried. It was said to be haunted. After discussing the strengths and weaknesses of the three places we decided that we would make a three-pronged attack. I would take the settlement in the east. It had been the home of Prince Buthar. Karle would take the one in the south and Karljot the western one. We chose the last day of Gói for the attack. Spring would just be beginning and when we had defeated them, we had time to prepare defences to welcome King Harald. Karljot agreed with me that he would come. By then he would know that Pasgen was dead and as he would have to sail the same route we had taken, then the depths of winter might cost him ships. He would come from the north and that meant Fótr's stad might be the first one to feel the full force of the vengeful Norwegians. When a warrior put his first foot on the vengeance trail then he had to stay on it until the very end. The Clan of the Wolf and its land would have to pay a price for the rescue of my family. The prize would be freedom and a return to life as it had been before the invaders came. We would be fewer in number and would have to mourn good men but freedom always has a price and we warriors would pay it.

We sailed back after dark. Normally this would be a risk but Aed knew the waters well and we judged it a risk worth taking as we could avoid the dangers of an attack. It was a swift voyage back as we had favourable winds, and most people were abed when we landed. The next day I spent some time with Fótr and Ebbe for I needed my plans finalized.

"I will send men to sail our drekar down to Whale Island. Erik can begin to improve the defences and train some men to sail them."

Fótr said, "And I have spoken with Reginleif and my children. They are happy to move to Whale Island. Some others wish to return with me. Now I see that the unfriendliness we felt was not to do with the Clan of the Wolf but part of King Harald's schemes. We will sail south when you send men to take the drekar and that will allow Erik to come back to Hawk's Roost. I am sorry that I did not tell you the true reason we moved here. Had I done so then Pasgen's evil rule might have been ended sooner."

131

"No, my friend, the sisters enjoy making us grope around in the dark. This is for the best but Ebbe will need to have the defences of this stad so strong that King Harald will land his fleet elsewhere."

"We have already begun. We have carted much stone down from the pass. We will have stone walls to deter him. We intend to divert the sea and the river to make a defence he cannot cross easily. The pass to the east is a difficult one. King Harald will choose an easier route. I think that we will be in more danger in Whale Island."

"And there we are also improving the defences. Do not worry, Fótr, I will not be idle over the winter. The borders are being actively patrolled, and men will be trained. We might not be able to field an army the size of Dragonheart's, but we will have one which will make King Harald question his need for this land! We will make his army bleed so badly that he will seek easier conquests."

We headed back towards Hawk's Roost. The weather deteriorated as we rode east and soon the pass to our home would be difficult to negotiate. The men I would send to man the drekar would need to wait until Þorri. I guessed that they would reach what they were now calling Ebbe's Point, by the middle of the month. That would give them six weeks to prepare the drekar for war.

I was chilled to the bone by the time I reached my home and it was pitch black. The snow had come and while it would not yet lie it was a foretaste of the next months. The weather prevented my home being forewarned of our return and I was forced to bang upon the gates. The blizzard had made us all but invisible and I knew that we needed an extra defence against a surprise attack. We had no dogs and that was easy to remedy. There were always pups we could acquire from farmers and noisy dogs would warn us of an enemy. While Ylva was keen to know about Erik, Ragnar was more interested in my meeting with the men of Dyflin. He knew the importance of such a meeting. My wife was just glad that I was home. The hall now felt like a home. When I had lived alone it felt like a place I ate and slept. Now it welcomed me.

I answered Ylva's questions first, "Erik will rule Whale Island for me until Þorri. Then Fótr will take over and Erik will return home, but it will be a brief stay only for I take the clan to war in Gói. The men of Dyflin and Veisafjǫrðr will join us." I smiled for that answer seemed to satisfy both of my children's questions. There was more to it than the simple answer I had given but I was tired from my journey and the details could wait. What I needed to know was how safe was Hawk's Roost? "And the defences, Ragnar, how do they progress?"

"Not as fast as with you and your oathsworn but Egil has the measure of these Danes and they seem to work for him."

"And you, my son, how do you find the labour?"

He smiled, "You are right, father, and I admit it. I can do more with my body than I thought. I just have to compensate for the lack of one leg. Egil Egilsson has asked if he can be my oathsworn." He smiled, "We get on and he is of a similar age. I thought, at first that he was just taking pity on me, but I now know that he was the youngest of his band and he found we have much in common. With him on my lame side, we can be a formidable combination."

I saw Aethelflaed put her hand to her mouth and I said, "This is good, wife. An oathsworn or shield brother makes any warrior stronger and safer."

"War!" She shook her head, "Why is it always war?"

"Wife, we did not make war on King Harald and what good did it do? He came to try to take what he wanted. So long as there are greedy men then good men must fight and die! The only way to be safe is to make your enemies fear you. We have to make the Norwegians choose another foe."

She made the sign of the cross and we ate in silence for a while.

"After the winter solstice is a good time to hunt the wolf, Ragnar. The wolf skin of Fótr helped you on the voyage home and you are of the Clan of the Wolf. I have hunted one; it is a family tradition that we wear the skin of the animal we kill. Your great grandfather, Wolf Killer, was much younger than you. This might be a good test for your leg and your new oathsworn."

He smiled, "I am ready although my leg may not help, and I might fail."

"It will not be a failure, it will simply be a measure of what you can and cannot do."

That night as we lay in bed, Aethelflaed expressed her doubts once more and I tried to assuage those fears, "Your son will not die when we hunt the wolf. I cannot guarantee that he will not suffer a wound but my oathsworn and Egil Egilsson will provide a human shield for him. He needs to do this. He has to face danger and defeat it himself. When he was in Moi he could not do so and now he can. I have done this as did my father and grandfather. My great grandfather did so whilst protecting an old, crippled man and he was younger than Ragnar."

She squeezed closer to me and kissed me, "I know that you will do all that you can to protect him but he is my son and after what the Norwegians did to him I worry."

"And it is right that you do."

We celebrated the solstice and Christmas. I found it easy to do both and I found no problem with celebrating the birth of a man who tried to

133

change the world for the good. I could find nothing bad about the White Christ. He was a good man, but he was not a warrior. Turning the other cheek did not work for there were evil men in the world who would take advantage of what they deemed to be a weakness. Men could admire him but to follow him was an invitation to death. As soon as the celebrations were over, we prepared to hunt. My intentions were to head towards Úlfarrberg and hunt there but on the day we left we heard wolves howling closer to home and so we followed the lone howl. It was as we neared Skelwith that one of Egge's thralls found us.

"Lord Sámr, Egge asks you to come. There are wolves north of the Loughrigg. He fears, not for himself, but some of the others who live by the tarns and waters. He says they came there on the day of the winter solstice."

We had many families who chose to live by water as it made life easier. When there were wolves it was an invitation for the animals to hunt. As much as I wished to hunt at Úlfarrberg the lives of the clan were more important and so we headed for the cave of Myrddyn. In many ways, this was appropriate for it was there that my grandfather had killed his wolf. The snow which had fallen before the shortest day had now frozen solid and the air was so cold that our breath appeared like fog. We followed the howls and by the time we reached the cave, we saw the tracks. There were wolves and they were close. We paused at the cave for all knew who lay beneath the rockfall. The legend of The Dragonheart and the sword was known throughout the Viking world and my family knew that Ylva and her spirit lived in the cave which had been the home of the wizard Myrddyn.

After we had paid homage I said, "Now we hunt. Ráðulfr Ráðgeirsson, Danr Danrsson, Ulf Olafsson and Gandálfr Eriksson form a line of beaters before the three of us."

We all had swords, but our main weapons were the long ash spear and the throwing javelin. As we reached the top and saw the white world before us, I heard the howl again. There was something odd about this howling for it was not one wolf howling for another. There was just one howl and it seemed to come whenever we reached a place where we could take one route or another. If I had not known better I would have said it was directing me towards the den.

Danr was a good hunter and he stopped and waited for me to close up with him, "Lord Sámr, I do not like this. It feels as though we are being led into a trap."

I nodded. Wolves were as clever as men and were perfectly capable of ambush. Haaken One Eye had spoken of such ambushes. I looked around and spied to the east of us a jumble of snow-covered rocks. The snow had fallen heavily but the jagged rocks still showed through in places. In summer the scrubby shrubs would have hidden them. I did not fear an ambush and I knew why. Ylva was directing us. I could not hear her voice in my head, but we were close to the place her spirit rested and my eyes had been drawn to the mound of rocks. She wished us to go there. I would not risk another on my assumption and so I said, "Oathsworn flank Ragnar. Ragnar, walk in my footsteps."

Almost as though it had heard me the wolf's howl sounded, and it came from the direction of the place I had seen.

"Ready your weapons."

"Lord Sámr, this is a trap!" Danr's voice was urgent and filled with fear.

I felt supremely confident as I answered, "And that is why I will be the one to go first!"

As soon as we began to climb the slope to the rocks, I saw the frozen paw prints. There were wolves yet the snow-covered mound did not look large enough for a pack. "Ragnar, have your spear ready!"

"Aye, father!"

I smelled the wolves before I saw them, and my spear was ready but this was Ragnar's hunt and I was there just to protect him and to strike only if he faltered. It was as we climbed up the mound that the single wolf attacked. It was an old one, but it still had power and it knocked me from my feet. I had the wit to brace my two hands against the spear haft and I used it to hold the savage jaws from my throat. Ragnar acted swiftly. He rammed his spear into the ear of the wolf. Driving through his skull it killed it instantly. As my men raced to help me, Ragnar climbed up on the rocks to peer down into the den. The wolf's body was taken from me and I stood. I went to peer down into the den. There were two wolf cubs and a dead she-wolf. She must have died recently for the cubs were still trying to get milk from her. Like the old wolf Ragnar had slain, she was emaciated.

Ragnar looked confused, "What is this?"

"It is the spirits. Ylva sent us here for we were meant to care for these cubs. The old one and the she-wolf must have been separated from the pack. The old one sacrificed himself but Ylva had us come to rescue the cubs. This is *wyrd*. We sailed the seas to rescue you, Ragnar, and now we have climbed our land to rescue these cubs. I had intended to use dogs from Cyninges-tūn to guard our home, but these will be better. You can hand feed them with milk. Dragonheart trained a wolf and we can do the same." I turned to the oathsworn. "Fetch the two wolves. We can skin them both and Ragnar can wear his wolf skin but

135

the she-wolf's fur will give comfort to the young. Ragnar and I will carry the cubs. This is meant to be."

Danr nodded, "It is, lord, and now I understand why I was suspicious. The old one was close to death too, but he had an honourable death and he served his family to the end. It is all that a warrior can do and this one was a warrior." He pointed to the marks on the fur. They were old wounds, some were made by man and some by other animals.

It was after dark when we reached our home. Aethelflaed was waiting anxiously and I saw her examine first, her son for wounds, and then me. The old wolf had not harmed me and that was down to the prompt action of Ragnar. The teeth marks on my spear would be a reminder to me of the encounter. The spear was even more special now. Ragnar and I put the cubs in one of the rooms we used to store weapons while he organised the thralls to build a cage and help him skin the two wolves. Danr assisted and advised him how to make a feeding sack from the wolf's teats.

I sat and told Aethelflaed and Ylva of the hunt. Aethelflaed was sceptical for she was a Christian. "You are saying that the wolf was commanded by the spirit of Ylva to summon you?"

I shrugged, "Perhaps the old wolf was summoning help from other wolves, I do not know but I felt Ylva's presence. We needed animals to guard our hall and what better animals than wolves for we are the Clan of the Wolf?"

My daughter nodded, "I believe that it was the spirit of my namesake. I will help Ragnar to feed them. That way there will be two of us who they will regard as their family."

My wife threw her arms in the air in exasperation, "This is what I get for marrying a pagan! I have given birth to two pagans!"

It was only during the first few days that the cubs howled at night but the fur of their mother and the love and attention they had from Ragnar, Ylva and Danr soon won them over and their training began. I forgot about them almost immediately for I had plans to finalise. I sent four of my oathsworn in two pairs to visit with my lords. I would not take all of their men, but I needed at least half for the raid on Man. I would not use my Danes yet. I wanted my defences built and I needed them for the fight we would have with King Harald. While they were away, I visited Cyninges-tūn. This was always the heartland of the warriors I would use, and it was not just warriors I needed. The young could also be utilised. Viking boys know that they will be warriors and from an early age begin their training. They would be of no use in a shield wall, but they could be ships' boys and slingers. When I reached

Cyninges-tūn I went to Bacgsecg and commissioned him to make twenty special seaxes. I had plenty of coins from Dragonheart's hoard. I asked him to put a wolf on the handle of each one. I would give one to each of the twenty best slingers. I had Haaken assemble all the warriors and boys and spoke to them by The Water. It was an icy day and the wind made it feel even colder, but they were all happy to stand and hear my words.

"Cyninges-tūn is the heart of the Land of the Wolf. Its warriors always form the most dependable shield wall. We go to war soon and we will end the threat of Man. You have until Gói to prepare! When Man is no longer a threat, we will then await a war with our real enemy, the King of Norway."

They began to cheer and shout insults towards the Norwegians as though they were actually present. It was a cacophony of noise, but it heartened me. The time they had spent under King Harald's domination had not disheartened them.

"And you boys will also go to war. Practise your slinging. Find the best pebbles from The Water and hone your skill. You will all fight before the shield wall and you will learn to hide close to the shields of our warriors and, while we fight, you will use your daggers to slash and stab at the legs of their warriors. The twenty most accurate slingers will be awarded a special dagger I am having made. I will return in a fortnight to see who will be given the blades." I pointed to Hawk's Roost. "I will be over there with my oathsworn. If any of you wish to come and practise with us, then you may do so but time is short and daylight would be better used in learning to fight better rather than sailing across The Water. Now begin your preparations!"

I spent two hours with the leaders of the warriors. They needed to know what I expected of them as leaders. "Haaken, you and the other greybeards will not go to war. I will not leave Cyninges-tūn defenceless. The young must learn to shoulder their share of the fighting and rowing a drekar is a young man's lot in life! I want the women arming for they can help to defend the walls. We need as many arrows making as we can manage. We may not need them when we go to Man but we will need them when Harald comes!"

Haaken beamed, "This is better, lord! When you stayed behind the walls of Hawk's Roost, we feared that King Harald had won. Now that you have your family back, we see the old Sámr Ship Killer!"

As I headed back to my home, I saw that the title, Dragonheart's Heir, was not simply given. It had to be earned and I had spent a year or more doing nothing; now I would earn the accolade or die trying. I had a son again and he could follow me.

Two days later Erik arrived and Ylva's face was filled with joy; that gave me much satisfaction as did Erik's news. He told me that the ships had arrived along with Fótr and the people who would be living at Whale Island. Erik had travelled along the Water alone and it had been not without incident. He told me that as twilight descended, he saw the figure of a woman rise from the middle of The Water. She seemed to float on its surface, and she came to the beach. Erik said that although the spectre did not speak, he heard words in his head.

'Tell Sámr that he should use the land and sea to defeat his enemies. Make the rivers into warriors and have the trees fight as men.'

"I did not understand the words. What do they mean?"

I drank some of the ale as I considered the question and the vision. He and Ylva looked at each other while Ragnar and his mother stared at me. Aiden and Kara had often explained dreams to Dragonheart and I had heard those explanations. I knew how to look beyond the words to the practicality of an action. When I spoke I had translated the words Erik had spoken. Although I might have got it wrong I knew that the idea would work.

"I think that the spirit who spoke to you was Erika, Dragonheart's wife and my great grandmother. The river which flows along the side of Úlfarrston is sometimes shallow. If we were to build a dam to hold the water, then when the Norwegians come we can release it. We cut the trees down to make the dam and they will fight for us. They will flood down to be as spears." I put an arm around him, "I am glad that you are back, not just because it will make my daughter's life joyous, but you bring news that the spirits are active still. We may not have a galdramenn, but they will find ways to talk to us. Now speak with Ylva. She has awaited your return." The two stared at each other and then disappeared to be alone. The hall was still not fully filled and they could do so.

The days were short but even had it been midsummer they would not have been long enough for all that we had to do. We were in a race and we had to act before any of our enemies did. We won the race to build the defences of Hawk's Roost but that was mainly because of Ragnar and Egil who drove the men on. As I had promised I gave the thralls their freedom. The Saxons headed across The Water to work for Bacgsecg and the Danes accepted my offer to guard Hawk's Roost. Many might have thought it a risk but I knew that warriors would never break an oath which was sworn on a sword. Ragnar, his oathsworn,

138

Egil's men and the Danes, along with the two cubs on leashes, came with me when I went to inspect the slingers and to review the warriors who would be marching to Whale Island with me. I left Erik at Hawk's Roost. When we went to Man he would stay with Ragnar and my family.

There were more warriors waiting for me than I had expected. Some had been absent or lived on the fells but they were all ready to show me their weapons, shields and helmets. The twenty-five slingers were also ready to win the weapons I had promised. The seaxes were arrayed on a table by The Water. Haaken had placed a boat a hundred paces from the shore. He grinned when I asked him its purpose, "There is little point in asking the boys to hurl stones at a static target. When did warriors stand still? We have made one hundred and fifty small boats. They will be released from the anchored boat and they will be the target. It will be like trying to hit a warrior's face but the water will make them bob up and down."

I looked at the boys who were waiting. They had obviously been told their task. I nodded, "Very well. Let the competition begin."

The first ten took their places and Haaken waved to the crew of the boat. Twenty of the tiny boats were released. The breeze and the current made them bob up and down. The boys impressed me. Nine of them hit the target with their first stone and some even managed to hit a second one before the targets either sank or disappeared from view. The one who had missed with his first stone hit one with his second but he knew he had failed and he left. The other nine were marshalled by Haaken's son. The second ten came and this time only eight sank one with their first stone. Once again, some managed to hit a second and in one case, a third target. The eight joined the first nine. There were three places left and five boys. If all five were accurate then we would have to hold a second round. I think that Haaken must have organised the boys into their groups with some knowledge of their ability. Three of the last five hit their targets and the other two did not manage to hit a single one. The gods had chosen the twenty and I gave each of them a seax. I was not sure which gave them the greatest pleasure: the knife was being presented to them by the Lord of the Land of the Wolf.

I sent for the ones who had not been chosen, "I make a promise to you. When you fight before my shield wall, I will give those who have not yet received a seax one from my collection in Hawk's Roost!"

That brought a cheer from them all. Haaken had provided ale, mead, bread and cheese. We ate in the open and it was the beginning of the birth of my new warband. The next time we were together we would be marching to Whale Island.

Chapter 13

We spent the night before we were due to leave for Whale Island at Cyninges-tūn. I had said my farewells to my family, and they had been tear filled. Ragnar and Erik would have to defend my home with just the servants and Egil Egilsson. I slept in the hall where I had spent so many years with Dragonheart. It was the perfect start for my war for the hall had nothing but good memories for me. Dragonheart had died on the walls but his hall had never been touched by his enemies. I did not ride to war, I marched at the head of a column of one hundred and ten men and twenty-seven boys. More boys had joined the ranks of my slingers and we made a merry band as we marched south. It was the mothers of the ships' boys who shed tears. As we marched, the warriors and boys of the clan sang and it was a song of the clan which helped them to maintain such a good pace. The snows had gone but the weather was worse for it had rained heavily and added to the snowmelt we trudged through the mud. The song helped to keep up our spirits.

Through the stormy Saxon Seas
The Ulfheonar they sailed
Fresh from killing faithless Danes
Their glory was assured
Heart of Dragon
Gift of a king
Two fine drekar
Flying o'er foreign seas
Then Saxons came out of the night
An ambush by their Isle of Wight
Vikings fight they do not run
The Jarl turned away from the rising sun
Heart of Dragon
Gift of a king
Two fine drekar
Flying o'er foreign seas
The galdramenn burned Dragon Fire
And the seas they burned bright red
Aboard 'The Gift' Asbjorn the Strong
And the rock Eystein
Rallied their men to board their foes
And face them beard to beard

Heart of Dragon
Gift of a king
Two fine drekar
Flying o'er foreign seas
Against great odds and back to back
The heroes fought as one
Their swords were red with Saxon blood
And the decks with bodies slain
Surrounded on all sides was he
But Eystein faltered not
He slew first one and then another
But the last one did for him
Even though he fought as a walking dead
He killed right to the end
Heart of Dragon
Gift of a king
Two fine drekar
Flying o'er foreign seas

The boys soon learned the words and the stories of warriors past would help them to become warriors themselves. I was pleased with the choice of song for we would be sailing in the two drekar we had taken from the men of Man. That they were not ships of the clan would not matter once our shields were along the side and our chests on the deck. As we marched, I was able to look at the faces I knew and the faces I did not. I marked their shields, helmets and weapons. On the battlefield that would be important.

Fótr showed that he was now in command at Whale Island. He had men posted north of the port and they sent word to him that we were on our way. They waved to us as we passed but I saw the rider heading south to inform the new Lord of Whale Island of our proximity. He was showing that he was cautious. I liked that. There would not be enough room for us all in the warrior hall and so the boys would sleep aboard the three drekar. That too would help them. They would be curious about their ship and their play and adventures would make them familiar with their new homes. There might be falls, cuts and injuries but they would only serve to make them better at their job. Some of the younger men, often the brothers or fathers of the boys, also volunteered to sleep aboard. The rest of us marched to the stronghold and my father's hall. Fótr greeted us there and clasped my arm when I arrived.

"The two drekar have been completely cleaned. All taint of the men of Man has gone. We have not yet cleaned the weed from her hull, but

142

speed will not be as important on this raid. When we defeat the men of Man, we will have time to haul her ashore and clean the bottom."

I could not help myself and I burst out laughing, "You are so confident that we will win?"

He gave a self-deprecating smile, "When they sent men to raid us, they sent their best men and they were slaughtered by a handful of warriors. The ones we find will be the warriors who wish others to fight for them. The Norwegians will be a harder test but the men of Man will not." He frowned as he led me to the hall, "My main worry is that we will not have enough time to become proficient at the oars."

"As you say that is not important. We can land to the north or south of Duboglassio unseen and then march along the coast. It will be the steel in our warriors that will determine the outcome."

I saw that Reginleif was happy to be living in such a magnificent hall. She beamed as she greeted me, and she had her servants take my chest to my chamber. She had not been there long, but I could see her influence already. My mother had made it a home and Reginleif had returned it to that state after Halgerd tried to make it a palace. Fótr's wife had many qualities that she shared with my mother. She was a mother first and the wife of a leader second. The spirits would approve of her.

I needed a bath after the muddy journey, but it would have been rude to ask for water to be heated. I would rise early and have the servants do so. Instead, I followed Fótr to the feasting hall where we would eat and finalise the details for the raid. The bees in this part of the world made fine honey and I knew that once Reginleif was settled then they would begin to make their own mead. They had brought some from Ebbe's Point and the taste of it reminded me of Fótr's people. I knew his parting from them would have been hard. He and Ada had been close as had he and Helga. He had been the one who saved them from the sea and was their leader. That he had accepted my offer showed his true character. I saw that Bear Tooth and his family had followed Fótr and that was a good thing. The three of us stood before the roaring fire to warm ourselves. I knew that when we went to sea, even though it was a short voyage, we would be even colder. Winter still gripped the sea.

"Did we find the names of the two ships?" It did not do to change the name of a ship for it was unlucky.

I saw Fótr shake his head. "There were none left alive to tell us. Ada and the women of the clan wove spells and spoke with the spirits. We looked at the figurehead and Ada thought that one looked a little like Bear Tooth's people. We named that one *'Skraeling'* and the other had

143

a dragon carved, albeit badly, so Æimundr Loud Voice suggested *'Dragon's Bane'*."

"And they did not object to their names when they sailed south?"

Fótr gave me a wry smile, "They are not well-made drekar, Sámr. They will do to take us to Man and fetch us home but the ones I will begin to build will be better."

It was as honest an answer as I could expect. He was right and it would be a short voyage to Man. We would sail at night and simply follow Fótr on *'Gytha'*. Surprise would be everything. Of course, I was reliant on the Vikings of Dyflin and Veisafjǫrðr doing their part. I did not think that Karljot would let us down but if he did then our raid would still hurt the men of Man and pay them back for their attack on Fótr. Our biggest problem would be the lack of information about our enemy and their stronghold. We did not know how many men we would have to face nor, more importantly, who led them. Had we had Ulfheonar then they would have gone ashore first and we would have had a very accurate picture. I was happy to express my fears to Fótr and Bear Tooth for, despite their relative youth, I knew them both to be reasoned warriors with good minds. It was the Skraeling who pointed out the obvious, reiterating what Fótr had said.

"Lord Sámr when they raided our home, they were either led by their best leaders and we slew them or the ones they considered the best stayed at home. Would you fear such men?"

"They might have thought to have an easy victory and did not need to sail and raid."

"And, again, would you fear such men? We will have on *'Gytha'*, young and untried warriors. This raid will make men of them for I see sterner tests in the future."

"The Norwegians?"

Bear Tooth was a warrior and he knew war, "We left too many men alive in Moi. That was not our fault for we had too few men, but they will seek revenge and from what I have been told King Harald Finehair will not be a happy king. When he comes, perhaps I should challenge him to single combat!"

I laughed, not because I thought it was a foolish suggestion, but because I knew that while Bear Tooth meant it such a thing could never happen. "King Harald Finehair sees himself as a king now and he would only accept such a challenge from another king. Believe me, the thought crossed my mind. You are right he will send warriors to punish us and, you are correct, this will be a hard fight but this time we will be prepared for whatever cunning he attempts."

144

We then spoke, while we ate, of the plan of attack. Fótr and Bear Tooth would lead one warband, I a second and Ráðgeir Haakensson a third. Enough of my warriors had sailed close to Duboglassio for us to have a good idea of the layout. The port had a wooden dock and the settlement's houses spilt out from the water and nestled below their stronghold. It was no longer the fortress it had been in Prince Butar's time. We had a simple plan and it involved the destruction of the houses rather than a bloody assault on their walls. We did not have enough men to waste in such a costly attack.

"So, Lord Sámr, we have two days for the men to get used to their new ships and then we sail?"

"Aye, Fótr, but unless we wish the men to be exhausted when they fight that two days is a day and a half in reality. They will need to rest on the afternoon of the second day and prepare for the battle."

Fótr nodded, "And that is why you lead and not I. I had not thought of that."

I took the steering board of *'Skraeling'*. Fótr and his people had cleaned her up as best as they could but Fótr had been correct, it was not a well-made ship. I put those thoughts from my mind. Ada and her witches had spun and the drekar was protected, all that we had to do was to learn to sail her. Ráðgeir had *'Dragon's Bane'* and we took our two ships to sea. Getting in and out of Whale Island was never easy. We had chosen the site because it was a hard approach for any enemy. That made it hard to get to sea but that was a good thing for a captain and his crew could not be complacent. I was luckier than Ráðgeir. I had the men who had sailed with me to Moi. Egil and my oathsworn were triple crewed on the front oars. The twelve ships' boys we had were too many for such a small ship, but they were keen and took my commands well. We rowed out of the anchorage to clear the land. We could have used the sail, but I wished to get the crew used to rowing together. This was not *'Gytha'* and I needed to get to know how she responded.

She was quite quick in a straight line but there had to be weed on her keel for her turns, especially to larboard were laboured. She was shallow drafted and that was a good thing. We had not had time to make a new sail and when we ceased rowing and used the sail I saw that it was not the best sail. The boys scampered up and down the sheets and stays. They swarmed up and down the mast and along the cross trees. To the younger ones, it was a game and, as in all games, there were accidents. The most serious was when Leif Larsson fell from the mast. He was lucky and just sprained his ankle. He could have broken his back. Of course, he was distraught as it meant he would have to stay in Whale Island and would not be sailing to Man.

We were all exhausted when we returned and negotiated the tricky passage back into port. That night, Fótr spoke with Ráðgeir and me about the two drekar. He nodded his agreement to our comments about the sailing properties, "It is as we found when we came south. I did not tell you of their idiosyncrasies for it is better for a captain to discover them himself."

"And it does not matter a great deal. We have to follow you and then ground them on the beach south of Duboglassio."

Ráðgeir asked, "Is that wise, Lord Sámr? What if we need to get off in a hurry?"

"Do not have such negative thoughts, my friend. You and your crew need to believe that we will win. My plan might not be as good as one devised by Dragonheart, but I believe that it will save lives and that we will emerge victorious. At the very least we will weaken the men of Man. Remember that the purpose of this is to win the island for Karljot and his brother. We need the southern approach to our land to be guarded. We do not have the men and Karljot is ambitious."

"And if he chooses to take the Land of the Wolf?"

"Ráðgeir, I have eaten with this man and I have looked into his eyes. He has no such ambitions. I am not replacing one enemy with another. We need allies. The war with Norway cost us men. I have spent long hours thinking this through and I believe it is the only solution."

"Then I am happy!" His words belied his eyes.

It had been some time since I had steered a drekar and I was glad that all I had to do was to follow the light hung from the stern of *'Gytha'*. Fótr knew his business. We left as the sun set ahead of us and gave us a point at which to sail. Man lay due west from us. The forty-five miles would take just over five hours for us to row. We had enough oarsmen to be able to change them every hour and we kept a steady rhythm. We had a light burning in a clay pit hanging from our stern so that *'Dragon's Bane'* could follow. I had one of the ship's boys watching her and he had strict orders to tell me if she began to fall back. The oarsmen were not perfect, and they made mistakes. It did not matter we had almost eleven hours of night time and even if the journey took twice as long we would still reach the beach in darkness. I missed Erik, Ebbe, Bear Tooth and Fótr. My oathsworn were a comfort but I felt that I could speak more easily with the four men who had sailed to Moi with me. The steering board was a lonely place. Perhaps I should have brought Ragnar and then I dismissed the thought. He had grown stronger since our return and the wolf hunt had helped but he was not yet ready to fight and certainly not on Man. The day would come when he would have to face enemies with a sword in his hand and I hoped

146

that he would be ready, but I feared for him. Standing on one leg and fighting was a risk. Was he good enough?

Although the sea was not lively it was far from a flat calm. The winds were from the wrong direction else we might have made better progress. We had no hourglass on my drekar and there was no measure of time except for the changing of the oarsmen. I kept the boys busy serving ale and dried fish to the men who had been rowing. I knew from experience that boys will skylark if they are not kept busy. As the oarsmen were changed, I saw that they were all sweating. Many were rowing in their byrnies and the ones who did not have mail byrnies had leather ones, some studded with metal. It was necessary for we would have to fight but it was not the best way to row. That set me to thinking. If King Harald's Norwegians came by ship, they would not come in mail. They would expect to land first, make a camp and then change into fighting gear. They would have sailed all the way from Norway. If we could attack them before they had mailed and prepared, we could hurt their ability to attack us. The plans I made kept my mind occupied as I stared at the glow that was the light on *'Gytha'*. Great grandfather and Aiden had prepared me for such diversions. They had taught me to play chess when I was very young. At the time I had wondered why but now I saw the reason. It was training for my mind. It showed me how to see a problem and then find a number of different solutions.

The signal that land was close almost took me by surprise. The ship's boys designated to watch the stern of *'Gytha'* ran down to me, "Lord Sámr, three flashes."

I nodded, "Galmr Galmrsson, send the signal to *'Dragon's Bane'*."

"Aye, lord!"

As he did so I gave my orders, "Single oars, we are close to land!" Although it was unlikely that we would be opposed I wanted two-thirds of the warriors ready to leap into the water, if it was necessary. I could see nothing ahead for it was too dark and there were too many men between me and the coast of Man. However, when I looked off to steerboard I saw a thin line of white. It was the waves beating on the rocks north of Duboglassio. I moved the steering board slightly to steerboard for I did not wish to run into *'Gytha's'* stern. The beach we had chosen, north of the town, was long enough to accommodate all three ships. Fótr began to turn north a little and I mirrored his moves. Glancing astern I saw that Ráðgeir had also turned. As I did so I saw the faintest of lights on the horizon. It was a false dawn and the voyage had taken longer than we had anticipated. We would still land in darkness, but I knew that there would be people awake. It could not be helped.

When I looked back, I saw the beach which looked like a line of white. When I saw Fótr's oars begin to back water I knew that he was slowing his drekar so that it did not damage itself on the beach. "Jumpers, be ready to leap ashore. Rowers, on my command back water." I saw the waves breaking and shouted, "Back water!" I wondered if I had misjudged it as I felt sand beneath our keel but when we came to a gentle stop, I knew that more by good fortune than anything, I had judged it well. Not only the ship's boys leapt ashore but also fifteen men who wore no mail but had their shields and spears at the ready. They were to protect us from an attack. None materialised. I concentrated on my drekar and assumed that Ráðgeir and Fótr would do the same on their ships.

Men stacked their oars on the mast fish as more of my men jumped into the sea. Bear Tooth and Fótr would be already making a shield wall in case the worst had happened and men were waiting for us. The four ship's boys who were to wait with the drekar came to the stern. They were not happy at the duty but knew that it was necessary. "Remember, you keep this safe for us. If disaster strikes and we have to flee back here, then you will be the ones who will offer us protection." I saw that they all wore their new seaxes in their belts. They would be desperate to use them!

I donned my helmet and strode to the prow. Ulf Olafsson and Gandálfr Eriksson were waiting on the beach with my shield and my spear. It was the spear with the teeth marks of the dead wolf. My oathsworn were ready to form a shield around me. It would take some time for Ráðgeir to land his men. With my shield over my arm and the spear in my hand, I headed for Fótr. Bear Tooth was not there. Fótr was also armed and mailed. He said, "Bear Tooth has gone with your scouts."

I nodded as Ráðgeir appeared, "Most of my men are ashore."

"Then let us go!"

I led my oathsworn and the other two captains at a steady jog down the beach. There was a little more light from the dawn and I saw, ahead, the shapes of the houses and the masts of the ships tied up to the wooden quay.

Bear Tooth and his scouts were waiting for us at the edge of the settlement. I saw two dead men and a dog. I nodded and waved my sword. Everyone knew what they were to do. Fótr's men ran to capture the ships and make them ours. My men and Ráðgeir's would attack and fire the houses. The warriors of Duboglassio lived largely in the stronghold but the levy and the bulk of the men were in the town. It was ruthless but if we were to eliminate the threat from the island then the

148

men had to be killed! We would drive the women and children away. Their fate would be a decision when we won. As the men from Cyninges-tūn began to rampage through the houses I stood with my oathsworn and faced the stronghold. We were just two hundred paces from it. The land between the wooden stronghold and the settlement had been cleared. It gave them a killing ground, but it also gave us somewhere to deploy! Behind me and my wedge of oathsworn, I heard the screams and the cries as the killing began. I felt no sympathy for them for they had tried the same thing at Ebbe's Point. The difference had been that we were waiting, and they were not. Had they kept a better watch from their towers then it might have made a difference, but it was only now that I saw men appear on the fighting platform and a bell tolled. It was still dark and until the buildings were fired then the warriors behind the wooden walls would not see how many men had attacked them. Our boats were beached more than half a mile from the stronghold and were invisible.

My men had been right when they said that their attack on Ebbe's Point showed how weak was their leadership. Instead of ascertaining the threat, the gates opened, and some warriors rushed out. If I had more men with me, we could have taken advantage. There was just a wedge of us but I was confident. Twenty odd men hurtled towards us. I could smell smoke and I heard the crackling of flames as the buildings were set on fire behind me and I heard the shouts as men died and the women and the children were chased south. The warriors from Duboglassio came at us as a mob. Had I been leading seasoned warriors then I would not have been worried but all of my oathsworn were young. We had fought at Moi and Ebbe's Point but they were still raw.

"Brace! Let them break upon me."

The light was improving all the time but as it was behind us I could not tell how far from full sunrise it was. I braced the wolf spear so that the butt was next to my right foot. With my shield protecting my right hand and body the only place the men of Man had to strike was my head and I wore a good helmet. The first warrior to die simply ran on to my spear. His shield was held before him and he was thrusting at me with his own spear. My spear did not move and, often, the lack of movement made weapons seem not to be there. I easily deflected the thrust of his spear which slid off the metal boss of my shield. His shield nearly caused me problems as he was punching with it but by then the tapered head of the six feet long ash spear had driven through his mail byrnie, padded kyrtle and up under his ribs. I flicked his body from my spear, and it fell into the path of the warrior trying to get at Ráðulfr Ráðgeirsson. He naturally spread his arms to stop himself

149

overbalancing and Ráðulfr Ráðgeirsson had all the time in the world to ram his spear into the warrior's face. It was at that point that a horn sounded, and a voice called, "Back to the walls!"

Most of the men who had attacked us realised their folly and obeyed but three of them were too busy trying to kill my oathsworn. Ulf, Gandálfr and Danr slew their opponents and then reformed the wedge. Seeing the gates slam behind the survivors I risked a look over my shoulder. I saw that the butchery was over. The men of the settlement were dead. The ships were ours and Fótr's men guarded the quay. Fótr, Bear Tooth and Ráðgeir Haakensson were leading their men to join me as were the slingers. They had not had the chance to show their skill yet but that would come. Fótr and his men formed a wedge to our left and Ráðgeir Haakensson to our right. We had practised this move after a morning of rowing, and I hoped that they would all remember what they were to do.

Ráðgeir Haakensson said, "Eight of my young men are chasing the women and children south." He laughed, "I am guessing that they are heading for their southern stronghold. If Karle has done what we hope, then they are in for a shock."

"Good. Dragon's teeth!"

The two wedges moved sideways, banging their shields with their spears as they did so. It helped to keep time and I knew it would intimidate those inside the stronghold. The three wedges had a total of forty-five men in each one and now they were joined by a double line of warriors. The slingers raced to form a line before us. Then we waited. Behind us, I could hear and smell the burning. As the wood burned so parts fell with a crash. Some tumbled into the sea where they hissed. Those inside the stronghold found themselves in a dilemma. If they did nothing, then we could simply take their ships and sail home. There were two small drekar and five knarr as well as three snekke. This was their main settlement and a most important port. Could they afford to let us take it? I guessed that there was a debate going on inside the fortress. I knew that we were not a large warband. The Clan of the Wolf used to be able to field six times the number we had and still have reserves. Times had changed.

I began to sing, I chose a song which I knew would annoy the men who were within the stronghold. If they decided not to come out, then we would have to think of something else. I had one or two ideas in my head. The song would also put heart into my men.

The storm was wild and the gods did roam
The enemy closed on the Prince's home

Two warriors stood on a lonely tower
Watching, waiting for hour on hour.
The storm came hard and Odin spoke
With a lightning bolt the sword he smote
Ragnar's Spirit burned hot that night
It glowed, a beacon shiny and bright
The two they stood against the foe
They were alone, nowhere to go
They fought in blood on a darkened hill
Dragon Heart and Cnut will save us still
Dragon Heart, Cnut and the Ulfheonar
Dragon Heart, Cnut and the Ulfheonar
The storm was wild and the Gods did roam
The enemy closed on the Prince's home
Two warriors stood on a lonely tower
Watching, waiting for hour on hour.
The storm came hard and Odin spoke
With a lightning bolt the sword he smote
Ragnar's Spirit burned hot that night
It glowed, a beacon shiny and bright
The two they stood against the foe
They were alone, nowhere to go
They fought in blood on a darkened hill
Dragon Heart and Cnut will save us still
Dragon Heart, Cnut and the Ulfheonar
Dragon Heart, Cnut and the Ulfheonar
Clan of the Wolf, warriors strong
Clan of the Wolf, warriors brave
Clan of the Wolf, fierce as the wolf
Clan of the Wolf, hides in plain sight
Clan of the Wolf, Sámr's wolves
Clan of the Wolf serving the sword
Clan of the Wolf, Sámr's wolves
Clan of the Wolf, serving the sword
Clan of the Wolf, warriors strong
Clan of the Wolf, warriors brave
Clan of the Wolf, fierce as the wolf
Clan of the Wolf, hides in plain sight
Clan of the Wolf, Sámr's wolves
Clan of the Wolf, serving the sword
Clan of the Wolf, Sámr's wolves
Clan of the Wolf, serving the sword

Each time the warband sang '*Clan of the Wolf*' we all gave a double bang on our shields. It was most effective. We finished the chant and although we cheered there was no sign of the gates being opened. I handed my shield and spear to Ulf and Danr. "I will go to speak to them."

"We will come, lord."

"No, Ráðulfr Ráðgeirsson, for that will make them think that I fear them!"

As I stepped forward, I touched the golden wolf I wore around my neck and intoned, "Ylva, Erika and Kara, protect your blood!"

I stopped one hundred paces from the gates and shouted, "We have told you who we are and who I am. In case you did not hear, I am Sámr Ship Killer and I am the one who led the warband which destroyed two of your crews. Whom do we face? What is the name of the nithing who skulks behind these wooden walls because he fears us?"

The arrow which was sent from the walls was well aimed. It came straight for me and was so fast that I did not have time to move out of the way. As events proved that was a good thing. The arrow hit me in the throat, but it had to travel through mail and a padded kyrtle. Even so, it might have killed me. In fact, I thought that I was a dead man as I reeled backwards, barely keeping my feet. The men in the stronghold cheered and I heard an angry wail from behind me. Then I realised that I was not dead and I could not even feel blood. I knew I had been hit but why was I not dead? I reached my hand up to the arrow as I raised my head. The arrow had hit the golden wolf and Dragonheart's gift had saved me. I left the arrow there and stepped forward. When I was confident that I could speak I laughed, "I should have expected nothing less from the treacherous spawn of Man. It has ever been thus, but do you not know the story? Odin protects our blood! A treacherous arrow will not end my life! Who commands here? Speak lest I bring the wrath of the Allfather down upon your head."

A warrior took off his helmet and shouted, "I am Jarl Finbarr the Fearless, and you are nothing, Sámr Ship Killer! You were held prisoner by King Harald, and he took away any power you might have had! Quit this land for when my brothers see the smoke rising in the sky they will come and destroy you!"

"Then Finbarr the Fearless, if I am nothing come forth and fight me. I challenge you to single combat. Let the Allfather decide. When you place my head upon your walls then you can crow. Until then you are a nithing!" This was a crucial moment. Would he take me up on my offer of single combat?

152

Chapter 14

Jarl Finbarr the Fearless was a coward. When he stood and said nothing I knew that he feared to fight me. I waited for a suitable length of time and deliberately turned my back on him. I walked back to my men who were banging their shields and chanting my name over and over. I waited for the thud of an arrow in my back, but none came. Bear Tooth and Fótr came towards me and Fótr showed his concern, "How are you still alive?"

I lifted my helmet for I was sweating, "I was lucky. It hit the wolf amulet I wear around my neck." I took the arrow and prised it from the wolf. I slipped the arrow into my belt. It was a good luck charm!

Bear Tooth said, "If that was my people then they would have surrendered already. What will these warriors do?"

I turned back to face the walls. "I do not know but I suspect that if there are real warriors inside, they will demand that they come to fight us. If they do not then they are all scared of us and we will risk an attack on their walls."

I saw that they had left just a few men on the walls and that suggested that they were holding some sort of meeting. Finbarr the Fearless had not earned his name; perhaps he gave it to himself; some men did. I was about to order our archers to light fires so that we could rain fire arrows on them when the gates suddenly opened. They were coming to fight. This time, however, they were not going to charge us recklessly. They formed up in a shield wall and I saw that they outnumbered us. The difference was that we had planned this battle and every man knew what to do. Those led by Finbarr were reacting to our tactics. We would have the edge.

I shouted, "Slingers, be ready to advance. We keep the same formation! Dragon's Teeth!" I allowed them to form up and then shouted, "Slingers, now is your time! Make your fathers proud!"

They needed no urging and they ran to within fifty paces of the enemy and began hurling their stones. This time the target was just moving steadily towards them. There was neither current nor waves to put off their aim. Even when the men of Man dipped their heads the ring of a pebble on metal told me that they had hurt a warrior. Four warriors dropped from the line. I had told my slingers to fall back steadily and they did so. None were reckless enough to risk being run down by a maddened Viking. It mattered not that only a few men were badly wounded or killed, the slingers threw so many stones and hit so many of our enemies that all of their front rank would be weaker. I saw that Finbarr the Fearless was in the second rank. If we did lose, I doubted that he would be jarl for much longer. A leader had to lead.

This time I held my spear overhand for the fighting would be shield to shield. I had height and I intended to use it and strike down over the shields. If I could I would threaten Finbarr the Fearless who had shown that he lacked the courage or, perhaps, confidence. If I could make him run, then the battle might end.

"Slingers, fall back!"

They all hurled one last pebble and then ran back to hurl themselves at our feet. We had practised this and both warriors and slingers were comfortable. The ones who were at the tip of each wedge were in the greatest danger. All the slingers had protection from our shields and if any of the men of Man chose to try to spear them then they left themselves open to attack from our spears.

"Archers, release!"

We had a thin line of archers behind the shield wall. They all had a shield and spear too but the twenty of them would release their arrows over our heads and only use their shield and spear if our line was breached. Now that the slingers were safe, they had free rein. As the first arrows fell, I saw men hit. I did not see any killed, but I saw arrows sticking in arms and shoulders. The men would be able to fight but they would be weakened, and combat would make them even weaker. The first point of contact would be Bear Tooth, myself and Ráðgeir Haakensson. We were well protected by our oathsworn and their best warriors would be drawn to us. The archers could continue to send arrows at the enemy and if only a few hit then the odds would gradually increase in our favour.

I shouted, "Lock shields and brace!" when they were just ten paces from us. I knew that they would charge the last few paces. Some would hurl themselves in the air and attempt to break our line with their bodies while those who were mailed believed that their weight would carry them through. Against our three wedges, they would have little success as each wedge consisted of fifteen men and we were all mailed! With my two oathsworn's shields locked against my sides and their bodies pushing against my back, we were solid. I took the black-bearded warrior's spear on my shield and it slid along, first mine and then Gandálfr's. As I jabbed down over his shield Stig Snorrison, the slinger who crouched beneath my shield, stabbed upwards with his wolf seax. The warrior screamed and his back arched as his hamstring was slashed and I rammed my wolf spear into the black-bearded warrior's screaming mouth. It came out of his back and raked the face of Jarl Finbarr the Fearless who stood behind him. Their attack overlapped ours but before they could use their advantage our shield wall between the wedges struck and our lines were still solid. The line of the men of Man was a ragged one. It is in those first encounters that battles are lost and won. They tried jumping at the spears and shields to knock holes in them but our shield walls were double-banked and the young warriors there were determined. As warriors fell to the ground the slingers' hands darted out and their seaxes found flesh.

I was still assailed on both sides by warriors desperate to kill me and end the shame of my words. Their jarl had let them down. The two men who battered at my shield and helmet would be two potential rivals to become the new jarl. Finbarr the Fearless stood behind them and allowed them to attract my attention. I wondered if his name was meant as a joke. Stig Snorrison was doing his best with his seax but the two men wore sealskin boots. Gandálfr and Ráðulfr were having their own battles and for the first time since the battle had begun could not come to my aid. I took drastic action. My shield was still before me and I turned the wolf bitten spear horizontally and punched with both at the same time. The spear of Finbarr the Fearless darted forward for my eyehole. I was committed to the blows and could do nothing. My foot caught on Stig and as my head went down a little the spear scratched and scraped along the side. The two warriors who had been fighting me fell back and I threw the spear into the face of one while drawing Wolf Killer. The second warrior I had punched roared at me and lunged with his spear. He, too, came for my head. Dropping slightly, I raised my shield and thrust Wolf Killer blindly up. I found the flesh beneath his chin and beard. Driving upwards the blade emerged through his helmet, spattering Finbarr the Fearless with blood, bone and brains.

He reeled backwards and shouted for more of his men to come to his aid. For the briefest of moments. I was not assailed and I did two things, I glanced around the battlefield to see how we fared. Our shield wall was bowed in places, but the three wedges held firm like rocks upon which the enemy broke. The archers were now having more success as their arrows fell upon those without mail at the rear. The line of men before us was thickest around the wedges as the men of Man tried to slay our best warriors. The second thing I did was to shout, "Stig Snorrison, are you hurt?"

His voice came back, "No, Lord and I have put my wolf seax to good use!"

It was time and raising my sword I shouted, "Clan of the Wolf, attack!"

The last rank of our wedge with Ketil Arneson, Asbjorn Ulfsson, Lars Rolfsson, Buthar Faramirson and Fámr Ulfsson had not yet had much to do and as the five of them pushed I had to step over Stig as I was propelled towards Finbarr the Fearless. Gandálfr and Ráðulfr must have managed to miss the slingers too and we began to march towards the enemy. I now had Wolf Killer in my hand and I preferred a sword to a spear. Blocking the axe from one of Finbarr's oathsworn with my shield I hacked at the warrior's thigh. His byrnie was a short one and I felt the edge, as yet unused, slice deep into flesh and grate along the bone. He dropped and in doing so exposed Finbarr the Fearless. He still had his spear and he thrust again. I was not constrained by warriors attacking me and I simply moved my metal covered face out of the way. The rear rank of the wedge was still pushing and the weight of fifteen mailed men was too much. Finbarr scurried and danced away from me but his men still tried to stand and hold us. They could not do so and were knocked to the ground where they were easily slain. Our swords raised and fell on men who could not defend themselves properly.

Finbarr turned and ran. In a normal battle that would have signalled the end but none of the other enemy warriors had been watching him and they carried on fighting. Honour was at stake. The clan had a bad leader, but he led brave men and they would fight to the end. They might be brave, but we had the weight of numbers now and with the slingers now risen and hurling their stones, along with the archers who had clearer targets we began to win the battle.

I shouted, "Oathsworn! Finbarr the Fearless is escaping. With me!"

There were just four warriors who stood in our way. As we broke the wedge the four found that they were each attacked by two of my oathsworn. Viking Killer was not needed, and while my men killed the four, I ran after Finbarr. My oathsworn stayed behind me. Their job was to protect me. I knew what Finbarr intended. He would find a horse and ride to one of the other settlements. He did not know that this was a coordinated attack and that Karljot and Karle had, hopefully, already taken the other strongholds. He would run to the stables. Although I did not know where they were my nose and ears would tell me. Behind me, my ears told me that the men of Man were dying. I suppose if I had been my great grandfather, I might have asked them to surrender and given them the chance to join my warband, but I was not The Dragonheart. The men of Duboglassio would all die and the threat from Man would be over.

I saw that three men had run with the Jarl and I had no idea how many men remained within the walls. "Use your shields and watch for tricks and treachery. We do not fight an honourable man! We fight a snake!"

156

As we ran through the gates, I had my shield above my head, and it was good that I did for a rock was hurled from the fighting platform. "Ketil Arneson and Asbjorn Ulfsson, clear the gatehouse."

If the defenders had any sense they would have tried to bar the gates of the stronghold. The Norns were spinning. There had been people left inside the stronghold but now, seeing us pour through the gate, the majority fled. There would be a second gate on the opposite wall. They would be racing for it. From my right, I heard a neigh and pointing Viking Killer I gestured towards it. The stable doors were open, and I wondered if we were too late. Had they fled? I was answered almost immediately as two ponies galloped towards us. I used a horse when I could and if they had done the same then things might have been different. I stood with Gandálfr and Ráðulfr and we blocked the path of the two ponies with our three shields. The animals were terrified and as they reared the two riders fell from their backs. I ran between the ponies for the two men were oathsworn and not Finbarr the Fearless. I saw him and his last oathsworn as they levelled their spears and rode at me. I was not afraid. I wanted Finbarr and so I stepped to the side so that he could charge at me. He had never used a horse in combat, and it showed. Leaving the last warrior to be dealt with by my own men I put my left leg forwards and leaned into my shield. The ash spear wavered up and down, but he managed to hit my shield. He would have been better to have missed. The spear hit my shield, but my shoulder absorbed the impact and he was not using stirrups. He was thrown from the saddle and landed heavily on his back, winded. As the pony raced off, I ran to him and had my sword at his throat in an instant.

"Do not kill me! I have information!"

I laughed and pushed so that a little blood trickled down his neck. My oathsworn flanked me. "What information do you have that is of any use to me? I was right for you are a nithing. You could have saved many brave men's lives this day but you chose to hide behind your walls and not face me like a man, a warrior!"

"King Harald is coming for you! That is valuable information is it not?"

"All the world knows that he will come, and we will be ready."

"But you know not when he will come! I do for we are to join with him. Take me with you to Whale Island and I will be your man!"

"I would rather take a viper to my bosom."

"Then come the summer solstice you and all your family will die!" he spat the words out and I do not think he realised what he had said until I grinned. He said, "I will curse you! I…"

157

Curses did not worry me, but I had heard enough and I ended his life.

Gandálfr said, "Then we now know when they will come."

I shook my head, "We know when they planned to come but that was when Man was an ally and they would have helped. He would have brought his fleet to Man to prepare for an invasion. Now he will have to think again but we know that he will not come before summer and that gives us time."

I saw that there were just eight of my oathsworn with me. More men were flooding through the gates; the majority were my men. "Who did we lose?"

Ráðulfr said, "Just two of your oathsworn: Einar the Unlucky and Windar Leifsson. They died well."

"Good."

Just then some of the slingers ran up to us. I saw that Stig Snorrison was one of them, "Here is the hero who saved his lord. Would you have the sword, helmet and dagger of Finbarr the Fearless?"

His eyes widened, "Aye lord!"

"Then take them and the scabbard. I would offer you the mail, but we have a battle with the Norwegians to fight and I will need every mailed warrior that we can muster."

He nodded, "There will be other mail and this day has shown me how to fight!"

I took off my helmet and sheathed my sword. I saw that we had prisoners. Fifteen men were captured. Ten had been slightly wounded and five realised the folly of fighting for a faithless leader. While our wounded were tended, and men sought out the treasure I spoke with them. "Why follow such a craven coward as Finbarr the Fearless?"

The man who spoke had lost the end of his nose in the battle. Gandálfr had sealed the wound with a burning brand and the warrior, we learned his name was Gurt the Dane had not made a sound. "His brother was the real leader. Fámr son of Faramir was a warrior but you slew him when we raided your land. I was away, raiding the Hibernians, and when I returned Finbarr was chosen jarl by his oathsworn. I did not like the choice but what could I do?"

"And now?"

"We are your prisoners. You will take our heads and hurl our bodies into the sea. We just ask that you let us die with our swords in our hands."

I nodded, "Or you could swear an oath and fight for the Clan of the Wolf."

Ráðgeir Haakensson said, "You cannot do that, lord. These men are not to be trusted!"

I turned and glared at Ráðgeir, "I am the heir of The Dragonheart and if a man swears an oath to me then he will keep it. Is that not right, Gurt the Dane?"

"Aye, lord, but I will happily fight this warrior with the big mouth who judges a man so quickly!"

"Peace! There has been enough bloodshed. So," I took out my sword and held it before me, "will you swear?"

Gurt the Dane nodded and gripped the blade so hard that it cut him, "I swear to serve Lord Sámr Ship Killer until death." He glared at Ráðgeir Haakensson, "And this is a blood oath!"

The others all swore although none took the blood oath. "Ráðulfr, take these and some other warriors who are unhurt. Fetch the drekar here to the port."

"Aye, lord."

"Ráðgeir Haakensson, take your men and make sure we have all the warriors accounted for."

He nodded. He was not happy either with my reaction or the insult from Gurt the Dane. By the time Fótr and Bear Tooth arrived I was with my oathsworn in the Great Hall. We had taken a great deal of treasure and supplies. The supplies had been taken from others that they had raided.

"A great victory, Sámr."

"Aye, Fótr, and we have learned much," I told him the information I had gleaned and about the fifteen recruits.

"Is that wise?"

I laughed, "You and your brother showed me the way."

"My brother?"

"When you captured Bear Tooth you did not kill him but made him a warrior. Is he not now the best warrior in the clan?"

They both laughed and Fótr said, "I can see that I have to become wiser before I can emulate you. And what now?"

"We wait here until Karljot and Karle have sent word that they have completed their task. If not, we fight again. While we wait, we will divide the plunder and then, if you wish, I will take you to the place where the god touched the sword of Dragonheart!"

In the event, we had no time to visit the place of legend that day. By early afternoon the three drekar were safely moored in the anchorage and the dead warriors were burning. Just as we were about to leave to visit the place of legend the women and children began to return to the port. My young warriors did not know what to do. The group was led by Mara Arnesdotter. She was a young unmarried woman of perhaps twenty-five summers and that was unusual but as I came to know she was a strong-minded woman. She stood before me with her hands on her hips. She was not intimidated by the Lord of the Land of the Wolf.

"Lord Sámr Ship Killer," she was, at least, respectful when she spoke, "you have burned our homes and killed our menfolk. What will become of us?"

I realised that I had hoped they would simply disappear, and I would not have to worry about them. I was not Dragonheart for he would have had a plan for them. "What is it that you wish to happen?"

She laughed and shook her head, "That you have not come and not be as strong as you are." She shrugged, "But we cannot change the past and the sisters have spun. We are the women and children of the town. My father, Arne the ropemaker, was killed. Your men gave him little chance. Others here gut and preserve fish or make ale for the sailors who visit. There are net makers and pot makers. We do not farm, and you have taken away our existence."

"More men will come, and they will need your services. Be patient!"

She stamped her foot, "Are you not listening to me?"

Ráðulfr growled, "Woman, curb your tongue."

I held up my hand, "Let her speak. Other men will come here. They will come from Dyflin."

"But when? What will we eat until then? You are responsible for us, Lord Sámr. You have to provide!"

I knew that my men were angry, but the woman was right and I was responsible. Fótr and Bear Tooth were close and it was Fótr's suggestion which gave me a way out. I saw now that their coming had been necessary. Had they not sailed across the Great Sea then the Clan of the Wolf might have been no more.

"Mara Arnesdotter, would you be happy to live in the Clan of the Wolf?" She looked at him as though he was speaking Walhaz.

Bear Tooth smiled, "What my friend means is, if Lord Sámr took you to our home, would you be happy to be part of our clan and to live alongside us, to swear allegiance to the clan?"

She snorted, "Swear allegiance? We are not warriors!"

I saw the point that my two allies were making and I clarified the point, "But your children, the boys will grow up to be warriors and in our clan, the women also fight. When your menfolk came to raid us there were women who were happy to stay in the village to fight them."

She looked around at her small band. There were fifteen or so women and about seventeen children. Two of the younger women were nursing babes. None of the children was older than eight summers. "There will be work for us?"

"You make ropes? She nodded, "Then Fótr here, our ship maker, will need ropes and buy all that you can make on your rope walk. My men drink ale and mead, your alewives will be kept busy. At Ebbe's Point, the place your men raided, there are fishermen. They need fish gutters." I saw hope on their faces, "But Bear Tooth is right, we need to know that we will not be murdered in our beds."

She smiled for the first time and I saw that she was not unattractive. I wondered why she had not married. "Then you have our word. On what would you have us swear?"

"Have you heard of the legend of the sword touched by the god?" Her hand went to the charm she wore around her neck. I smiled, "I see you have. Then tomorrow, when I return for a visit to the place where that happened, I will bring a piece of the wood which Odin himself touched. Will you swear upon that?"

She realised, I think for the first time, that this would be a real oath with all the consequences that came with such an oath. She nodded, "I can see that you are wise. Yes, we will swear such an oath,"

"Good, then come into the stronghold. We are hungry and while there is food, I know that you will make a better fist of cooking it than will we." That was not true, but this was a test. Would they cook food for us or try to poison us?

"Aye, we will do as you ask so long as we eat first! That way you will know that you are not to be poisoned."

I nodded, "That seems reasonable."

Neither Ráðulfr nor his father was happy with my decision, but they would live with it. By the time everything was organised it was too late to ride to the Garlic River and climb the hill to the place I sought. I had been there once, with The Dragonheart, and it had had a profound effect upon me. I wondered what it would do to my oathsworn, not to mention Fótr and Bear Tooth.

That night we kept a good watch on the boats. The gates were barred and the walls were manned. We had not had word from Karljot or his brother. For all we knew an army could be marching over Snaefell or coming from the south to fight us.

I dreamed and the dream was not of Dragonheart as I had expected but an old, wise-looking man and a Saxon woman. They said nothing but I saw that they were bouncing two babies upon their knees. They smiled at me and, somehow, I know not how, I knew that it was Prince Buthar and Myfanwy, The Dragonheart's mother. Did that mean that my children would have children of their own? I did not know but it gave me comfort.

Word had not reached us by dawn. We mounted the ponies and I led them north along the shore until we came to the deserted settlement with the handful of graves. I knew the story and I knelt at the graves to ask permission of Myfanwy and the others who had died there, to pass through the graveyard. The tower which had stood on the hillside had been burned down when the lightning struck it, but the burned remains had been left. None had dared touch it. I felt that I had the right to do so. There were no warriors left who were descended from Cnut who had been with The Dragonheart and it was my decision. We climbed to the top and I saw that the grass had not grown back. That might have been because the rock was close to the surface, but I believe that the gods left it that way. I chose a piece of burned wood which was about the size of a short sword.

As I picked it up Bear Tooth shivered and said, "The spirits are here, Sámr. You have more courage than I do. I would not have touched the wood."

I nodded, "It is a solemn thing that I do but I believe I have the right."

We stood in silence and looked at the place all had heard of but not yet seen. I had been here before and heard the story so many times that I could visualise the storm and the battle,

When all were ready, we descended and made our way back to Duboglassio. As we neared it, I saw ponies there and I recognised Karljot. They had arrived while we had been on our pilgrimage. We dismounted and he came to speak with me. I held up my hand, "Before you tell me your news, I have something to do which cannot wait. Mara Arnesdotter, bring your people. I have the sacred wood from the burned tower."

Karljot could not help himself. He grabbed his hammer of Thor, "The tower where the god touched the sword?"

"Aye, this is it." He and his men looked at the burned piece of wood. Mara and her folk arrived. "Here it is, now would you swear?"

Mara nodded and stepped forward, "I will swear for my people." She touched the burned wood and intoned, "I swear that the people I shall lead will be loyal members of the Clan of the Wolf." She suddenly pulled out a seax and before any of my men could react she had cut her palm and held the bleeding wound over the wood. "Now it is a blood oath, Lord Sámr. I may be a woman, but I know the power of such an oath. Are you satisfied?"

"I am!"

When they had gone and I was alone with Karljot he shook his head, "I can see that the blood of The Dragonheart flows in you."

I shook my head, "It is the power of the spirit of Dragonheart which makes people act the way that they do. I bear the name is all. Did we win?"

"Aye, the island is ours, but they fought hard and I lost men. Thank you for taking this stronghold and now we will be your allies. It will take us time to make this stronger but when you need us then send one we know and trust."

"I will." I nodded to Gandálfr, "You know this warrior?"

"I do."

"If any other than Gandálfr comes then it is not a message from me. The Norwegians had planned on bringing their fleet here at the summer solstice. We have upset their plans but they may try to take the Island of Man from you before they attempt to attack us. If that happens then send to me and I will come to your aid. We now have more drekar and by the summer we will have more."

He clasped my arm, "The Dyflin and the Wolf are as one again. It has been many years since the offspring of The Dragonheart lived on the island but we will rekindle those days. Together we will show King Harald of Norway that there are still Vikings left who will oppose him."

Chapter 15

We sailed home two days later. Some of Mara's folk, the ones who were fisherfolk, went to Ebbe's Point. Bear Tooth went with them and they took one of the captured drekar and a knarr. We had done well from the battle. The slingers were all rewarded for their courage. When they became warriors, they would have weapons. There were some small chests of treasure and they were distributed. I took the new warriors with me on my drekar and when we landed, they marched back to Hawk's Roost. I realised that I had a large number of new men who had sworn an oath to me and yet were not of my clan. I intended to go to my steam hut and dream. I would let the spirits advise me.

Fótr was happy to have the women and the children with him. He saw it as a positive thing and did not feel threatened. As Lord of Whale Island, he would be a good leader. I now had a rock to the south of me. The last time the Land of the Wolf had enjoyed that level of security it had been when my father had lived there, and before the falling out with Gruffydd. Gurt the Dane was curious about my land.

"When I grew up in Denmark, we had all heard of Dragonheart, his sword and this magical land. It is why so many of my people came here to try to take it from you."

I nodded, "And yet it is that very attraction which helps to protect us for the magic is the land." We were just passing The Water. "The spirits live there, and they guard the land. Soon you will see Old Olaf, who lived on Man and he watches over it too. At Úlfarrberg the spirit of the wolf protects us and in the cave of Myrddyn lies the body of Dragonheart guarded by his granddaughter Ylva. When the Norwegians tricked us and caused great pain they did not win. The land waited and it was the coming of Fótr the Wolf which brought it to life again. You should know this, Gurt the Dane, for once the land has bitten you then you belong to it forever."

He nodded and touched his hammer of Thor, "Aye, Lord, I feel it now."

We left the majority of the warriors at Cyninges-tūn and then took my treasure around the north of The Water to Hawk's Roost. I knew that Aethelflaed would know of my arrival. A boat would have already sailed across the narrow stretch of water to take her the news. Food would be already prepared as well as ale and mead. She would have been told the numbers who would be arriving. Valborg would have put fresh straw down for the new warriors for my people knew their business. It was always a comfort to come home. Before I did anything,

I went with Gurt and Egil to the warrior hall. I wanted them all to know that they were now my warband. When I had sailed to Moi I had just a handful of oathsworn. Now I had Egil's folk, the Danish mercenaries and now many more new men. I took them into the warrior hall.

"This is your home and we have some time before we need to go to war again. Until you choose to farm or to leave me then we spend each day training for war. Whatever differences you had before you joined me are in the past. We do not live in the past we live in the present so that we all have a future. Egil Sorenson is master of this hall for he is the oldest and the wisest. His word is my word." I then smiled, "Welcome to Hawk's Roost. You will all be rewarded for serving me. When time allows, I will share with you the treasure from Duboglassio. I know that there will be food, ale and mead. Enjoy!"

I realised that all would not be smooth. Every warrior has rough edges. There would be bloody noses and knuckles. That was to be expected but there would be no blades and when those rough edges had been smoothed, we would have a warband which, while it was not Ulfheonar, would give a good account of themselves upon any battlefield.

They were all waiting for me when I entered the Great Hall. I saw that Erik and Ylva were holding hands. I had been away for a short time, but things had changed and moved on. I was pleased. Ragnar looked more confident too and he came to clasp my arm. "We heard of your great victory! The next time you fight, your son, Ragnar the Lame, will be at your side."

"You gave yourself that name?"

"It was good enough for Karl, and Haaken One Eye celebrated his affliction. I bathed myself in self-pity and it does not leave a man clean. Honesty is the best way to scour away the pain."

I hugged Aethelflaed and said, quietly in her ear, "And here is a change!"

She laughed as she kissed me, "I will tell you later but first, Erik has something to ask you."

I knew what it was, but I kept a straight face.

"Lord Sámr, I would wed your daughter. Ylva and I wish to be together."

I looked at my daughter, "You are ready?"

She came to kiss me on my cheek, "When I came back from Moi I was not and sought to end my life by hiding from the world. I am still uncertain if I will ever give you grandchildren or that I am ready to try but Erik is kind and he is gentle. If any man can give me happiness, then it is he."

165

I hoped that she was not settling for Erik but when I saw them look at each other then I knew that the sisters had been spinning. "Then I am happy, and you can be wed as soon as you wish!"

If I thought preparations for war were hard then preparations for a marriage showed me I did not know the meaning of the word hard. I thought they could have just married at Hawk's Roost and the simple ceremony would have been over in a heartbeat. I did not know my wife. She saw it as something to unite the clan and wanted the best of food and the best of ale and mead. I decided to use the wedding to my advantage, and I invited all of my leaders. We would have the wedding feast to plan for the arrival of Norway and his men!

The sparing of the lives of Gurt and the men of Man came home to me when they gave me much information about the alliance between Man and Norway. I learned the names of the leaders who would lead the attack.

"It will not be King Harald who is at the fore. He is not a fool. If he leads and he loses then it is his reputation which suffers. He will let others lead and when they win, he will take the credit and if they lose they will be sent home to Norway. Finbarr told us that the initial plan was to sail from Man and make two landings: one to the east of the river which runs by Úlfarrston and the other to the west of Whale Island. They could then drive up to Cyninges-tūn. The attack on the place you call Ebbe's Point was intended to weaken the defences there."

This fitted in with my dream. When the wedding was done, I could go with my warband and we would prepare the dam which would unleash the power of the river.

To see my daughter who had come back from Moi broken and in pain now to be so happy almost moved me to tears. Erik Black Toe might not be a mighty warrior or a hero to most people, but to me, he was both. I would not put Erik in a shield wall but if I had to descend into a witch's cave in Syllingar then the one I would choose to protect my back would be Erik Black Toe. Our ceremonies are simple. I think Aethelflaed would have preferred a priest and a blessing but Ylva and Erik were pagans. They believed in the spirit world and so it was our own ceremony and as such over quickly. The main celebration consisted of drinking. Aethelflaed accepted that because there was such joy in Hawk's Roost that she could not be angry. There were ladies from Cyninges-tūn to entertain and so I was left to speak with Ragnar and my leaders. Ragnar sat and listened, and I was reminded of myself when I had sat with Dragonheart. I hoped that he would learn better than I had.

I discovered much and most was to our advantage. Bjorn Asbjornson had learned that the Danes of the east, what the Saxons called Danelaw, were now busy fighting with the Northumbrians. They had sent peace emissaries to Bjorn to ask that the Clan of the Wolf not interfere. I was not offended that they had not sent to me for they had thought I still sought my family. That meant we did not need to have so many men guarding the east and the north. Ketil Sigibhertson confirmed that his border was at peace and Ulf Ulfsson said that the men of Strathclyde were too busy fighting King Harald's men who were trying to move from the islands to the mainland. For once their wars would make them ignore us. It also explained why King Harald had waited so long and why the men of Man were so important to him. I told them of our small war and brought out, for them, the piece of burned wood. I suppose it could have been any piece of wood I showed them but my oathsworn had been with me as well as Fótr and Bear Tooth. They knew it was the truth.

"So, I would ask you all be ready to send men when I call for them. Do not leave your borders unguarded but I do not wish to have to retake the land as we did the last time the Norwegians came."

"Aye, better to beat them in the south so that our people are not hurt." Bjorn knew better than any the price we had paid when we had lost the last time. His mother and sisters had died.

Ulf said, "It is a pity we do not have Kara and Aiden. When they were here, we always felt safer. Even when The Dragonheart went to Miklagård we were not threatened."

"Their spirits are here but the time of our witches and galdramenn has passed. We were lucky to have had their power for so long. Now we have them watching out for us, but we have to win the battles. We need to use swords, shields and mail. It is we who will shed the blood and I am happy that we have young warriors like Stig Snorrison." I told them the story of the contest, the seaxes and the battle of Duboglassio. Every one of them could remember when they went to war as a slinger or fought their first battle as a ship's boy. There was hope in the young. We ended the night singing the songs of The Dragonheart. Bjorn's father was celebrated as well as Ketil's grandfather and Ulf's father. I confess that I drank too much. There was a good reason for I was comfortable, and I was safe. I was amongst my warriors and family. What else did a man need?

I put off moving south for I was enjoying life and then I remembered my indolence. I moved south at Harpa. This time Ragnar came with me. He brought his mail, helmet, shield, sword and spear. He also brought the horn which the Ulfheonar had used. None had used it since my great

167

grandfather and Haaken One Eye had died. It was right that my son should think to bring it. We left six men under the command of Erik to guard my home, but the borders were still safe and no other had left their stad. Hawk's Roost and Cyninges-tūn were the last places which would be attacked. We did not travel lightly. We had not only weapons but also tools. We would be labouring for a month at least.

The shipyard which Bolli had built was south of the junction of the River Crake, which was fed from The Water and the River Leven which was fed by Windar's Mere. It was Ragnar who pointed out that we could double the effect of rushing water by building two dams.

"Father, the Crake is but ten paces wide where it meets the Leven. We could build a sluice there easily and the dam would be simple to build. We build that first and then go upstream and do the same on the Leven. A mile west of Haver's Thwaite it is just one hundred paces wide and there is a large loop, like an oxbow. We would not need to build a sluice. The water will flood the land and make a huge tarn. It might even improve the land. If they do not come this year we simply let the water out."

"How did you know this?"

"I spoke with Erik for he lived here with Erik Short Toe who took him up the river and showed him."

I gave him a searching look, "You are asking for a great deal of work. A dam one hundred paces wide is unheard of."

He did not look daunted, "Then Erik can write a saga about it."

My men all seemed happy to try and so we began to work on the small dam. Fótr sent some of the men he was using to build his first drekar in this old world. They had completed the hard part and hewn the timbers; the keep was laid and Fótr could begin to shape and fit the ribs which would add to the strength of the keel. They were now making the pine tar and shaping the strakes. It was time-consuming and did not need much labour. The first dam and sluice took just six days to complete. We were lucky for the water of the river was low and we learned much. There was a family who lived by the river. The father was one of the warriors who had sailed with Fótr and although his son had not been with us, he was keen to help. I gave the two of them the task of opening the sluices if the level of the river upstream became too high. The actual breaking of the dam would be the task of two of my warriors.

While the river levels were still low, for we had not had rain lately, we built earth dams on both sides of the river. When Fótr came to inspect the works, he told us how the bjorr built dams in the New World and we used the technique he described. We used small branches and shrubs intermixed with longer branches to gradually build out from the sides. While we worked, he also told us that he had cleaned the hulls of the two drekar. They would now be far quicker than they had been. With fresh pine tar, they would be better ships. We learned from our mistakes but, after a week of hard work, we had a small gap in the dam left to fill. The water rushed through it. We used larger trees and branches to fill in from the sides and use rocks to help anchor it. We tied a rope to a keystone and branch in the middle. That would be the way we broke the dam. It was Gurt the Dane who came up with an ingenious idea.

"Your aim is to destroy the drekar?" I nodded, "Then if we cut down trees and sharpen one end we can float them on the water which will fill the dam. When the dam breaks the logs will race down the river and if they hit a ship, they might hole it. They would be like giant spears."

I had already had the idea but it was good that he had come up with it himself and I sent the Danes, under his command, to cut down the trees. We then finished the top part of the dam. We dropped stones from the top to gradually fill the hole we had left and then watched as the water level rose. As I had expected it took a long time for the water to reach the top of the impressively high dam. The low-lying land around absorbed the water and the oxbow filled. By the time Gurt and his men had hewn the timber and placed it by the side of the water, it was Skerpla. I was not sure they would still come at the summer solstice, but we had watchers all around the coast. There would be so many ships that the Norse would not risk coming at night time and a fleet big enough to bring all the men they wanted could not be hidden. Leaving a few men to watch the dams and to add more stones and trees, I took the rest and we boarded *'Skraeling'*. Gurt told me that her original name was *'Helga'*. He liked the new name and we had not suffered bad luck. We kept the new name. I sailed north and west to the channel between Man and the coast of the Land of the Wolf. Bear Tooth and Fótr would relieve us after a week. Ráðgeir Haakensson would bring down the men I had summoned while we patrolled. The crops had been sown and the animals had calved and lambed. We could go to war knowing that we had food for the winter.

We saw no fleet that week when we sailed up and down but it was not wasted time. The warband became a crew and that would be reflected when we fought. I learned about Gurt and his homeland in Denmark. Men who rowed together became brothers of the oar and that could only help when they became shield brothers. We stopped every ship we saw but we did not do so aggressively. We merely asked them if they had seen a large number of ships and we received intelligence of

169

variable quality. The secret was to tease out the elements which were useful and gave us hints about the bigger picture. It was towards the end of the week when a ship which had been to Føroyar to hunt for seals said that they had seen sails to the east as they were heading south past Ljoðhús. He said that they were dots on the horizon and there were many of them. I wondered if this was the enemy. The next day our stint was over, and we headed home. I told Fótr what we had seen. He had *'Gytha'* and his crew were his own men. Some were from Ebbe's Point and the rest were the men he had brought to Whale Island. I was confident that they could deal with any problem which came their way and he would be accompanied by the snekke, *'Jötnar'*. Aed and Padraig knew the waters better than any and the shallow snekke was fast.

After we had been relieved, I sailed to Duboglassio where I spoke with Karljot's wife. Karljot was raiding the Mercians and I gave her information which would help him. "I may not be able to send Gandálfr to summon the jarl for we believe an attack is imminent."

She smiled, "He is keen to repay you, Lord Sámr, and if he is returned from his raid then he will come!"

I left the port feeling more confident but worrying, nonetheless that the Norwegians would attack before Karljot returned. All depended upon the Norns. What would their spinning produce? When I was back in Whale Island, I began to organise the defences. We now had more warriors, and some were sent to Úlfarrston to bolster the garrison there. The men with mail and experience I would keep with me but any who had weapons but no mail would guard our two strongholds. The men from Ketil, Ulf and Bjorn had yet to arrive and, along with my men, would be the backbone of the army. My whole plan depended upon defeating the fleet. To that end, we prepared the two drekar we had and made ready for war. I wanted them to think we would fight a sea battle. After five days we saw *'Gytha'*. As she was returning early, we knew that she had news. The men from Ketil had still to arrive and I wondered if the Norse had caught us out. The rest of the warriors were mustered and readied. We had over sixty archers and I was keeping them with the main force of warriors. We also had forty slingers. They had proved to be a real asset and might yet win the battle for us.

To my great relief Ketil finally arrived with his men as *'Gytha'* negotiated the harbour entrance and I sent his men directly to the camp close by Úlfarrston so that I could talk with Ketil at Whale Island. I had stayed to await the arrival of Fótr.

He had news which was of great importance and I saw the Norns at work. The Clan of the Wolf had friends. There was a family of Saxons who lived on the high ground which ran down the length of the country.

170

They had a hard and perilous existence, but they were our friends. It had begun with Carr who had married a woman of our people. They often visited Eoforwic or Jorvik as it was now known. They had been friends with the son of Windar, Ketil. My great grandfather would have known of the connection, but I had either forgotten or shelved it in the dark places of my mind. Whatever the reason, when the rider came from the north telling me that he had had a message from Carr's family, I did not know what he meant. It was Ketil's third son, Karl, who brought the message. Ketil looked at his son in surprise for he had just told me that his second son had been left with the young and the old to defend his lands.

"Lord Sámr, father, Eystein said that he has had a message from Carr. He is sorry you did not get it sooner. King Harald has sent men to Jorvik. The Danes there have been bought off and a warband of two ship's crews and more are heading here from the east!"

Ketil shook his head, "Eystein is my wife's father. He was all I had to leave in command."

I stared east. King Harald had outwitted me. To the east, we had no defences. His warband could tear through the valley of Windar's Mere. Hawk's Roost and Cyninges-tūn would be defenceless. He had fixed us here in the south and was now marching west. "Ride back to your grandfather. Ask him to muster as many men as he can and head to Hawk's Roost."

"Aye lord."

Ketil said, "Wait my son." He turned to me, "Eystein is an old man, lord. Karl, when did he get the message?"

"Four days since, father. It came the day after you left but he did not tell me until yesterday. He did not send the message straight away. I am sorry. I saw Carr arrive and I should have known that his words were important. Eystein is old and forgets."

I saw Ragnar's face fall. He knew our plans were well made and to see them undermined in such a short time unnerved him. I smiled. The young warrior was loyal to his family and that was good, "The Norns spin, Karl, and we are tested. Let us see if the Land of the Wolf can outwit this Norwegian." He nodded. "When you pass through Cyninges-tūn tell them there and at Hawk's Roost that there is a Norse warband on the loose to the east and it may be better if you lead the men from your stad!"

Ketil said, "He is a good boy. Perhaps I should have left him in charge. Eystein's wife died and he forgets things but…"

"As I said to Karl, the sisters spin. The question is what do we do now?" I was not asking Ketil for advice. He had been a young warrior

171

in the war where I had been captured and his father had died. He had the experience of one campaign, the one which retook our land. This decision was mine but I would use Ketil to hear my ideas and to comment. "If we take the army north then the enemy fleet can land unopposed. Our dam can hurt them, but it will take steel to defeat them."

"Aye, lord, and the men are tired after their march and we do not know where they will reach the land. It could be anywhere from my land to the land which borders Mercia."

"You are right and that shows that whoever has planned this is clever for they keep us guessing."

"Surely it is their King."

"King Harald is sly and cunning, but he has not shown me yet that he is capable of such a strategy. From what Gurt the Dane told me he leaves battles to his underlings." I rubbed my chin. The Viking fleet lay to the north of us, somewhere, and could arrive at any time. A warband on foot could reach our borders within the next day or so. Then it came to me. He would not attack further north. He knew we had taken Man and was making a flank attack to allow his ships to land his men in the land which had once been ruled by Sigtrygg and, latterly, Gruffydd. Few of our people lived there.

"Ketil, go to the camp. I want the army moving close to the river by Úlfarrston. There are a couple of bridges and I would have them guarded. We will have three drekar moored there."

"But Lord Sámr, suppose they land to the west of here? Your stronghold will be defenceless."

"We have made the walls strong and it can sit out a siege." I pointed to *'Gytha'* as she negotiated the narrow entrance. The one place I knew that Harald would not land his men would be here for it was a hard place to navigate. "Fótr returns and that means he may have news. Have the army ready and ask Bjorn to send scouts east to see if they can spy the warband."

My oathsworn were armed and mailed already. We hurried down to the quay to await Fótr and Bear Tooth. Ragnar said, "Does this mean that we have been outwitted?"

"No, Ragnar, it just means that the enemy has given us another problem to overcome. When I leave here, I want you to stay and help defend this stronghold."

"I can fight with you!"

I shook my head, "You are now a warrior and have learned to fight well but you cannot fight from the deck of a pitching drekar and besides it will give the folk of this town more confidence if they have one of Dragonheart's blood on the walls."

I saw Mara and the others at the ropewalk. The ones they had made were coiled nearby. She saw me waiting and the approaching drekar. "We fight soon, Lord Sámr?"

"Perhaps, Mara. King Harald has sent ships to take this land."

She pointed to her gear and I saw a sword, "We will fight them! I did not fight you at Man, but we will fight here! I like the Clan of the Wolf. My people will fight!"

"Then get your ropes inside the walls. I think my drekar brings us dire news."

"Aye. May the Allfather be with you." She turned to her people, "Pick up the ropes and let us go within these walls! The Norwegians are coming!"

I nodded to my son as she left, "And, Ragnar, you have good people here. If the worst comes to the worst and I fall in battle, then you and these folk must fight beyond the end. We make this Norwegian king pay such a price that he decides to choose somewhere easier to devour!" He was wearing the wolf cloak we had taken from the old he wolf. "It is good that you wear the cloak. Do so in the battle. When the Norse see it they will think The Dragonheart has been reborn. It may draw men to you, but the wolf will protect you. There was once a wolf who died here protecting the blood of The Dragonheart!"

I could see that they had news for Bear Tooth held on to the forestay and balanced on the gunwale as the drekar edged her way in. He would not shout the news, but he could not wait to tell me. He leapt down and landed next to me. "They come, Lord Sámr. *'Jötnar'* captained by Padraig, spotted them and came to tell us. There are more than thirty ships. We would have been back sooner but Fótr wished to find a knarr to send a message to Karljot."

I nodded. The biggest flaw in my plan and the alliance with the Vikings of Dyflin was that they could not come until we knew where the Vikings would land. We had a contingency plan in case they tried to take Man. I now knew that would not happen but Karljot and Karle would have to wait until the Norwegians landed on the mainland before they could come to our aid. We would have to fight a battle on two fronts until our allies arrived.

"Bear Tooth, I wish you to command here." He cocked a head to one side, and I told him the news of the warband. "I need to attack the fleet and draw them up towards Úlfarrston so that I can use the waters of the dam to hurt them."

"But the dam will damage our ships too!"

I shook my head, "Úlfarrston was used to land ships long before Whale Island. There is a wooden quay which will protect us. The ships will be safe although they might need work afterwards."

"And what do I do?"

"I leave you here with my son, Ragnar. You will fight on these walls and make any of the enemy who come bleed to death! Hold out here until Karljot comes and then bring them to the river!"

He was actually grinning as he clasped my arm, "Do not slay all of these Norwegians, lord, save some for us!" Bear Tooth was a warrior.

I boarded the drekar with my men, "Fótr, we need for you to leave this anchorage and head for Úlfarrston."

Fótr had survived the Great Sea. He was a hard man to shock. I told him our news and he merely nodded. "The Norns spin. Of course, the Norwegians do not know about the new water which lies in their path. That may confuse them but when the dam is broken, and the water is released, then they can cross it."

I had not thought of that, but it made little difference to my plans. We would still draw the fleet to Úlfarrston and try to win the war at sea so that the people would not be hurt. Even if the three drekar were sacrificed their loss might mean that the Land of the Wolf was safe and I was Dragonheart's Heir, that was my responsibility.

174

Chapter 16

It was dark by the time we reached the camp. There was a sea of campfires. We were one army but men liked to sleep close to those with whom they would fight. After my oathsworn and I were dropped at the quay Fótr took the drekar to moor in the river. My leaders were all waiting anxiously for me to arrive. Ketil had given them the news.

"The scouts will not be back until morning and the fleet is on its way. This is my plan. I will join Fótr and take '*Skraeling'*. Ráðgeir Haakensson, you will crew *'Dragon's Bane'*. We will wait just off the coast. King Harald will not try to land at night. He does not need to for he believes that he has the advantage of a warband making a surprise attack from the east. Bjorn Asbjornson, we know the size of the warband. Do not be tempted to march to fight them. If they come, then let them attack. I want riders ready to head for the dams and open them. As soon as you see our ships approaching then send riders and open the dams immediately!"

"Is that not a risk, Lord? What if you are damaged?"

"Then my sacrifice will be necessary. If that happens then the army must be ready to fight the survivors of the Norwegian army. Protect Whale Island and the road to the north. My son Ragnar and Bear Tooth hold Whale Island. We may be outnumbered but we have heroes amongst our numbers. The Norwegians just have ambition. Now let us part." I clasped each of their arms in turn. I said nothing for the words were in my eyes and in my grip. I had been asleep, but the wolf was now awake. The plan was improvised and could fail but I was confident that we would hurt the Norwegians and by the time Karljot came he would be able to send them home. Our sacrifice would be worthwhile if the land and the clan were saved.

We boarded the drekar. Amongst the ship's boys was Stig Snorrison, "It is good to see you, defender of my shield. We go to war again. Are you ready?"

"Aye, lord, and this time I hope for more treasure. Do the Norwegians have good weapons?"

"Not as good as ours and their men do not have the heart of even the boys of the Land of the Wolf!"

The whole crew cheered and I felt buoyed! With warriors and boys like this behind me, what could we not achieve? I waited in the estuary with my drekar close to *'Gytha'*. We waited for *'Dragon's Bane'* to join us. "Fótr, we will sail to wait a mile south of the coast. When we see the enemy, we close with them in line abreast and rain arrows on their leading ship. We will all turn to steerboard so that they think we are heading for the safety of Whale Island. Then we turn and flee north as though we fear them. You lead the way and I will bring up the rear. We must tie up quickly when we return here for I have ordered the dams to be broken once they see us. I want the Norwegians as close to us as we can manage."

"Do not worry, Lord Sámr, the plan is a good one. You are using the land and the waters to defeat the enemy and the spirits like that."

I pointed beyond him to the increasingly darkening land, "But what of the warband? Where will they land?"

"You cannot worry about that. We have made preparations and I believe that they will work but we both know that we are pieces on a chessboard. We do what we can but if some higher power takes against us then we are doomed." He patted his heart, "In here I do not believe that we are doomed!"

When the other drekar joined us, we rowed south. It was an easy row for the current was with us. I was heartened by the fact that even though we had dammed the rivers there was still enough force to move us south.

The snekke, *'Jötnar'*, found us before dawn. I had not slept but I had ensured that all of the crew had enjoyed at least five hours of sleep. Padraig first went to *'Gytha'* and then came to me. He hailed me, "The fleet beached themselves north of the river the Walhaz call Ēa Lōn."

That was just a few miles north of Larswick; *wyrd*. "Did they land and then march north?"

"No, Lord Sámr, they camped. They will sail north!"

That made sense for it was almost forty miles by foot yet by sea it was a mere fourteen miles. With the wind behind and rowing, they could reach us within two hours of dawn.

"Then be our hunting hound and lead them here to us. After you have led them to us then carry on to Úlfarrston where you can tie up and watch the power of nature."

"Aye, Lord Sámr! Jarl Karljot was summoning his drekar when we passed Man."

"But he will not reach us this morning."

"No lord. There was just one drekar in the anchorage."

I roused the crew so that they could make water, drink ale and eat before the Norwegians arrived. That we would be outnumbered was obvious, but I had made some assumptions. The ships at the fore would be their best men. The men aboard them would be mailed, and they would be seasoned veterans. If we could hurt those men, then the odds would become slightly more even in the land battle which would

176

follow. I also hoped that the leader of this expedition would be there. It was a good plan. The warband, however, was a real threat for we could not hurt them with the dam. When I landed, we would have to march north and west to meet that threat and that would leave Úlfarrston still in danger. Ráðulfr and Gurt joined me at the prow. We peered south into darkness.

Gurt said, "It does not sit well, lord, to run from a Norwegian."

"Yet the wolf scout will often run before hunters, will he not, to lead men into a trap? We are the Clan of the Wolf, Gurt, and we fight like the wolf. We might run but it is only to turn and bite when we are ready. I want our archers and slingers to annoy them so much that they hurtle after us and then they will be blind to the dangers of doing so. Even without the dam, our waters can be treacherous. You may not know but the reason we moved our port from Úlfarrston to Whale Island was because of the treacherous waters. Your tree spears will be the surprise that no one expects."

We watched the sunrise and it was as we did that I saw the first light sparkle from metal. There were men. "Stig Snorrison, you have good eyes, get up the mast and tell me what you see."

A few moments later he shouted down. "There are perhaps a hundred warriors marching up along the shoreline."

I wondered if this was the warband and then dismissed the idea. It was coming from the wrong direction. These were men from the fleet. They still had more than twenty miles to march but they were reinforcements for the warband. Even if we destroyed the fleet, we would have more than two hundred men to fight us and these were all mailed. As the rays of the sun bathed the coast in blue light I could see byrnies for they all carried their shields upon their backs.

A short time later Stig, who had remained at the masthead shouted down, "Ships, Lord, Sámr, I see ships."

"Man the oars. Ship's boys and archers prepare for war!"

I reached the steering board. Olaf Jenson was there. He was a ship's boy, but this would be his last voyage for he was ready to begin to train as a warrior. He had my shield and his job was to protect me from any arrows the enemy might send our way. I did not look at the other two drekar. We did not need to strike at the same time. "Down oars!" The oars came down as one. "And row!"

I began the chant. This was a chant of war for we needed speed. It was the saga of Sigeberht whom my great grandfather had slain in Lundenwic.

The Dragonheart looked old and grey.

177

He fought a champion that cold wet day.
A mountain of a man without a hair
Like a giant Norse snow bear
Knocked to the ground by Viking skill
The Saxon stood and struck a blow to kill
Saxon champion, taking heads
Ragnar's Spirit fighting back
Saxon champion, taking heads
Ragnar's Spirit fighting back
Old and grey and cunning yet,
The Dragonheart his sword did wet
With Ragnar's Spirit sharp and bright
He sliced it down through shining light
Through mail and vest it ripped and tore
The Saxon Champion, champion no more.
As he sank to the bloody ground
Dragonheart's blade whirled around
Sigeberht's head flew through the air
Dragonheart triumphant there
Saxon champion, taking heads
Ragnar's Spirit fighting back
Saxon champion, taking heads
Ragnar's Spirit fighting back

We surged forward as the rhythm helped to speed us up. The other two drekar would have their own chants. I shouted, "Stig, how many ships can you see?"

"There are at least twenty drekar, lord. There are four at the front but the one which leads them has twenty oars on each side and a red sail with a dragon upon it." The tone of his voice told me that he was fearful. He was right to be afraid. Twenty oars a side meant there could be a hundred men aboard the drekar.

The wind was with them and they were moving quickly. We too were travelling fast across the waters which were sheltered by the land. I would have to judge this to perfection. "Archers and slingers, as soon as you can hit anything then release. Ship's boys, be ready to loose the sail."

I saw for myself the huge drekar which, had we been alongside, would have dwarfed us. The ship to larboard was also a large one with eighteen oars on each side. That one would have to endure the slings and arrows of all three of us, the larger one just two. The arrows and stones flew. Some were short and missed. I knew that the enemy would jeer the attempts but as we raced together more stones and arrows hit. I left it as late as I could and then turned to steerboard. "Loose the sail!" The rain of stones diminished as the slingers lowered the sail and then secured the stays. I saw that Ráðgeir had turned before me. I wondered if I had misjudged it as the eighteen oared drekar with the witch as a figurehead, came racing towards us. Fótr had done a good job with *'Skraeling'* and with no weed on her hull she skimmed over the waves. We were so close to the figurehead of the witch that, as we passed, I saw the carver had given her three eyes! The closeness of our vessels meant that the slingers and archers were hitting men and I saw four of our enemies pitch overboard. A ship's boy fell from the enemy cross trees and when the drekar with the witch figurehead lurched to larboard I knew that a stone or arrow had hit the helmsman. These were small victories, but they were successes nonetheless.

Fótr had turned and so I maintained my north-easterly course until he was behind *'Dragon's Bane'*. I followed her wake and I would be the rearmost drekar. No longer in danger from arrows and stones, I said, "Olaf, put down the shield and watch the drekar with the red sail. I want to know the distance between her and us."

"Aye, lord. She is five lengths astern, lord." I allowed the rowers to keep rowing. Ahead I saw the thin smudge that was the coast. It would soon grow. "Six lengths, lord."

"Rowers slow the beat." Ráðulfr and Gandálfr were at the front oars and they controlled the speed. The coast became clearer and Olaf had not changed the distance. I would entice them. "In oars!"

It was a risk but it proved to be one worth taking as, a short time later, we spied the dwelling on the headland and Olaf said, "Lord, they have run out oars. The whole fleet has oars out! They are going faster!"

"Good! Oars on the mastfish."

"Five lengths lord!"

I knew that we would now be visible from Úlfarrston and a message would be speeding its way to the dams. I turned the steering board to take us slightly north and east. It was not a mistake. The Norse would think that I was taking the safe channel but as the wind came from the south-east I was merely giving my drekar the chance to race the last few hundred paces into port and to have the Norse beam on to the flood of water and tree spears as they turned to follow me into the harbour.

"Four lengths, lord!"

I turned the steerboard to aim the drekar at the entrance to the harbour. The other two ships were already there and with sails reefed would be tying up and disembarking their crews.

"Three lengths, lord."

179

We were just one hundred paces from safety when I saw the wall of water and sharpened timber heading for us. It was more terrifying than I had expected. The top of the white water looked to be higher than a snekke's mast. It was though it was a watery wall of spears. I saw, as the harbour mouth drew closer, that the larger and heavier tree spears were at the bottom of the wall of water.

I had just shouted "Reef sail!" and begun to turn when the log hit our stern. It pushed us around. I felt the vessel beginning to fill with water. "Everyone forrard! We are sinking! Olaf, go!" I could not resist turning and, as I did so, I saw logs smash into the side of the red dragon drekar and then the eighteen oared drekar. Both were turning to follow me and I heard, first the crash, and then the shouts and screams as warriors at the oars were speared and crushed by the trees of the Land of the Wolf.

Gandálfr shouted, "Lord Sámr! Run!" I saw that we had just made the entrance to the harbour, but the water was lapping around my ankles and we were sinking quickly. I picked up my shield, spear and helmet and ran. Fótr had run a gangplank from the quay to the prow and my crew were racing over it. *'Skraeling'* was settling in the water by the stern as I passed the mast and I was having to run uphill. When I hurled myself on to the dock, I saw that the danger was not over. The tree spiked wave which had hit us and the Norwegians was now followed by the rest of the water from the dam. Both the drekar already tied up would be in danger from the water as it lifted them higher than the ropes which secured them to the quay and I saw the army ready to fight the Norse scrambling to the higher ground. My oathsworn waited for me as we ran over the flooded quay to reach the road which led to safety. We almost did not make it as the river water came up to our chests and threatened to drag us back to the now flooded harbour. Ropes were thrown to pull us to safety and like so many drowned rats we staggered on to dry land.

I turned to look at the result of our flood. Four enemy drekar had been sunk and another four were sinking, their crews trying to beach them on the far shore. All the ones on the Úlfarrston side of the estuary had been hit. That meant that up to fifteen drekar might be able to land their men and join the two hundred who were already there. It was a victory but not as great a one as I had hoped. Even as I watched a few logs, obviously entangled upstream suddenly smashed into a drekar which, until that moment, had been unharmed. They smashed into the strakes of the drekar along its length for it was beam on. As they punctured it the hull began to fill with water and as the water lapped and flowed to the undamaged side of the drekar, the ship turned on its side and sank. Arms came up from the water but there was no one to save them. The threttanessa went to the bottom of the estuary and there was not one survivor.

Fótr came to give me a hand and pull me from the muddy hole in which I found myself, "I think, Lord Sámr, that you have made somewhat of a mess of the estuary but I believe you have saved your land."

I shook my head and pointed across to the other bank. It was almost a mile away, but I could see the undamaged drekar disgorging warriors. The damaged ones would join them. Some drekar made it to within eighty paces before grounding. As the waters receded, they would be able to land. "There are more than five hundred men now on the other side. True, they are more than twenty miles away but at least two hundred have not endured this defeat. We still have the battle to win. The difference is that we now have a chance and before we used the land, we had none!" Slinging my shield on my back I shouted, "We head north to Greenodd. We hold them there."

When we had been building the dams, I had realised that Greenodd would be the best place to intercept the Norse. The nearest bridge was a mile north of the small hamlet but that had been weakened when the water we had used for the dam had risen above it. The Norwegians had a choice. They could fight a battle against us there or head north to Cyninges-tūn. If they chose the latter, we could use the better road on our side of the River Crake and reach The Water before them. I was confident that if my small army arrayed before them then they would fight. It would be a race, but we had less than three miles to travel and the advance warband of Norwegians had more than six.

Bjorn and Ketil along with Ulf, led my men. They had seen what we had done and they were running the men the short distance to the River Crake. As much as my men and I tried to overtake those before us we could not for we were all soaked and we had rowed and fought. This army had heart. The men who had released the Crake dam were there already and, as my men formed their lines, I saw the ten men from the Leven dam racing towards us.

It was Einar Squint Eye who led them. He was out of breath for they had been running, "Lord Sámr, before we released the water, we saw the warband we were warned of and they were coming around the flooded land. As we headed here, we saw more men crossing the side of the muddy ground to join them. They will be here within the hour."

That gave me a dilemma. Did I attack them piecemeal or wait for them all? The problem would be that these would be their best men and while I might defeat them, I could lose our own, better warriors in the process. I looked at the River Crake. The dam had flooded the ground

181

on both sides. We could not cross it easily and that meant heading north to the bridge. I took the decision to abandon our position and march north. It would add to the distance the Norse had to travel, and we had time to make a more defensible decision. It was just over a mile, but the dam had done its work and the mud clung to our boots. The Norwegians would have it as bad!

We reached the bridge before the Norse. The water had damaged it but not enough to prevent it being used and the river was now shallow enough to ford. Of course, warriors clambering up the banks would be easy prey to spearmen.

I set men to hacking down some of the smaller trees to make stakes to protect our flanks. The Norse would have the advantage of numbers and I did not want them to spill around our flanks. The slingers would not have a problem with the mud and so I had them line the river bank. I divided the archers into three uneven groups. The largest number would be behind our triple lines of warriors. The other two would guard the flanks. I chose the dragon's teeth formation because it had worked so well at Duboglassio. The difference this time was that there would be seven teeth and the men between each tooth would be fewer. Those with mail were in the front two ranks and it was only the third, the rear rank who had no mail at all. They did have javelins and when the slingers ran back for shelter, they would hurl their javelins at the advancing Norse. We were on drier, more solid ground and I hoped that the Norse would slip and slide. I was the middle tooth and I was flanked by Bjorn on one side and Fótr on the other.

It was the middle of the afternoon when the Norwegian army finally arrived. They were led by a leader who had a crested helmet. Those types of helmet were rare and they were valuable. I had hoped he would have drowned in the river. The problem with such a helmet was that it attracted attention and a blow to the crest could knock it from a warrior's head. The advantage was that it could be seen from a distance and encourage those in the rear ranks. The enemy army stopped a hundred paces from the river for more men were arriving. It was a metal snake which headed towards us. They sent a few scouts to examine the ground, but our slingers were too good not to take advantage of the lightly armed men. Eight died before the dragon crested warrior brought shielded men to examine the ground. The pebbles which rattled against mail, helmets and shields must have disconcerted them for they did not stay long, and I saw the leaders retire to consider their options.

Bjorn had ensured that we had ale and food. As they debated, we ate and drank. We could have done so earlier but this would madden the enemy as it would be an insult that we were not worried by them.

182

Ráðgeir had thought it a foolish idea but as Bjorn had agreed he went along with it. Egil was standing in the line to the left of me and he suddenly shouted, "Lord Sámr, it is he! It is Jarl Rognvald Larsson! He is the one with the red skull on his shield. The Allfather smiles on me and now I can avenge my people!"

I turned, "Egil, you swore an oath to me. Obey orders for we have few enough men as it is."

He laughed, "Do not worry, Lord Sámr, you destroyed his drekar, he will come for you and I will have my chance."

I looked at the warrior Egil had identified. He was right, of course. When I had killed Uddulfr the Sly I had killed a friend of the jarl. Added to the loss of his ship and men he had to try to kill me. I doubted that he would even know which of my men was Egil. He would have a shock when he attacked for Egil had become a better warrior since he had joined me. Practice with my oathsworn and my Danes had improved him. I looked due south. My hope still lay with Karljot and his brother. They were fresh warriors and they were veterans. I had counted the enemy and knew despite the men they had lost they still outnumbered us. Úlfarrston lay four miles away, Whale Island almost twelve. If we began to lose I had a plan to pull back to Úlfarrston and shorten the journey our allies would have to make to come to our aid.

The enemy had a plan and I saw them form up their lines. The river was shallower to our left and the enemy leader, Dragon Crest, sent a quarter of his men there. He had a handful south of the bridge and the rest were lined up opposite me and to my left. Those on my right might not have an enemy to fight. On the extreme right was Ulf Ulfsson backed by the small number of archers. When it became clear I had their dispositions right I shouted, "Ulf Ulfsson, Bring your men and join mine. Have your oathsworn make my wedge larger. Archers move up to support Bjorn Asbjornson."

It would be Ketil and Ráðgeir who would be in danger of being outflanked. I could use Ulf and his men to swing around and form a new defensive line if they were broken. Once in their line the enemy began to bang their shields and chant the name of their leader. It was not King Harald!

'Barekyr Wolf Killer
Barekyr Wolf Killer
Barekyr Wolf Killer
Barekyr Wolf Killer
Barekyr Wolf Killer
Barekyr Wolf Killer'

183

If it was designed to frighten us it did not for my grandfather had been named Wolf Killer. In reply, my men chanted too. We chanted the song of Dragonheart

From mountain high in the land of snow
Garth the slave began to grow
He changed with Ragnar when they lived alone
Warrior skills did Ragnar hone
The Dragonheart was born of cold
Fighting wolves a warrior bold
The Dragonheart and Haaken Brave
A Viking warrior and a Saxon slave
When Vikings came he held the wall
He feared no foe however tall
Back to back both so brave
A Viking warrior and a Saxon slave
When the battle was done
They stood alone
With their vanquished foes
Lying at their toes
The Dragonheart and Haaken Brave
A Viking warrior and a Saxon slave
The Dragonheart and Haaken Brave
A Viking warrior and a Saxon slave.

Haaken One Eye had no sons but I knew that some of his grandsons were present and even a great-grandson. They sang as loudly as I did. The Norwegians stopped singing first and that was a small victory to us. Their chant was repetitious but ours told a story. Dragon Crest held up his sword and when he waved it forward his men raced in one line. I say raced but that was not quite true. The ground was slippery and slick. They hurried as fast as they could manage. The ones who ran across the bridge were eight men wide and twelve men deep. Under normal circumstances, they would have knocked us from our feet but the mud from the dam made the ground slippery and even before they reached the bridge two had slipped. The archers and slingers began to send arrows and stones at the enemy. I saw one warrior whose helmet was smacked by a pure white pebble. He tumbled from the bridge and into the river. The ones who intended to ford the river had two techniques. One was a mighty leap and the other was to lower themselves into the water and wade. The former had mixed success. Those who managed the leap reached halfway across but the ones who failed slipped on the mud. When they lay floundering, they were an easy target for both stone and arrow.

I forced myself to concentrate on the battle before me. Dragon Crest was not leading but it was not the same reason as Finbarr the Fearless. This warrior wanted to watch the battle and decide where he needed to send reinforcements. The leader who was in the front rank was Jarl Rognvald Larsson. Egil was right he was coming for me. Now that we had Ulf and his oathsworn behind me we had a chance of halting the nearly one hundred men who would be charging at us.

The slingers and archers were now hitting with every throw and draw of their bows. Few men fell for these were Norse warriors and as tough an enemy as there was to be found anywhere. Despite arrows in their arms and stones which broke noses and cheekbones, they came on. However, even the best of warriors could not fight as well if he was wounded.

"Brace!"

I felt the reassuring pressure of metal and wood behind me. My wedge would feel the first full force of the attack as those who had crossed the river were struggling to get out. As Jarl Rognvald led the men from the bridge I shouted, "Slingers, withdraw!" Hurling one last stone at the enemy they threw themselves at our feet. Some would be small enough to squirm to the second rank where they could still inflict damage but be less likely to be speared by an angry warrior. Two of the last stones, allied to the mud made three of the leading warriors slip and the jarl was thrown to my left as he stumbled across their bodies. He kept his feet, but he would no longer be facing me. He would have Gandálfr and Egil to deal with. The Norse frontage widened to twelve warriors as they left the bridge and that suited me as it dissipated the weight that they could bring to bear. Once again, my wolf bitten spear was braced against my foot. Not all of the enemy had spears for these were the best that the enemy could muster. With good mail, fine helmets and charms bought at great expense they would all have a named weapon as did I. The warrior who would have the first swing had a three-legged design on his red shield and he wielded a war axe. It was not a weapon to be dismissed easily but he had to negotiate my wolf spear first.

Disappointingly for him, as he raised his axe to smash it upon my shield he ran into my spear. He had good mail but it unbalanced him and he lost his footing, I quickly raised my spear and stabbed down at his right shoulder. The head came away bloody and I braced it again for the next man. Then I heard a scream as Stig rammed the seax up

185

between the stricken warrior's legs to emasculate him. The second warrior could not make a direct attack because his wounded companion lay bleeding. He came at my right and Ráðulfr and I had our two spears there. He blocked my spear but ran on to Ráðulfr's.

To my left, Egil and Gandálfr were fighting the jarl and his oathsworn. Egil's companions, not to mention Danr and Qlmóðr the Quiet were jabbing their spears at them. I heard a triumphant shout as Egil's spear darted forward to drive into the nose of the jarl and through his skull. He was dead and, in their eagerness to protect their lord, his oathsworn soon followed. The place I had feared we might suffer, the bridge wedge was holding its own. The slippery ground and the enemy dead slowed down their attack and stopped them simply pushing us back. The archers were whittling down those at the rear and I wondered what Dragon Crest would do next. When I saw him and forty warriors run north along the river, I knew that he had found another place to cross.

Sometimes you make a decision because of a feeling and I had one then. It may have been the spirits in my head warning me or perhaps I did have some innate ability. I shouted, "Ulf, they will try to flank us. Move your men and make a new line at right angles to us. Archers of the right, stand to the west of Ulf Ulfsson. Bjorn keep your men where they are but anchor the archers!"

"Aye, Lord! It is the right thing to do."

What it meant was that until we had defeated the enemy left, we would be in danger of being surrounded. "Men of Windar's Mere, avenge Jarl Asbjornson, push those before you back into the river and let them drown."

The vengeance trail is a powerful one. It had led me to Norway and now, years after his death, Asbjorn's warriors avenged him. They roared his name and simply charged. The Norse were not expecting it. They had seen mailed warriors move away and thought we were retreating. Suddenly swords, axes and spears tore into bodies. Even the slingers joined in. Some used their slings while others helped the warriors by slashing their seaxes at the thighs and calves of the Norse. When the Norwegians tumbled into the river the slingers hurled stone after stone at them until none remained alive.

I could hear savage fighting to the north. Ketil and his warband as well as the men of Cyninges-tūn were being forced back and I was glad that Fótr supported them for he had a wise head and would not panic. We were still far from victory for more than half of the many hundred men remained but the warriors at the fore had all been slain and I shouted, "Oathsworn we will charge. Egil swing your line and anchor it on the river."

"Aye, lord!"

I raised my spear and shouted, "Dragonheart!" We ran. All of the training when they had first come to me paid off and despite the slippery, body covered ground, we did not falter. I made for the men on the bridge. Gandálfr and Ráðulfr stabbed and thrust with their spears but I had no target. A warrior stood with legs astride to deny me the bridge. I did not slow and as his spear was thrust overhand at my shield, I aimed mine at his middle and when it struck mail I kept on running. Perhaps the he-wolf which had bitten my spear had given it power, I do not know but the huge man was not only knocked to the side but he crashed through the wooden sides to fall into the river. My wedge was perfect for the task and the men on the bridge were either killed where they stood or knocked into the river.

I risked looking around and saw that the rest of my men were in danger of being surrounded. They had done as I had asked but Ketil, the men of Cyninges-tūn and Fótr were in disarray as they fell back, it was a fighting retreat but the Norse had more men and they were whittling down those on the outside.

"Oathsworn, we must run and form a new left flank! I know you are weary, but we go to save the Land of the Wolf."

I turned and ran wondering if we were too late for our lines were now broken and when I saw the bodies of some of the slingers, my heart sank. I saw that Dragon Crest was mimicking my move and running with his own oathsworn to get around our flank. Ulf was holding the line against the more lightly armoured men the Norwegians had sent. The elite of the Norwegian warband could well break Ulf and wrap up our line. The sight of the dead slingers made me forget my weariness and I ran harder. My oathsworn were younger than I was and had no trouble keeping up.

We won the race and I shouted, "Form a double line!" Dragon Crest and his men were twenty paces from us by the time my men were next to me and behind me. Buthar Faramirson and Fámr Ulfsson locked their shields with the edge of Ulf Olafsson's wedge. We were fighting veterans for they did not slow to form a line or a wedge, but they showed that they were used to fighting together and Dragon Crest, flanked by two men, came at me.

I heard, from my right, Gurt the Dane shout, "Hawk's Roost, to me!"

We then braced for the attack. I still had my spear and as he swung his sword at me, I thrust my spear at him. The move was a trick as I feinted to his chest and he was forced to move his shield to block the blow. I was not aiming at his shield, but the dragon crest and I hit it so hard that the helmet was knocked from his head. He brought up his shield and smacked my spear with such force that it flew from my hand. Both sets of oathsworn were now fighting and there was no quarter to be had. Men would fight to the death for this was a matter of honour. Each was protecting their lord. I blocked his next strike although it was not hard as he was still reeling from my spear thrust. Viking Killer was drawn and ready as I stared into his blue eyes. They were as hard and piercing as a glacier, but he was not as young as I had expected. There were flecks of white amongst the blond.

He spat out a tooth which had been dislodged when the helmet had been struck from his head, "I was told that you were tricky. Now let us see if you are good for I cannot believe that you have the skill of Dragonheart."

"Aye, for we had a leader we could follow! Where is King Harald? Is he waiting for you to return to decide if you live or die?"

I must have struck a nerve for he rushed at me and smashed at my shield with his sword. The blow was so powerful that it hit my left shoulder and I heard something crack. I was wounded. I thought that with just Hrólfr Haakensson and Ketil Arneson behind me I would be pushed from my feet, but not only did I not move, I felt Hrólfr's shield in my back as I brought my sword from on high.

As I struck him, I heard Gurt shout, "Push!" He had brought the men from Hawk's Roost to reinforce us and as they pushed, I found myself face to face with the Viking leader.

It was too good an opportunity to miss and I brought my head back to butt him. With no helmet for protection, my full-face helmet smashed his nose and his teeth. Blood filled his face and tears ran down his cheeks. He had to take four steps backwards and as we moved, I swung my sword sideways to hack through the back of the neck of the warrior fighting Gandálfr. The Norwegian leader and his oathsworn were falling back. We had not yet won the battle, but we had defeated Dragon Crest and his oathsworn.

His voice sounded strange as he shouted through a broken nose and with shattered teeth. "Form a shield wall." Even as he gave the order more of his men died. He raced back to the safety of more men who had made their way around from the river. I saw that both sides had lost many men. The difference was that they could afford to lose men for they still outnumbered us.

Then I heard a sound I had last heard on the walls of Cyninges-tūn on the day that heroes died. It was the horn of the Ulfheonar, and it came from behind the Norsemen. Every warrior on the battlefield knew that it had to be men from the Clan of the Wolf. A few moments later as the battle froze in expectation I saw Ragnar riding a horse and leading the men from Whale Island. Running next to him was Bear Tooth and Karljot. The men of Dyflin had kept their promise. The Norwegians were caught between us and fresh warriors.

Dragon Crest raised his sword and shouted, "Back across the river!" I was actually disappointed. I had thought that they would fight to the end, but they did not. They ran and that, I think, was a measure of their King. I suspect that had he been there then they might have fought on. They ran.

Less than half of them made the river for Ragnar or whoever had conceived this plan had men coming along the riverbank. The half who made the river then had to negotiate its already bloody and muddy banks. Unencumbered by mail the archers and the slingers were there to rain death on the Norsemen who tried to clamber out. The ones who made it were the ones without mail. They ran as fast as their legs would take them. They were racing back to their ships.

Dragon Crest and his oathsworn along with thirty other survivors found themselves trapped at the river. They formed a half-circle. I felt obliged to offer terms, "Surrender and you shall live!"

It was still hard to make out Dragon Crest's words, "Surrender? And be held prisoner?"

I shook my head, "We will send to King Harald and he can buy you back!"

He laughed, "If King Harald bought back Einar Golden Hair it would only be to punish me in public. He does not reward failure. No, Sámr Ship Killer, we will end it here. The Norns have spun. Lay on and we will die like warriors!"

I nodded and shouted to my men, "Kill them and do so quickly!"

I did not participate. That honour went to Karljot, Karle, Egil Sorenson and their men. The best of Einar Golden Hair's men lay dead already, but they all fought until their heads were hacked from their bodies. They were brave men. In the silence which followed every eye was drawn to me and then my son shouted, "Sámr Ship Killer, Dragonheart's Heir!" The cry was taken up and warriors banged shields and cheered. Against the odds, we had saved the Land of the Wolf.

Epilogue

We had paid a high price and there were many men who would not return home. I had lost oathsworn amongst them Ráðulfr Ráðgeirsson. That his father Ráðgeir Haakensson had also died would break the heart of Haaken Ráðgeirsson and his wife. That he had other sons who had survived would be of little consolation. Ulf Olafsson had died along with all of his oathsworn, but they had held the left flank and their death had been honourable. Haldr the Dane had survived as had Gurt but two of Haldr's mercenaries had died. It was Gurt who later told me that they had stopped many of the enemy fleeing back across the river until they were slain. Haldr said that they had died as happy men.

Karljot and the men of Dyflin pursued the Vikings for two days and were rewarded by the capture of two drekar. The survivors managed to crew a threttanessa and they would take the news back to King Harald. The Norns were spinning. We did not know it then but the enmity of King Harald shifted from the Land of the Wolf to Karljot and the Isle of Man. He made it his business to take the island and make Karljot pay the price for what he termed his interference. It was King Harald who took the vengeance trail. The Land of the Wolf had proved too great a mouthful for him and Man was more easily digested. This was many years in the future when Ragnar ruled the Land of the Wolf.

That day was like the rebirth of Ragnar. It was Bear Tooth who told me all, as we celebrated the victory at Whale Island. "It was as we walked the walls of Whale Island, Lord Sámr, that it came to him. I was speaking of the horse and the pony. I told him that we did not have such animals in my land and that if Fótr and Erik had had them then they would have been unbeatable. It was as though my words had suddenly lit a fire in his eyes for they burned and sparkled. He said that he would ride to war! He did not need two good legs if he had a horse with four! I confess, Lord, that I was confused and then he told me, as we hurried to the stables, of a story you had told him. The story of Hrólfr the Horseman who had served with The Dragonheart and then gone on to become a great leader of the people who lived over the water in Frankia."

I nodded. "Göngu-Hrólfr Rognvaldson!"

"Aye, that was the name. He said Göngu-Hrólfr Rognvaldson led Vikings who fought on horses as well as on foot and carved out an empire bigger than the Land of the Wolf!"

The threads of the sisters were long. Hrólfr had left the Land of the Wolf when he was still a young man but we had told the story and its

190

telling had helped Ragnar realise that he could be a warrior. He had mounted a horse and when Karljot and his men arrived he was the one who told them that they had to march north to attack behind the enemy. That battle was his first and it created a new leader for my people. It was my last battle. The blow from Einar Golden Hair had broken my collar bone. The bones healed but they ached in winter and made it hard for me to use a shield. When Ragnar married and told me that he was happy to lead the clan I gave him the job. I enjoyed hawking and hunting with my son, Erik and my grandchildren.

As for Fótr and the Clan of the Fox, they survived the battle and his people lost only two warriors. Their coming had been necessary to save the Clan of the Wolf. It was not just the saving of my family which had been their doing, their bjorr dam and drekar not to mention the warriors they had brought were the difference between success and failure. If Bear Tooth had not mentioned the horse would Ragnar have thought to ride to war? If Ragnar had not ridden to war would we have won? That is the past and we now live in a present which has a future. The Danes in the east are more concerned with the Saxons of Wessex. King Harald will not risk his reputation by losing to us again and we are left alone. The mountains and the waters protect my land. The skeletons of the drekar lost in the flood were left where they sank as a reminder that the Land of the Wolf could defend itself. The only ship which was removed was *'Skraeling'*. We dragged her ashore and, after removing the mast and figurehead she was inverted and became a home for fishermen. Úlfarrston was a port no longer but the inverted drekar was a visible reminder to our enemies of the price they would pay if they tried to take our land from us. Ylva and The Dragonheart were long gone but their spirits still lived in my land. I had my family back and Viking Killer hung from the wall of my hall. I would not need it again. I had stepped on to the vengeance trail just once and I would never need to do so again for our enemies could not bear the cost in blood of trying to do the same to us. We were left alone, and the Clan of the Wolf became a legend. When the day of the Viking was long over my people still lived as they had in the time of The Dragonheart, never conquered, never enslaved they and the land were as one.

Wyrd!

The End

Norse Calendar

Gormánuður October 14th - November 13th
Ýlir November 14th - December 13th
Mörsugur December 14th - January 12th
Þorri - January 13th - February 11th
Gói - February 12th - March 13th
Einmánuður - March 14th - April 13th
Harpa April 14th - May 13th
Skerpla - May 14th - June 12th
Sólmánuður - June 13th - July 12th
Heyannir - July 13th - August 14th
Tvímánuður - August 15th - September 14th
Haustmánuður September 15th-October 13th

Glossary

Afen- River Avon
Afon Hafron- River Severn in Welsh
Beck- a stream
Blót – a blood sacrifice made by a jarl
Bondi- Viking farmers who fight
Bjorr – Beaver
Byrnie- a mail or leather shirt reaching down to the knees
Chape- the tip of a scabbard
Cyninges-tūn – Coniston. It means the estate of the king (Cumbria)
Drekar- a Dragon ship (a Viking warship) pl. drekar
Dyrøy –Jura (Inner Hebrides)
Dyflin- Old Norse for Dublin
Ēa Lōn- River Lune
Eoforwic- Saxon for York
Eyin-Helha -Eynhallow in the Orkney Islands
Føroyar- Faroe Islands
Fey- having second sight
Firkin- a barrel containing eight gallons (usually beer)
Fret-a sea mist
Fyrd-the Saxon levy
Galdramenn- wizard
Hersey- Isle of Arran
Hersir- a Viking landowner and minor noble. It ranks below a jarl
Hí- Iona (Gaelic)
Hoggs or Hogging- when the pressure of the wind causes the stern or the bow to droop
Hundred- Saxon military organization. (One hundred men from an area-led by a thegn or gesith)
Hwitebi- Norse for Whitby, North Yorkshire
Jarl- Norse earl or lord
Joro-goddess of the earth
kjerringa - Old Woman- the solid block in which the mast rested
Knarr- a merchant ship or a coastal vessel
Kyrtle-woven top
Ljoðhús- Lewis
Mast fish- two large racks on a ship designed to store the mast when not required
Mockasin- Algonquin for moccasin

193

Midden- a place where they dumped human waste
Miklagård - Constantinople
Njörðr- God of the sea
Nithing- A man without honour (Saxon)
Odin- The "All Father" God of war, also associated with wisdom, poetry, and magic (The Ruler of the gods).
Orkneyjar-Orkney
Ran- Goddess of the sea
Roof rock- slate
Saami- the people who live in what is now Northern Norway/Sweden
Sandaigh -Sanda Island
Scree- loose rocks in a glacial valley
Seax – short sword
Sennight- seven nights- a week
Sheerstrake- the uppermost strake in the hull
Sheet- a rope fastened to the lower corner of a sail
Shroud- a rope from the masthead to the hull amidships
Skjalborg- shield wall
Skeggox – an axe with a shorter beard on one side of the blade
Skíð -the Isle of Skye
Skreið- stockfish (any fish which is preserved)
Skræling -Barbarian
Snekke- a small warship
Stad- Norse settlement
Stays- ropes running from the masthead to the bow
Strake- the wood on the side of a drekar
Suðreyjar – Southern Hebrides (Islay)
Syllingar Insula, Syllingar- Scilly Isles
Tarn- small lake (Norse)
The Norns- The three sisters who weave webs of intrigue for men
Thing-Norse for a parliament or a debate (Tynwald in the Isle of Man)
Thor's day- Thursday
Threttanessa- a drekar with 13 oars on each side.
Thrall- slave
Trenail- a round wooden peg used to secure strakes
Tynwald- the Parliament on the Isle of Man
Úlfarrberg - Helvellyn
Úlfarrland- Cumbria
Úlfarrston- Ulverston
Ullr-Norse God of Hunting

Ulfheonar-an elite Norse warrior who wore a wolf skin over his armour
Verðandi -the Norn who sees the future
Veisafjǫrðr -Wexford
Vreinihala -Wrynose pass
Volva- a witch or healing woman in Norse culture
Waeclinga Straet- Watling Street (A5)
Walhaz -Norse for the Welsh (foreigners)
Waite- a Viking word for farm
Withy- the mechanism connecting the steering board to the ship
Woden's day- Wednesday
Wyddfa-Snowdon
Wykinglo- Wicklow (Ireland)
Wyrd- Fate
Wyrme- Norse for Dragon
Yard- a timber from which the sail is suspended
Ynys Enlli- Bardsey Island
Ynys Môn-Anglesey

Historical Note

King Harald Finehair is a figure as mysterious as Dragonheart himself. The only references to this power-hungry Viking from Norway come from Iceland. There are no records of him in Norway which is strange, for the rumour is that he was the first King of Norway. The Iceland sagas talk of men who left their homes rather than submit to King Harald. The lack of information was too good for me to ignore. I apologise to any descendants for blackening his name but my story needed an enemy and it is he.

This, I hope, will satisfy those who demanded another Dragonheart book. There will be no more but if you wish to imagine another adventure then be my guest.

There will be another story involving Erik and Laughing Deer but it will be a novella or long short story in the anthology-Tales From The Sword III due out in 2021.

Griff Hosker
August 2020

Other books by Griff Hosker

If you enjoyed reading this book, then why not read another one by the author?

Ancient History

The Sword of Cartimandua Series
(Germania and Britannia 50 A.D. – 128 A.D.)
Ulpius Felix- Roman Warrior (prequel)
The Sword of Cartimandua
The Horse Warriors
Invasion Caledonia
Roman Retreat
Revolt of the Red Witch
Druid's Gold
Trajan's Hunters
The Last Frontier
Hero of Rome
Roman Hawk
Roman Treachery
Roman Wall
Roman Courage

The Wolf Warrior series
(Britain in the late 6th Century)
Saxon Dawn
Saxon Revenge
Saxon England
Saxon Blood
Saxon Slayer
Saxon Slaughter
Saxon Bane
Saxon Fall: Rise of the Warlord
Saxon Throne
Saxon Sword

Medieval History

The Dragon Heart Series

Viking Slave
Viking Warrior
Viking Jarl
Viking Kingdom
Viking Wolf
Viking War
Viking Sword
Viking Wrath
Viking Raid
Viking Legend
Viking Vengeance
Viking Dragon
Viking Treasure
Viking Enemy
Viking Witch
Viking Blood
Viking Weregeld
Viking Storm
Viking Warband
Viking Shadow
Viking Legacy
Viking Clan
Viking Bravery

Dragonheart's Heir
The Vengeance Trail

The Norman Genesis Series
Hrolf the Viking
Horseman
The Battle for a Home
Revenge of the Franks
The Land of the Northmen
Ragnvald Hrolfsson
Brothers in Blood
Lord of Rouen
Drekar in the Seine
Duke of Normandy
The Duke and the King

New World Series
Blood on the Blade

Across the Seas
The Savage Wilderness
The Bear and the Wolf

The Reconquista Chronicles
Castilian Knight
El Campeador
The Lord of Valencia

The Aelfraed Series
(Britain and Byzantium 1050 A.D. - 1085 A.D.)
Housecarl
Outlaw
Varangian

**The Anarchy Series England
1120-1180**
English Knight
Knight of the Empress
Northern Knight
Baron of the North
Earl
King Henry's Champion
The King is Dead
Warlord of the North
Enemy at the Gate
The Fallen Crown
Warlord's War
Kingmaker
Henry II
Crusader
The Welsh Marches
Irish War
Poisonous Plots
The Princes' Revolt
Earl Marshal

**Border Knight
1182-1300**
Sword for Hire
Return of the Knight
Baron's War

199

Magna Carta
Welsh Wars
Henry III
The Bloody Border
Baron's Crusade
Sentinel of the North
War in the West

Sir John Hawkwood Series
France and Italy 1339- 1387
Crécy: The Age of the Archer

Lord Edward's Archer
Lord Edward's Archer
King in Waiting
An Archer's Crusade (November 2020)

Struggle for a Crown
1360- 1485
Blood on the Crown
To Murder A King
The Throne
King Henry IV
The Road to Agincourt
St Crispin's Day

Tales from the Sword I

Modern History

The Napoleonic Horseman Series
Chasseur à Cheval
Napoleon's Guard
British Light Dragoon
Soldier Spy
1808: The Road to Coruña
Talavera
The Lines of Torres Vedras
Bloody Badajoz

The Lucky Jack American Civil War series

Rebel Raiders
Confederate Rangers
The Road to Gettysburg

The British Ace Series
1914
1915 Fokker Scourge
1916 Angels over the Somme
1917 Eagles Fall
1918 We will remember them
From Arctic Snow to Desert Sand
Wings over Persia

Combined Operations series
1940-1945
Commando
Raider
Behind Enemy Lines
Dieppe
Toehold in Europe
Sword Beach
Breakout
The Battle for Antwerp
King Tiger
Beyond the Rhine
Korea
Korean Winter

Other Books
Great Granny's Ghost (Aimed at 9-14-year-old young people)

For more information on all of the books then please visit the author's web site at www.griffhosker.com where there is a link to contact him or visit his Facebook page: GriffHosker at Sword Books

Printed in Great Britain
by Amazon